HAIRLESS HASSLES

HAIRLESS HASSLES

A Mobile Cat Groomer Mystery

Ruth J Hartman

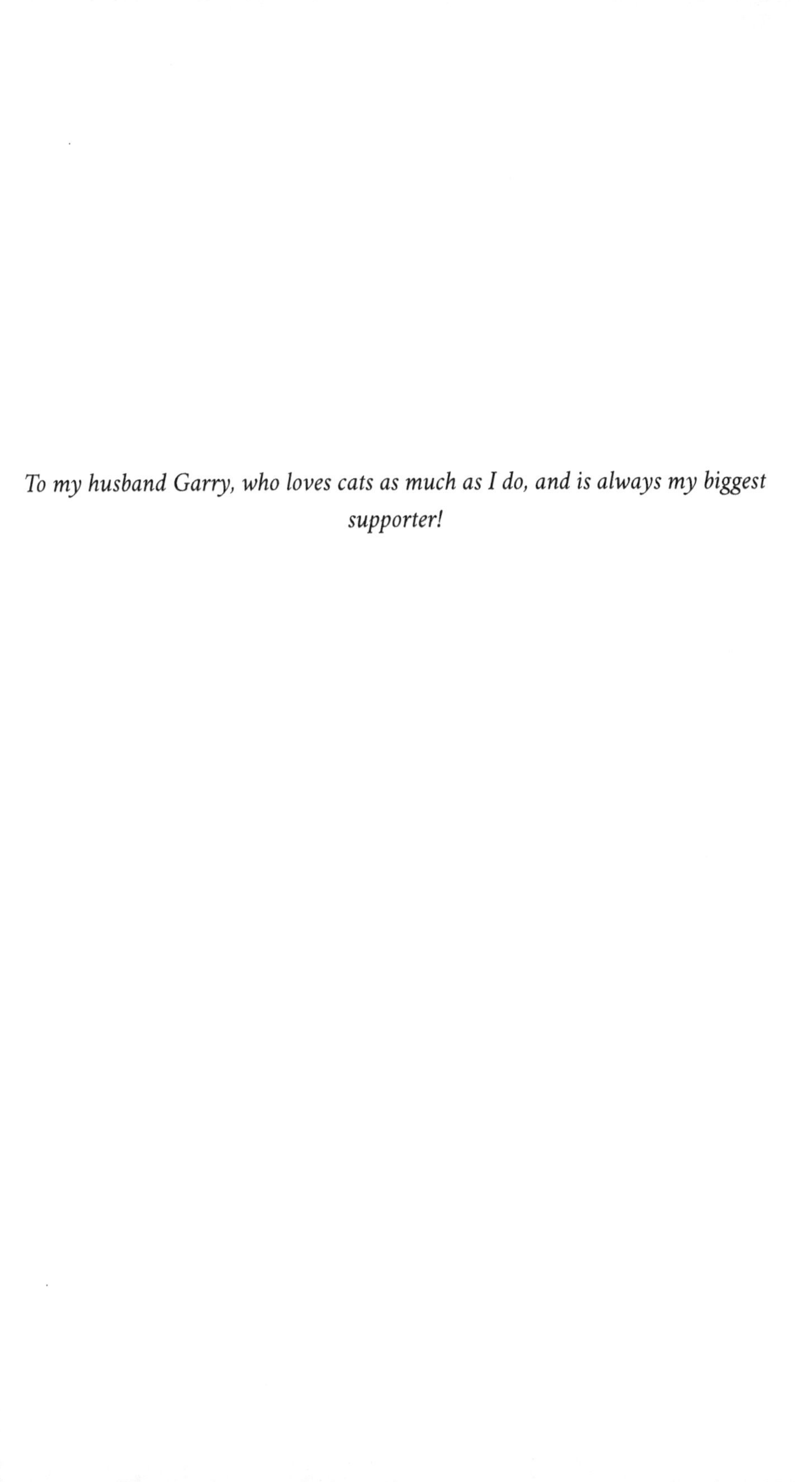

To my husband Garry, who loves cats as much as I do, and is always my biggest supporter!

Chapter One

I drove along Main Street in my mobile cat grooming van, through the tiny downtown area of Whitewater Valley, Indiana. Percival and Jasper, my two cats, stood on their hind legs as they peered through the passenger window, tails waving like slow-moving flags in anticipation of my next cat grooming visit.

"Hey, you two," I said, "we're going to two of your favorite clients, Helga and Eleanor, today. Are you ready to supervise?"

Jasper mewed, and Percival pawed at the air in my direction. I'd take that as a whole-hearted yes. It worked out nicely that my cats were usually well-behaved and got along with my feline clients. And that nearly all my clients liked them back. I did, however, leave Percival and Jasper at my shop with my assistant, Veronica Waters, when visiting the few kitties who didn't care for them tagging along.

I pulled onto the street where the cats' pet parents lived and stopped in front of the women's houses, making sure to keep my van positioned squarely in the middle of their driveways. The ladies, Florence Makes and Lottie Campbell, somewhere in their eighties, were very persnickety about whose driveway I parked in. I always left it up to them to let me know who the designated host for the appointment was that day.

The ladies were each standing in their own driveway, holding their respective Sphynx cats. The kitties were twin sisters, and their moms called each other every morning to ensure the cats were dressed alike for the day.

I put my van in park as I waited for the women to decide where we'd have the appointment. They gave each other hand signals and head nods, then both turned toward me. Lottie stuck her hand in the air and performed a reasonable princess wave, so I waited until she and Eleanor had retreated into her open garage before I pulled into her driveway.

Now that I was closer, I could see that the kitties were wearing lavender today—small bowler hats with chin straps to hold them on, and matching sundresses with a pattern of pink sunflowers on the fabric. The ladies must have been a dream come true for the woman who made all those tiny outfits for them, because the cats had on new clothes every time I saw them. I had to admit, they always looked cute.

I got out of the driver's side, then rounded to the back of the van to lower the steps. The women, now having decided where the grooming would take place, would have to choose which of the cats would have her appointment first. I turned, then walked to the ladies, who were standing side by side at the end of Lotties' driveway. And waited.

With eye winks, eyebrow wiggles, and side-to-side head movements, they once again faced me. The cats were twins, but their human moms might as well have been, with their special way of communicating without words.

"Eleanor will go first," said Lottie.

"Perfect," I said, the same as every time, no matter who the chosen cat turned out to be. I did my best to never seem to choose one cat over the other, or one lady over the other. Nothing good could ever come of that, and I wasn't about to start now.

I reached out to take both cats in my arms, smiling as they curled together in a single lavender-covered ball against my chest. The girls enjoyed being together any chance they got.

After several kitty head rubs against my chin, I placed first one cat, then the other, inside the van on the floor, until I could climb up the stairs myself. Next, I placed Eleanor on a thick towel beside my sink, and Helga on a blanket positioned on a nearby shelf.

A skittering noise came from my left. I smiled as Percival, then Jasper, climbed over the front seat to join us in the grooming area in the back. They jumped on the shelf, sauntered over to Helga, and gave her a sniff. She was so used to them, she barely opened one eye before snuggling down into the blanket.

A scraping noise came from the driveway as Florence set up two lawn chairs a few feet away from the back of the van. Lottie appeared with two glasses of something frothy, which, from past appointments, I knew to be some sort of adult beverage.

I ran the water in the sink, making sure it was warm enough but not too hot. Sphynx cats were normally cold, but also had very sensitive skin. I picked up Eleanor and placed her gently into the bath. She looked up at me and blinked, but otherwise gave no indication of anything much happening. She enjoyed her frequent baths and often even purred during the sessions.

As I massaged a small amount of specially formulated shampoo into Eleanor's skin, I turned my head so I could see the ladies. "So, what's been going on lately?"

Florence waved her hand. "Oh, you know, the usual. We had our weekly appointment with Miss Gibbons, the kitties' fashion designer, yesterday. There were so many outfits to choose from. That always takes the wind out of our sails, doesn't it, Lottie?"

She nodded. "Indeed, it does. Miss Gibbons is high energy, and she's only sixty. How can we compete with that?"

I smiled. "Your girls are always dressed so cute. Do you get to have any input into the fabric colors?"

Lottie snorted. "Well, I would be glad to, but someone"—she narrowed her eyes at her neighbor— "doesn't think we're clever enough to make those suggestions."

"I just feel like Miss Gibbons, being the professional, might just know a little more about what color schemes would go better with our babies' skin tone," said Florence. "I'd hate for them to go out and about into town, looking like a couple of circus clowns because their clothing clashed with their complexions."

I rinsed the shampoo from Eleanor's skin, making sure to cover her face as I did it. She held still until I was done, then waited until I'd removed my hands to shake her entire body, drenching me in the process. It was no wonder I went through so many aprons in my line of work. "However it happens, your babies are always the best-dressed cats in town."

The ladies beamed, so much so that their faces were shiny. But that might have been from the adult beverages they were both sipping.

After I dried the cat off, I checked her ears, eyes, and teeth, then I gently clipped her claws and redressed her. Once I was finished, I placed her on a blanket on the shelf where the other cats were napping. She settled down at once, walked in a circle, lay down in a ball, and closed her eyes.

Next, I picked up Helga, who squawked a little, but otherwise allowed me to carry her to a clean towel beside the sink. I let the water from the previous bath go down the drain, cleaned the sink, then refilled it with warm water.

As I repeated the bathing sequence with Helga, I turned to the ladies again. "Anything interesting happen lately? Aside from Miss Gibbons taking the wind out of your sails, I mean."

They looked at each other, gave some nods, then Lottie said, "We were in the nail salon yesterday, and that Trixie girl who works there was acting mighty strange."

"Trixie Torbeck? What was she doing?"

Florence narrowed her eyes as if in thought. "Let's see, she got huffy with a client, so much so that the woman left without paying."

"Oh no," I said. "I bet that didn't go over very well with Trixie."

"The person who really got upset was Carlotta."

"Why was that?" I asked.

"Because the client was hers, not Trixie's."

How awful and embarrassing for everyone involved. "Why would Trixie do that? Had the client said something mean or hateful?"

The ladies glanced at each other again. Lottie leaned forward. "We heard Trixie tell the customer that her nails were horrid and that she'd be better off having a rodent chew on them so they'd look better."

"Trixie said that?" If I talked to my pet parents that way, or to their cats, I'd soon be out of work.

"That's right." Florence nodded. "We were stunned. Weren't we, Lottie?"

"Absolutely appalled."

"I can tell you," said Florence, "that when Carlotta came back from fetching something from another room, found out what had happened from her other clients who were waiting there, including us, she really laid into that Trixie girl."

"Right in front of everyone," added Lottie.

I rinsed Helga off. "I bet that was embarrassing to watch."

Lottie giggled. "It wasn't embarrassing for us."

"That's right," said Florence. "We were fascinated. Haven't had such a show since Ricky the postman had a dream he was a circus performer, and the next day, attempted to do a backflip while wearing his mailbag, which didn't end well."

"Wow, uh…. So what happened after that?" I dried off Helga and redressed her quickly. I knew from experience that if one of the cats was dressed and the other cat wasn't, the ladies got quite indignant.

Lottie took a sip of her drink, then let out a burp. "We thought at first that Carlotta was going to attack Trixie. She had a ferocious look in her eyes. Like some wild tiger."

My mouth dropped open. "Attack? Like hit her?" Just what our town needed, a good old-fashioned cat fight in the nail salon, where everybody had extra sharp claws.

Florence shrugged. "Not sure. It didn't actually happen."

"Quite disappointing," agreed Lottie. "The show had only just begun, and it ended all too soon. After that, I was afraid I'd get so bored, I'd be forced to get my knitting out of my bag."

Florence blinked. "You've been knitting the same sweater for Eleanor for a year and a half. I doubt you'll ever finish it."

"It's not a sweater." Lottie wouldn't make eye contact with her friend.

"Then what is it?"

Her cheeks reddened. "It started out as a hat. But it sort of got away from me."

Florence snorted. "Keep going this way and Eleanor will have a knitted tent to nap in."

Normally, the ladies went out and about quite often all over town, so I'd assumed that took care of whatever boredom they might otherwise experience. But listening to them now, they sounded like young children who needed to be entertained. Gee, that also sounded like a couple of cats I knew. I glanced over at Jasper and Percival, who were watching my every move intently. "I'm assuming since the action ended too soon, that everything turned out okay for Trixie and Carlotta?"

"They argued some," said Lottie. "But we happened to be Carlotta's next clients, so there wasn't anything else to watch since it was time for our appointments."

Florence sighed. "Yes, after that it was business as usual as she did our manicures and pedicures."

"Well, one bad thing happened. Or, more to the point, something didn't happen."

Lottie scrunched her brow together, then nodded. "Oh, right. Normally, Carlotta gives Eleanor and Helga manicures, or is it pedicures?"

"Pretty sure it's pedicures since cats don't have hands," Florence pointed out.

I had to admit, that seemed above and beyond for a nail professional, but how could I say anything? I went overboard to keep the ladies happy with their kitties, too. Then why would they want their nail professional to trim the cats' toenails when I already did it? "You do realize that I always trim your cats' claws, right?"

I checked out Helga's eyes, ears, and trimmed her claws to emphasize my point.

"Certainly, Molly," said Florence. "But Carlotta applies nail polish to match whatever color they're wearing that day. It's quite the treat. And the cats always love having their nails done. They often purr. Or fall asleep. But either one works for us. On special days, all four of us have nails to match."

Huh. Well, they had me there. Nail polish for cats was one grooming service I didn't offer. "You'd said Carlotta normally does that for the cats. Didn't she give them, um, pedicures this time?"

Lottie slashed her hand through the air. It was the one holding her cup, and pink liquid dipped across her knees. "No, she didn't. She seemed too upset about what had happened with Trixie to care. She said she didn't have time. Can you imagine?"

Actually, I could. Sometimes my pet parents caused me to run over their appointment times, and it made me late for the following one. But I wouldn't bring that up now. The ladies seemed irritated enough. I redressed Helga and placed her on the towel next to her sister, who was still asleep. Percival and Jasper, however, were staring at something through the small window of the van. Probably watching some birds nearby. That was one of their favorite activities.

I picked up Eleanor and Helga, placed them near the open doorway, and climbed down the steps. Once I had the sister kitties in my arms, I headed toward where the ladies were sitting in their chairs.

As soon as each of the women had her respective fur baby in her arms, I was ready to say my goodbyes and move on to my next appointment. I'd stayed a little long, and my assistant Veronica, though having apologized to me profusely, had accidentally overscheduled me for this afternoon, so I needed to keep moving.

I jumped when something black zoomed past my feet and toward the grassy area between the women's houses.

It was a cat. One of mine.

Where was he going? "Percival, wait!" Before I got very far in that direction, a gray blur zipped in front of me, nearly tripping me. "Jasper? Come back!"

The cats ran several yards, then halted right in the middle of an area where the grass hadn't been mowed for a while. A young guy usually did the ladies' yardwork, but obviously didn't always get this part done. Wouldn't Florence or Lottie have said something to him?

I glanced back toward the driveway to check on the ladies. They were each cuddling their cats, whispering who knew what into the kitties' ears. Probably about the latest scandal they'd heard about happening in town. They loved to tell anyone who'd listen the latest gossip, even their cats. Had they even noticed that I'd run right past them as I trotted after my own cats?

Looking at the lawn again, I decided they might not have even paid attention to the patch of grass between their houses. Those two were all about their Sphynxes, daily adult beverages, and gossip. Anything else didn't get much attention.

I refocused on my cats, who were sniffing the air and pawing at the too-long swaying grass. "Hey, what's up with you guys? You know you're not supposed to run away from me like that. And you don't go outside without Mama and your leashes and—"

Percival let out a loud howl, followed by Jasper. I placed my hands on my hips in irritated Mama mode. "What in the world is wrong with you? You scared me nearly to death."

Was there a full moon coming up? That had been known to turn on the crazies in cats. Or had they heard something over here with their supersonic feline hearing abilities, like a mole or chipmunk hiding in the grass? Since they were indoor kitties and were only supposed to go out under my supervision, the local woodland creatures were safe from them.

Percival had run away from me one time before. But usually, he was good about keeping close to me and not going outside by himself. This was Jasper's first time running off, but he hadn't lived with me as long as Percival. And I knew that his previous owner had kept a close eye on the cat as well.

Grass rustled behind me. I turned to see the ladies carefully tiptoeing their way toward me. I'd hoped to grab the cats and hightail it out of here to make my next appointment on time, but if the ladies finally noticed I was missing and showed up to see what was going on back here, it would be difficult to leave.

I watched the women, keeping a close eye on them to make sure they didn't trip or stumble. Aside from their age, the fact that they'd consumed enough adult beverages to sink a ship also had me concerned.

Florence lifted her chin toward the yard. "Why is this grass so tall, Lottie? You should have Henry take care of that."

With a head shake and a hiccup from too many drinks, Lottie said, "Why is it up to me? It's on our shared property. It's your responsibility as much as mine. You really should be the one to—"

Both ladies yelped when Helga and Eleanor struggled out of their moms' embraces and leaped to the grass, rushing to join my two in their loud cacophony. The screeching got louder by the second.

"Where's my baby going?" asked Lottie.

Florence pointed toward the group of felines. "The same place as my baby."

This was ridiculous. Time to find out why all our cats were acting way out of character.

I crept closer to the four howling kitties, who were perched side by side, tails swishing through the lawn like windshield wipers, making the tall grass sway to one side, then the other.

When I was close enough to stand right behind the gawking felines, that's when I saw it.

A hand. Attached to an arm. Attached to the body of a woman.

I gasped. "It's Carlotta Sykes. She's been stabbed!"

Slow movements came from behind me as the women got closer.

"What's she doing in our yard?" asked Florence.

Lottie leaned closer to inspect the body. "And why is she wearing such ugly nail polish?"

Chapter Two

As soon as everyone had calmed down a little, I phoned the sheriff's office. He showed up a few minutes later, hat askew, pants hitched up too high, and walked in his ambling gait that I always assumed was his weird version of a rooster's strut.

Unfortunately, Sheriff Lawrence King wasn't the most on-the-ball guy. During two previous murders in town, he'd decided right away who the murderer was, and didn't bother checking other leads. He'd been wrong in both cases, so my friends, my cats, and I took on the task and discovered the real killers' identities. Much to the sheriff's annoyance.

"Well," he said, adjusting his hat, "what do we have here?"

"What we have," Florence pointed to the grass, "is a dead body straddling our two yards. What are you going to do about that? It isn't as if we can carry on our normal daily activities with a corpse lying in between our houses. I don't know of anyone else with a dead person taking a nap in their yard. Do you, Sheriff?"

Lottie tugged on Florence's arm.

"What?"

"You said straddling." Lottie's eyebrows lowered.

"Yeah?"

"But Carlotta's not riding a horse."

Florence huffed out an irritated breath. "It doesn't matter."

The sheriff watched the two ladies for a few seconds, wrinkled his large nose and narrowed his eyes. "Have you two been imbibing recently?"

"Of course not," said Lottie proudly. "We've been drinking."

With a roll of her eyes, Florence said, "That's what imbibing means."

"Oh. Well, then yes." She held up her index finger. "But we're over twenty-one, so it's not illegal right, Florence?" Her grin was wide, and she winked.

The ladies watched each other, and after their giggling started, it took a whole minute for them to contain themselves.

"Be that as it may," said the sheriff, "you do realize it's still the middle of the afternoon?"

Lottie tilted her head to one side. "I don't see a problem there." She turned to her friend. "Do you? Who watches the clock when you're retired? Those little hands on the clock just keep moving along. Why do they call them hands, anyway? There aren't any fingers on them."

"No," said Florence. "It's not a problem what time it is." She turned to the sheriff. "Can you elaborate on—"

Determined to get the ball rolling and stop arguing about imbibing, I held out my hand. "Listen, why don't we focus on the dead body here in front of us?"

Sheriff King's face reddened. "I was getting to that. Don't tell me what to do, Molly."

I refrained from grumbling out loud. If he'd do his job, I wouldn't have to.

Lottie pointed to the grass. "It isn't as if Carlotta is going anywhere, right? So what's the rush? We were rudely interrupted by murder and didn't get a chance to finish our daily refreshments."

Florence nodded. "Well said. We still have half a pitcher to drink and…"

Lottie tugged on her arm, then whispered to her.

With a frown, she said, "Oh, a fourth of a pitcher. Still…we'll need to refill that pitcher stat. A fourth won't last very much longer."

This wasn't going well. I jerked when I noticed all four cats—ears flat and tails down, as if sneaking up on live prey—creeping closer to Carlotta's body. Jasper sniffed her ear, and Percival batted at one of her hands. Helga and Eleanor had snuggled up close to Carlotta's side, like they were ready for a nap once they'd discovered the woman wasn't going to run away, so they could chase her.

No, that wouldn't do at all. No one else was making a move to do anything about it, so it seemed it was up to me to make the kitties behave.

I bent down and grasped both Sphinx cats beneath their tummies, turned, then placed them in their moms' arms. The ladies gave me bewildered looks, as if not sure what to do since their arms were now full up with feline, and they probably hadn't finished their discussion on the pros and cons of having a full refreshment container.

Next, I picked up my two cats, trying to ignore Percival's huff of irritation as I held them close, then took a couple of steps away from the crime scene. I bent close to my cats' ears and said, "You guys have to stay with Mama for a little while, okay? You shouldn't have run off like that. But you did find the body, so good job on that part."

When I glanced up, Sheriff King was staring at me with his mouth open. He snapped it shut, then took a step away from us. I knew from previous experience that not only didn't he like cats, they terrified him. I was surprised he was even standing here in the yard since four felines happened to be close by.

The sheriff must have finally decided to do his job and knelt in the tall grass beside Carlotta. He leaned closer. "She was stabbed."

"We already knew that," said Lottie, giving me a wink.

From behind, I saw his shoulders bunch together, as his neck took on the same shade of red as his face had been. Ignoring the comment, he said, "It's by an unusual weapon."

I peered over his shoulder. Even though I'd noticed blood on her neck and something metal protruding from it, I hadn't wanted to get close enough to see what it was once it was obvious she wasn't breathing.

Unable to help myself, I said, "Well, what is it?"

"If you must know, Miss Nosy, it's a fingernail file."

My eyes widened. That really was an unusual weapon.

He pointed to Carlotta. "Looks like it hit a major vein in her neck."

"Jugular?" I asked.

"What?"

"Her jugular vein?"

He flipped his hand. "Whatever. Does it matter? She's dead, all right."

Lottie leaned closer to me as she also peered over the sheriff's shoulder. "Did you say she was juggling? Why would a person choose our properties on which to juggle? Seems downright silly to me. And whatever she'd chosen to juggle, our cats would want to chase. Florence, remember when I dropped a tiny tomato and the cats chased it as it bounced across my kitchen floor?"

I shook my head, then noticed furious blinking and head tilts from the ladies. What was going on? That was one of their ways of communicating only with each other. They did it often. I never knew what they were telling each other, but they always seemed to get the message.

Finally, Lottie gasped and said, "That looks just like…"

"It can't be," insisted Florence.

"But I think it's"—

She scowled. "No. You're wrong."

Lottie's eyes blinked furiously. Was she trying to say something else? Was the grass pollen bothering her eyes?

The sheriff rose and pulled out his phone. After he placed a call to Tyson Berry, the funeral director, he stuffed his phone into his pocket. "That's done, I guess. We'll get Carlotta moved out of your yard and see what we find in an autopsy."

Lottie's face paled. "Autopsy?"

He crossed his arms over his chest. "That's right. Always have to do one when murder is involved."

"Maybe it's not murder. Maybe…" Lottie pointed toward the body. "Perhaps Carlotta fell at work and…"

His eyebrows shot up. "You think she fell on a nail file and accidentally killed herself?" His shoe tapped in the grass. "And just how would she have done it at work, all the way across town, then ended up in your yard?"

The ladies exchanged glances and gave a few shrugs.

The sheriff watched them with narrowed eyes. When they appeared to have stopped their movements, he pointed at them. "Hey, what's all of that supposed to mean, anyway?"

Lottie shook her head. "We, uh, don't know."

I repositioned Jasper and Percival in my arms. They were getting heavy to hold, but I didn't trust that they'd behave themselves around the body if I put them back on the ground.

A car door slammed from the driveway, and Tyson, along with another young man, approached, carrying a stretcher.

"Oh look," said Lottie, "they're going to put Carlotta in one of those black sleeping bags, aren't they?"

Florence shook her head. "I don't think that's what they're called. I'm pretty sure that's a stretcher."

"No, I mean the sleeping bag."

"That's not what they call it, " said Florence.

"Not what they call what?"

I refrained from rolling my eyes at first, but nearly went ahead and did it when I noticed the sheriff staring at the women. They were a bit daft, but I adored them. They were funny, sweet, and always seemed to know what was going on in Whitewater Valley when I needed help finding murder suspects.

Too bad that this time, their properties were right in the middle of an active investigation. Oh no. Surely the sheriff wouldn't consider them suspects in….

As soon as Tyson and his assistant had loaded up Carlotta, yes, in a black sleeping bag, er, body bag, the sheriff turned to us. "Now." He rubbed his hands together. "Let's get down to business."

"What business would that be, sheriff?" asked Florence.

"A woman was killed here and…"

Lottie raised her hand. "Her name's Carlotta."

He huffed out a breath. "Yes, I know that."

"Then why didn't you just say that?" asked Florence. "Then we'd all know what you're talking about and wouldn't waste time. Honestly, the way you drone on and on really makes everyone wait."

I pressed my lips together, laughter longing to escape. Those two ladies could out-talk anybody, and often did. Plus, the sheriff's face had gone red again, like he might explode.

"As I was saying." He gave a menacing look toward Florence, causing her to snap her mouth closed. "Now that the woman—Carlotta—has been taken away, I need to ask you some questions."

"Ask who?" said Lottie.

He pointed in their general direction.

She frowned. "You want to ask my cat questions? I doubt she knows anything about it, but I can check with her." She leaned down to her cat. "Eleanor, this man wants to ask you something. Is that all right with you?"

The sheriff gasped. "No! I don't want to talk to your cat."

"Why not? She's very personable."

"Don't you mean *purrs*onable," asked Florence.

The giggling commenced again, which caused the sheriff's eyes to nearly bug out.

I waved at the ladies to get their attention. "I think Sheriff King wants to talk to both of you. Not the kitties. Even though they are both quite personable."

Florence shrugged. "I guess so. Although, we are behind schedule."

"For what?" he asked.

She pointed toward the driveway. "Our refreshments. By now, we'll have to get clean glasses and refill them with fresh drinks."

"You're right," said Lottie. "A stale beverage can cause a multitude of bodily function issues. And I don't want that."

"No one wants that," agreed Florence.

Sheriff King looked ready to blow a gasket. He crossed his arms over his chest. "Now, back to some questions I have for you. For you *women*."

They nodded in unison.

I edged closer to my friends, hoping to give off positive vibes. I knew how being in the sheriff's sights felt, and it wasn't fun. When I stood next to Lottie, Percival reached out to pat Eleanor on the head, as if giving his support, too.

The sheriff grasped his hands together behind him and paced in front of us, back and forth several times, until Lottie said to her friend, "Are you getting dizzy too?"

Florence's eyebrows lowered. "No. Just look at the horizon and you'll be fine."

I leaned closer. "I think that only works if you're on a boat."

"What boat?" asked Lottie.

"Hey," said the sheriff, stopping suddenly. "Stop talking. I have questions for you."

"Then ask them," said Lottie. "We're a little wobbly over here and need to sit down soon."

Even the cats were drooping over their pet-moms' arms like hairless dust rags.

"Fine." The sheriff sighed. "First, I want to know if you ladies knew the deceased."

"Of course we did," said Florence. "We were regular customers."

His eyebrows rose. "Is that so?"

"Well, yes." Lottie nodded. "This is a small town, you know. And with only one nail salon, lots of citizens are customers there." She blinked. "Are you?"

"Am I what?"

"A nail salon customer."

He looked repulsed. "Of course not!"

Florence glanced down at the sheriff's stubby fingers with ragged fingernails. "Maybe you should be."

Knowing that my nails were in rough shape, as usual, I curled my fingers into my palms. Of course, that made it more difficult to hold my two cats, but I didn't want to end up getting a lecture on nail care from the ladies.

He glared at the women, then stuck his hands in his pants pockets. Maybe he wanted to avoid the same lecture I was hiding from. "So you admit you knew her. Do you have any idea why she might have ended up dead, stabbed with a nail file, in between your two houses?"

Florence whispered something to Lottie, who shook her head. What was that about? Earlier, Lottie had also tried to ask about the nail file and had gotten shushed. Did they know something about the murder weapon that they weren't going to tell the sheriff?

I didn't think they were guilty, but something was going on. Sheriff King seemed all too interested in them, which worried me. Would he want to arrest them for Carlotta's murder? I couldn't let that happen.

Chapter Three

My morning started off late at Fabulous Felines, since Melody Horn had a family emergency and couldn't bring in Prissy for her grooming appointment. Veronica would take care of things for me while I took advantage of the time to grab some blueberry tarts from Paula's Pastries and make my way to the library.

Jillian Wells, my best friend, was the head librarian and very good at her job. She kept everything in order and made it clear she'd have no roughhousing or loud noises in her place of business. I loved popping in to see her when I had the chance. Plus, she loved anything blueberry, and it always made her day to get a baked surprise. On top of that, she heard things from lots of patrons who came through the library daily. If people were saying anything about Carlotta and who might have killed her, Jillian would know.

I stepped into the quiet atmosphere, always amazed at the noise difference between here and my grooming shop. At my shop, people talking, sometimes loudly, was the norm, as well as various cat noises, some pleasant, some harsh, depending on the kitties' moods,

When I reached the main checkout counter, Jillian was standing behind it, her head bent over an open book. No surprise there. I placed the pastry sack a foot away from her, but she didn't appear to hear me. I edged it closer with my finger until it was a few inches away. She didn't budge. Finally, I ran my finger down the side of the sack, creating a crinkling sound.

With a small gasp, Jillian's eyes widened and she spotted first the sack, then me. "Oh! Molly! You startled me."

I pushed the sack closer. "Good thing I wasn't a thief or thug coming to hurt you. I've been standing here for like a half hour."

Her eyebrows lowered. "No, you haven't."

I laughed. "Well…maybe not quite that long."

"I'm hoping there might be one for me in there?" Her gaze dropped to the sack.

"Of course." I opened it so she could see.

She pressed her hand to her chest. "Oh, thank you so much. I'm famished."

"You're always famished."

"True statement." She reached in and snagged a blueberry tart. "These are so good. I love them."

"Yes, I know." I tilted the sack toward me and took one for myself, glad when Jillian produced a couple of paper towels from beneath her counter. They were good, but messy. If I showed back up at Fabulous Felines with sugary fingers, I'd never get my kitty clients to allow me to groom them since they'd be busy attacking my hands.

She sighed as she finished her treat. "I had the best day off yesterday."

"Oh, that's right. What did you end up doing?"

"Nothing."

"Really?"

"Yep, absolutely nothing."

"You didn't even read?" I asked.

She raised one eyebrow. "Now you know that's a silly question. I always read."

"But you said…." I shrugged. "Well, as I told you in my text last night, my day yesterday wasn't so calm.

"Yeah, so awful to hear what happened to Carlotta. I didn't know her well, but wouldn't wish that on anyone. Are Florence and Lottie handling it okay, since she was found between their houses? I'd be a mess."

"They're doing fine. You know them, only concerned about their cats and…"

She held up her hand. "Hold that thought. Someone's coming over here."

I turned to see a young woman I'd noticed around town but hadn't met. Jillian smiled at her. "Hi, Nellie. Need help finding something today?"

"Nope." She glanced both ways as if afraid someone might sneak up on her. "I wanted to show you something."

"Uh, okay," said Jillian. She glanced at me and gave a slight shrug. "What is it?"

Nellie raised her eyebrows and tilted her head toward me, as if she didn't want me to see whatever she had for Jillian. " What about…"

"I can leave, if it's something private." I hated it when one of my pet parents wanted to tell me something, and another person was standing way too close.

Jillian shook her head. "Unless it's something deeply personal, Nellie, may my friend Molly stay? If you're having some kind of issue, she's good at figuring things out."

My heart warmed, and I stood a little taller at her praise. "Thanks, Jillian. Yes, Nellie, I'll stay if you'd like me to."

She watched me for a few seconds. "Yeah, okay. It's something on my phone."

"A photo?" asked Jillian, as she glanced toward the woman's cell.

"No, a video." She reached into her small purse and pulled out her bling-covered phone. "I didn't see you here yesterday, Jillian. But I came back today because I really think you should see this."

My interest went sky high. This sounded too good to pass up. I picked up the sack and moved it a couple of feet away from us. There were two more desserts inside that Jillian could have later.

Jillian came around to the front of the counter to stand between me and Nellie. "All right, now you've piqued my interest. What's the video of?"

What would be so important that Nellie would need to come back into the library just to show it to the librarian? Had a patron tried to run out the door without checking out a book? That would really irritate my friend. I craned my neck around the side of Jillian's shoulder, the only way to see since she was taller than I was.

When the video started, I recognized the inside of the library right about where we were standing now. I could hear a few lower-pitched voices, normal for inside the building. It wasn't often people got loud, and that was thanks mostly to Jillian.

Her eyes widened. "When did you take this?"

"Yesterday. I wish you'd been here to see it in person, but—"

Jillian held up her hand to silence Nellie, the same reaction I often got from her. Being a librarian and shushing people was deeply ingrained in my friend. When we were little and played school, she always had to be the teacher. I'd been the subject of her raised palm for most of my life.

We watched the video, and nothing much happened. So far, it was kind of boring. But Nellie seemed insistent that Jillian see it, so I waited for more to happen.

A few seconds later, Valene Day appeared on the screen. She was Jillian's assistant.

"Hey," said Jillian, "that's…"

"Yep. Since I didn't see you here, I figured she was in charge for the day."

Jillian nodded. "That's right. But why were you filming her? I'm not sure that was a good idea. Does she even know that you…"

"Keep watching." Nellie's gaze was glued to the phone screen.

Jillian stiffened, surely not used to having someone tell her what to do in her place of work, where she was the boss. But she leaned down to see the screen better.

Nellie held the phone a little closer to Jillian, causing me to have to readjust to see the phone. "I got a really good view because I, uh, followed Carlotta over here toward the counter after she stormed by me. I figured something was up. I stood just across the lobby. They never even noticed me."

Suddenly, Valene's head turned to her right, and Carlotta came into view. I poked Jillian's arm. She didn't turn toward me, but nodded.

If this was taken yesterday, it couldn't have been much before Carlotta was killed, since the cats discovered her body in the late afternoon. "Nellie," I said, "what time did you take this video?"

Her brow furrowed. "Let's see. Right after the library opened, so about 9:30?"

In the video, Carlotta came around to the other side of the counter where Valene was standing.

Jillian's body stiffened. "What's she doing? She's not allowed back here."

I patted her arm, hoping to calm her down enough to continue watching. Since Carlotta was dead, it didn't make much difference if she broke a library rule.

I looked at the phone screen. Carlotta's face was red. She pointed her finger in Valene's face, making Valene take a step backward.

"You stay away from him," said Carlotta.

"From who?" asked Valene. She placed her hands on her hips. "And what are you doing? Only library employees are allowed back here."

Jillian nodded, as if agreeing with Valene.

Carlotta seemed to ignore Valene's library warning as she said, "You know who. I've seen you talking to him in here."

Valene stood up straighter, but was so short, it didn't seem to make an impression on Carlotta. "Listen, I can't help it if he likes me."

"He doesn't like you."

"Yes, he does. He's in here at least once a week. And he always talks to me." Valene pressed her fingers to her collarbone. It's become a regular thing for us."

"He's checking out books, you idiot."

Valene shook her head. "No, he… he flirts with me."

Carlotta sputtered out a laugh. "That's just how he acts. Believe me, he's only here for one thing."

"No, it's not true," insisted Valene.

"Yes, it is true. He only wants you for your books."

Just as Valene gasped in the video, Jillian did the same thing right beside me.

"How rude," said Jillian. "As if books were a bad thing." Her shoe tapped angrily against the floor.

"You can't know that," Valene continued on the video.

"Of course I know that. Because he loves me." Carlotta's smile was wide and confident. She slipped her long, dark hair over her shoulder.

Valene's eyes widened. "No, take it back." Suddenly, she reached out and shoved Carlotta, though the other woman was quite a bit taller and stouter, and the shove didn't move her very far.

"How dare you touch me!" screeched Carlotta. As quick as a cat, Carlotta swiped her fingernails at Valene's cheek. Bright red scratches bloomed on her skin.

"Oh no!" Jillian shouted, startling a couple of middle-aged men who'd just walked by the counter. But Jillian, so focused on what was happening with her assistant, didn't seem to notice.

Valene let out a howl and kicked Carlotta right in the shin, but that didn't slow the other woman down. She grabbed Valene's left arm with one hand and raked her nails down Valene's skin with the other.

My mouth had gone dry. I snapped it shut. Just how long had it been hanging open? But the spectacle we were seeing was almost too horrible to watch. Valene could be whiny and annoying but at least to me, she'd always seemed mild-mannered and harmless. Apparently, given the current circumstances, that had all changed.

Carlotta and Valene continued to claw and hiss at each other for another few seconds, then both jumped, acting startled at the same moment. An older woman had approached the counter, a book in her hand. She placed the book down, took one look at the appearance of the two women, and marched off in a huff.

"That was Mrs. Ferguson," said Jillian. "One of our most loyal patrons. What if she never comes back now? Or she starts spreading bad things about the library all over town?"

I patted Jillian's shoulder. "I'm sure she'll come back. She loves seeing you. You know that." I wouldn't comment on Mrs. Ferguson spreading rumors, because I didn't know her that well. Hopefully, she would keep it to herself. Although I had to admit, something like that would be hard to keep a secret, especially in a small town where everyone's business seemed to be fair game.

Jillian nodded. "True. She does seem to like me. But why couldn't I have been here yesterday? Why couldn't my day off have been at a different part of the week? Maybe I could have prevented the whole thing from happening."

I looked at the phone again. "I don't know, Jillian. It looked like a good old-fashioned cat fight. Both of them appeared mad enough to kill each other."

Kill each other.

Dead silence followed. All three of us widened our eyes at the same time. Carlotta had been murdered. Would it be a stretch to wonder if Valene had anything to do with that?

"Hey." Jillian's eyebrows lowered as she checked her watch. "I got so distracted watching the video of Valene, I just realized she's supposed to be here at work by now."

Nellie stuck the phone into her pocket. "I don't know about that, but wanted you to see the video. Listen, I have to get to work, so I need to run."

"Thanks," said Jillian. "You were right. I needed to see that."

Nellie waved goodbye to Jillian and nodded to me, then headed toward the door.

Once she'd left the library, Jillian turned to look at me. "What in the world just happened? I can hardly believe that was my assistant acting that way. I'm appalled. And here in the library of all places. It's embarrassing and inappropriate and…" She waved her arms, like she'd run out of words but still needed to express herself.

"I know. Maybe you should call and check on Valene? I realize that video looked awful. But maybe…" I held up my hands in the I don't know sign. "Sometimes there's a different explanation from what we've been given."

"What? You think it wasn't as bad as it looked?"

I bit down on my lip for a second, trying to decide how to answer. "Uh…"

She waved away my muttering. "Never mind. There's no way there was anything positive about what we saw."

"Sorry, but I think you're right."

Jillian checked around the library. Nobody was anywhere near us. She walked to her desk behind the counter, picked up her phone, and dialed. She rolled her eyes as she waited, then shook her head. "Valene's not answering. Where do you suppose she could be when she's supposed to be here?"

"Maybe send her a text?"

"Yeah, good idea." She tapped in a message, then waited. A few seconds later, her phone buzzed. "It's from her." She read it, her eyebrows getting lower and lower.

"What did she say?" I leaned forward, propping my elbows on the tall counter.

Jillian walked toward me as she read her text. "Valene says she isn't coming into work today. She doesn't feel well. And has a rash on her face. And arms. A rash? I don't think so."

"Huh. Well, if we hadn't watched the video, I guess that would be believable."

She blew out a breath. "Yeah, but we do know differently."

"What are you going to do?"

"I'm not sure. But one thing I know. I wasn't kidding when I told Nellie you were great at figuring out answers to problems. I'm going to need your help. Are you up for that?"

"For you? Anytime."

"Thank you. That means more to me than blueberry tarts, even though they were delicious." She winked.

Chapter Four

The next morning, my first client was Mrs. Kelper's cat, Cleo. I was in my mobile grooming van, a good place to be when I was on the hunt for information. People were sometimes willing to talk more about things they'd heard when I met them on their home turf.

As I pulled my mobile grooming van onto the street in front of her house, a memory hit me of the first time Percival had run away from me. He'd seen something that sparked his interest after I had groomed Mrs. Kelper's cat, and had leaped from the back of the van to investigate.

It had taken me quite a bit of time crawling around behind bushes to catch him, but in the end, it had allowed me to witness an important encounter that helped solve a previous murder. Unfortunately, because Mrs. Kelper had come back outside when she noticed my van still there, back door open, and my purse sitting inside, she'd called the sheriff. It hadn't been pretty, but we got through it.

Jasper and Percival were sitting in their usual place on the passenger seat, peering through the window. I wondered if Percival remembered running away from me here. Even if he did, I hoped he wouldn't do it again. Ever. A cat mom could only take so much stress.

Once I was at the back of the van and had lowered the stairs, Mrs. Kelper walked down her front steps, carrying Cleo over her shoulder like the cat was an infant. I smiled. I did that all the time with my two, and sometimes also cuddled kitty clients that way if they were apprehensive or nervous about their appointments.

Mrs. Kelper reached my van. "Hello, Molly." She peered up into the van.

"And I see Jasper and Percival are here today as well." She grinned as she turned Cleo around, then moved her cat's tiny paw in a hello to my kitties.

It was then I noticed her cat was wearing an apron. It was white with a red ruffle around the edges, and in red embroidered lettering said, *My Mom Won Again!*

My eyebrows rose. The apron was very cute, but I'd never seen that sentiment before. Usually, Mrs. Kelper's creations said something more like, *Meow is Your day Going?* or *I Purr for Belly Rubs.*

"I see you've noticed Cleo's newest outfit." She grinned.

My gaze snapped up to her face. "Yes, very cute. Did you make it?" I reached out to touch the red ruffle, always amazed at the superior workmanship that Mrs. Kelper's sewing projects produced.

"Why of course, dear. I make all of Cleo's outfits. As well as my own." She handed her to me, then did a little twirl in the long sundress she wore, which, I now noticed, was also white with red trim.

"You do an amazing job with sewing." I wondered what would happen if I matched up Mrs. Kelper's sewing skills with Florence and Lottie's need for so many kitty outfits for Helga and Eleanor.

She beamed. "Thank you very much. I do so enjoy it."

As I held Cleo against my chest with one arm, I reached up and tapped the words on the kitty's apron. "Did you recently win an award for something you sewed?"

She waved her hand. "No, dear. Well, I mean yes, I've won in the past. Of course."

Of course? She certainly had no problem with self-esteem. I nodded, encouraging her to go on.

She watched me for a minute. "Have you, by any chance, ever experienced Kelper-doodles?"

I opened my mouth to speak, then closed it. What the heck were Kelper-doodles? It sounded like either a type of puppy, or maybe a kid's artwork? "Um....not sure."

"Oh, Molly, if you'd ever experienced one, you wouldn't forget. Believe me. They are to die for."

I inwardly cringed at the word die so soon after Carlotta's murder. "Ah, okay. I guess…I never have experienced it."

She made a tsking sound. "Such a shame. I shall have to remedy that situation very soon."

Not sure what I was getting myself into, I said, "Um, sure, yeah, that would be great." As much as I liked dogs, I kind of hoped Mrs. Kelper wouldn't bring one into Fabulous Felines. The feline clients might not appreciate it. And I doubted the dog would either. That is, if that's what a Kelper-doodle happened to be. Was she going to tell me, or was I supposed to guess?

She pressed her finger to her chin. "As a matter of fact, if you'll wait right here, I'll bring one out for you."

I nodded, but tried not to panic. I glanced down at Cleo in my arms, then at my two cats who were now sitting at the top of the steps to my van, whiskers twitching in anticipation. If it were indeed a puppy, how would the cats react?

Deciding it might be better if all three cats were safely in the van for this, I held Cleo under one arm and climbed the short steps to the grooming area with the other. Once inside, I placed her on the towel beside the sink, ready to start her bath.

Footsteps approached. Was it Mrs. Kelper already? That was fast.

But a head popped around the corner, startling me. I yelped and clutched at my chest. "Oh, hi Ricky." Ricky Notts was Whitewater Valley's postman. Some people liked to use the term inept when describing Ricky's abilities to deliver the mail correctly. I tried to use the word unique instead. I liked Ricky. I really did. He just… well, he took a lot of patience to be around.

"Hey, there, Miss Molly. What 'cha doin?"

I glanced around. Considering I was in my mobile grooming van and had three cats sitting close by, I would have thought it was obvious. However, that kind of logic didn't always work with Ricky. "I'm getting ready to groom Mrs. Kelper's cat."

He chuckled. "That's fabulous. Good for you."

"Um, thanks." I glanced toward the front porch of Mrs. Kelper's house. Where was she, anyway? Whatever it was she was going to spring on me, I'd rather get the experience over with.

Ricky jostled the mailbag hanging from his shoulder. "Even though you didn't ask me what I was doing, I'll go ahead and tell you. I'm delivering the mail!"

"You know what? That would have been my guess."

"Really? You're smart, Molly."

"Thank you."

His eyebrows rose. "Hey, did you happen to hear about the body found between those old ladies' houses?"

I stared at him. First, I didn't think they'd appreciate being called old ladies, and second, if he knew about the murder, wouldn't he have also heard that I'd been there when Carlotta's body had been discovered?

He set down his mailbag, never a good sign because it meant he was ready to gab, and narrowed his eyes. "Say, didn't I also hear you'd been at the old ladies' places when the body of that crone had been found?"

Carlotta hadn't been a pleasant person, but to call her a crone now that she was dead seemed over the top. "Well, I…"

"Molly!"

I whipped around, glad to see Mrs. Kelper had returned. And that she didn't have a dog with her. Just a medium-sized, lid-covered bowl. Unless the puppy was in there? Surely not…

Ricky gave an exaggerated wave to Mrs. Kelper, which encompassed his entire arm. The movement looked a little painful. When she spotted him, she blinked, then gave him a head nod in return greeting.

When Mrs. Kelper reached me, she held out the bowl toward me. "Go ahead, don't be shy."

"Hey," said Ricky, walking closer to the back of the van. "What-cha got there?"

I opened my mouth to speak, then closed it. Since I didn't know exactly what I was holding, what could I say?

"Hello, Mr. Notts," said Mrs. Kelper.

"It's Ricky," he said. "Only my mother calls me Mr. Notts."

I widened my eyes. His own mother called him Mr.?

"Fine, um, Ricky," she said. "What I just proudly presented to Molly were some of my Kelper-doodles."

He tilted his head. "A what?"

"Cookies, Ricky."

I let out a breath, relieved that was all I was holding in the container. Although, to be fair, if it were a puppy, it would have jumped around in there. The cookies hadn't budged.

"Oh," said Ricky, nodding. "I know about those. All about them."

I stared at him. "You do?"

"Yup. Well, better go. See you ladies later." He winked, then picked up his mailbag and whistled off-key as he headed down the sidewalk. At least he didn't stay for two hours talking like he'd been known to do before. I'd take that as a win.

But what did he mean when he said he knew all about those? Her Kelper-doodles, or just cookies in general? And why had he winked? Was that code for something? Should I be worried?

"Well, shoot," mumbled Mrs. Kelper.

I turned toward her. "What's wrong?"

"Mr., er, I mean Ricky, forgot to leave me my mail."

That wasn't unusual for him. "Want me to run after him?"

She glanced in his direction. He was already halfway up the street. There was no way he'd delivered mail to the several houses he would have passed on his way. Would anyone get deliveries today on this block?

"Never mind." She flapped her hand. "I know you have a schedule to keep and you haven't even begun to groom Cleo yet." She crossed her arms and studied me, as if I were somehow negligent.

She was right about my schedule. But waiting on her to bring out her Kelper-doodles had been the holdup. While it was true I could have gone ahead and started with Cleo, the thought that a puppy might soon be joining the three cats in the van had made me pause. Or paws? *No, Molly, don't start that. Giggling right now at your stupid imagination will only make things more tense with Mrs. Kelper.*

"You're right," I said. "Let me get started right away."

Her face fell like that of a toddler who'd be getting a nap instead of ice cream. "Before you try one of my cookies? They did win an award, you know." She pointed to her cat.

It took me a second to understand why. Oh, right, the slogan on the apron. That's what Mrs. Kelper had won.

"While I do have several first-place ribbons for sewing projects at the county fair, the one I'm most proud of is my baking skills."

Reluctant to upset her even further, I obliged her by opening the container and choosing a Kelper-doodle. I had to admit, it did look yummy. One bite told me all I needed to know. It was indeed delicious. "Wow, I can see why you won a prize for these."

She held up her pointer finger. "Not any prize, mind you. First prize."

"Congratulations."

"Thank you. Lucky for me, everything worked out."

"Worked out?"

She waved her hand. "Never you mind. You have work to do."

I glanced down at the container. There were still at least a dozen baked delights left inside. "Don't you want your cookies back?"

"You keep them dear. I have more in the house. I can collect the container some other time."

"That's really nice, thanks."

"You're welcome. I need to run back to my kitchen and check on another batch. Give me a shout when Cleo's grooming is complete, will you?"

"Sure thing." Reluctantly, I set aside the container, making sure the lid was on tight. Cookies weren't on Percival or Jasper's menu, but the way they gazed longingly at them, I was sure they would have made an exception. And I wasn't sure if Cleo had a liking for the cookies, if maybe her mom ever gave her a taste.

With Jasper and Percival expertly supervising, I bathed Cleo, then clipped her claws before tying a yellow ribbon around her neck. I always did that as an extra fancy touch for the recently groomed cats.

I knew that lots of pet parents removed the ribbons and replaced it with the cats' collars once again as soon as they got their cats home. But that was okay. I felt the ribbons showed I cared. Plus, it gave the kitties something to play with later in the day if they got bored. When I got the ribbons ready before each appointment, I had to watch to make sure Percival and Jasper didn't run off with the whole spool. It'd happened before.

"Okay, guys, I'm taking Cleo back to her mom. I'll be right back. Stay here."

Jasper's eyes were round and guileless as he looked at me with an expression of innocence. Percival, however, refused to make eye contact and instead began washing his front paw.

I picked up Cleo, pressed her against my chest, and left the van. When I reached Mrs. Kelper's door, I knocked. A few seconds later, she opened the door and reached out for her baby. "Thank you, dear. She looks as wonderful as always." Then, she narrowed her eyes at me.

I checked out Cleo. Her fur wasn't messy looking, and she seemed content. "Is something wrong?"

"I thought maybe you'd return my Kelper-doodle container. I do need it back, you know."

Hadn't she just told me a bit ago to keep it and she'd collect it later? "Uh, sure. Let me just run and get it for you." I turned and headed down the walkway. I was nearly to the driveway when I heard her mutter, "Do something nice for a person and see where it gets you."

Good grief. Now I was sorry I'd ever accepted the cookies if it was going to be so much trouble for her. When I got to the van, my cats were checking out that very container.

"No, you don't." I climbed the steps, then hurriedly found a spare sack not in use and emptied the cookies inside. I didn't want to hurt her feelings in case I took it back still full, and have her think I hadn't liked them. Plus, I really wanted to eat more of them. They were amazing.

I grabbed the container, rushed down the steps, and trotted back up the walkway. Mrs. Kelper still stood in her doorway, holding Cleo. Her eyebrows were lowered in a frown. Now what? Did she think I hadn't moved fast enough?

Once at the doorway, I held out the container. "Thanks again for the cookies. They're delicious."

"You're welcome. You have a nice day, now." As she closed the door, I heard her say, "Cleo, can you believe Molly ate all those cookies in one sitting? Some people have no self-control."

With a groan, I headed back to my van. Mrs. Kelper was known to tell people things she found interesting about others, especially if it was something embarrassing. I closed the back of the van, made sure the cats had returned to their spot in the front passenger seat, and got in to head to my next appointment.

As I drove, I realized what had been bothering me during Cleo's grooming appointment. And it wasn't just Mrs. Kelper demanding back the container sooner than she'd originally said. What had she meant when she'd said things had worked out for her? Had something happened at the county fair that had allowed her to win when she might have otherwise lost?

Chapter Five

Later that afternoon, I had just finished grooming Essie Frame's cat, Cleopatra, and said goodbye to them, when the door opened again. It was Sunny Wether—yes, her real name—the accountant and receptionist for Second Hand Books, run by Jed Martin.

Sunny was all business with zero sense of humor. When I'd first met her, I'd tried to joke around with her, and was rewarded with a frown and crossed arms. With a name like Sunny Wether, I would have thought she'd be very used to kidding by now, but apparently not.

Not everybody had my weird sense of humor. But maybe that was for the best, since it did tend to get away from me at times and cause me trouble. Plus, it gave my boyfriend, Hank, additional chances to tease me, as if he needed more. Me, just living my life, seemed to provide people with laughter, usually at my expense. But everybody had to be good at something, right?

"Hi Sunny, how are you today?"

She approached the counter, arms hanging stiffly at her sides, her movements appearing more mechanical than natural. "I am well. Thank you, Molly."

Since Sunny worked for Jed, and he'd previously been married to Carlotta, would Sunny have heard anything useful about the recently deceased?

Just then, Veronica, my assistant, came from her grooming room and joined me behind the counter. "Hello, Sunny. How is the weather today?" She gave her a wide grin.

Apparently, Veronica still hadn't gotten the memo about Sunny's lack of amusement, or had tried to ignore it. I'd clued her in, but whenever she saw

Sunny, she couldn't seem to help ribbing her about her name. I'd always wanted to ask Sunny if she had family members named Stormy, Rainy, and Windy, but soon learned that would get me nowhere but scowled at.

She blinked at Veronica, then glanced over her shoulder. "It's a beautiful day. But then, you can see it for yourself if you look out your large front window." Her brow furrowed, confusion marring her pretty face.

Veronica's smile fell. "Huh. Well, yes, that's true."

Wanting to rescue my assistant from her most recent faux pas, I faced Sunny. "How can we help you today?"

She reached into her pocket. "I've brought over a check from Jed Martin for his cat, Regis', grooming."

I nodded and took the check she held out. Most people paid by credit card, but Sunny didn't think that payment method was a trustworthy way to go. Jed had tried to tell her it was all right to use them, but she'd refused. And because he'd needed a receptionist and accountant since his wife had moved out, and it used to be her job, along with being a nail technician, Jed tried to keep Sunny happy so she wouldn't leave him high and dry. But she was so odd. Did Jed have trouble dealing with that?

Veronica leaned against the counter. "How is Jed doing, anyway?"

Sunny shook her head sadly. "Not very well, I'm afraid. Even though he and Carlotta had separated and were heading toward a divorce, Jed took it hard when she died."

"That must be really hard for him," I said. "I'm so sorry he's going through this."

"Of course you're sorry." Sunny tilted her head to the side. "Why wouldn't you be? Any sane person would feel bad for Jed, would they not?"

Veronica and I gave each other a quick side-eye as she proceeded to write out a receipt for Jed's check. I was sure my assistant just wanted something to do other than to be scolded by Sunny again. I didn't blame her.

"Um, just thought I'd…" I shrugged.

Leave it to Sunny to misunderstand one person expressing concern for another. Wasn't that what most people did? Try to be understanding and sympathetic? But maybe she didn't possess those attributes. Or if she did, they were buried somewhere deep in her strange little humorless heart. I was of the opinion that she didn't know any different. That it was just her nature. Veronica, however, totally disagreed with my assessment.

I was saved from having to say more when Veronica gave Sunny the receipt. "There you go. You can always mail in payments, if you'd like. It would save you from having to come here every time Regis has a grooming."

Sunny's silver earrings glinted in the overhead lights as she shook her head. "No. It's more professional to bring it to you in person and physically place it in your hands. That way, I know it won't get lost in the mail and it won't keep me up at night worrying about where it might have ended up."

I had to agree that Sunny did have a point. With Ricky Notts in charge of making sure everyone got their deliveries on time, which they normally didn't, it did make sense to take matters into their own hands if the intended parcel was at all important.

"I appreciate that, Sunny." I smiled. "Thank you."

She bobbed her head. "You are quite welcome. Sometimes, I feel it's necessary to tell people how they should be doing things. It's only right. I mean, if I know a better way, it's my responsibility to pass that information along. It's for the greater good." She pressed her hands primly together in front of her chest. "People don't always know what's good for them. Sometimes they do things they shouldn't." She glanced away, as if embarrassed or upset.

Veronica tapped her fingers in a rapid beat on the counter, a sure sign she was getting antsy for Sunny to leave. My assistant preferred being around people who didn't make her feel as if she was being judged or lectured. No one really cared for that. However, Veronica's fuse was generally shorter than mine . Still, she should be used to Sunny's way of expressing herself by now.

I covered Veronica's fingers with my hand, stopping her rat-a-tat tapping. "Thank you, Sunny, for your advice. We appreciate it. Don't we, Veronica?"

My assistant mumbled something that sounded like, "Yeah, okay, I guess." I wasn't exactly sure if it was that, or something my grandmother wouldn't approve of, but I'd take what I could get.

Sunny pushed some of her shoulder-length dark hair behind her ears. "Anyway, back to speaking about Jed Martin."

I was glad she wanted to say more about her boss. And she liked to discuss what was on her mind, so it was best to just let her go on. Veronica blew out a loud breath but didn't say anything further. At least her fingers stayed still.

"Sure, go on, Sunny." I gave the clock on the wall behind her a peek. My next client was due soon and didn't like to be kept waiting. Maybe Sunny would get whatever she wanted to say off her chest quickly so I could hear what was going on, but still not be late for my grooming appointment.

"You see, Jed and Carlotta were in a legal battle over the house they'd shared." She frowned. "I guess it will be his now that she's gone?"

I nodded. "Yeah, that might be right. I hadn't thought about it until now."

Veronica's fingers started to drum on the counter again. I'd moved my hand away, but when I gave her a quick shake of my head, she sighed and stopped.

Sunny glanced at the ceiling, eyebrows lowered as if in deep thought. "You know, Jed hadn't liked Carlotta all that well."

"I guess that might be normal since they were separated and all," I said.

She waved her hand. "Oh, no. From what I've heard since I started to work at the bookstore, it goes way back."

Veronica stood up straighter, seeming to be interested now. "Is that right?"

"Yes, that's right. That's why I said it. You should show more respect when another person is speaking." Her eyes narrowed to slits. "

I gasped. This wouldn't end well if Veronica couldn't hold in what she'd inevitably want to say. Not that I'd blame her. Not only was Sunny all business, she appeared to have a testy side, too.

I gave Veronica another quick headshake, hoping to forestall any more finger tapping or possible future glares in Sunny's direction. I looked at Sunny. She might not have had a humorous bone in her body, but I'd discovered that she liked to talk. And usually about other people. With Carlotta having been Jed's ex-wife, maybe Sunny would have some insight into Carlotta's past.

I clasped my hands together on top of the counter. "What did you happen to hear about Jed and Carlotta?"

"It's quite the story, let me tell you." She moved closer to the counter, as if ready to give us all the facts.

The next thirty seconds were silent, except for the ticking of the wall clock and a couple of meows from cats waiting in their carriers to be picked up by their pet parents. I waited, but Sunny didn't say more.

Unable to stand the silence, Veronica waved her hand in front of the other woman. "What did you want to tell us?"

Sunny placed the receipt Veronica had given her into a pocket of her purse, laid the purse on the counter, looked first at Veronica, then at me. "Apparently, Jed and Carlotta hadn't been happy with each other since right after they got married. I happen to know that she was a terrible person. I'm not sure how he put up with her as long as he did."

"That's awful they weren't happy." What a letdown to marry someone, have such high hopes for your future, only to discover it was all a big mistake. Hank's handsome face crossed my mind. Would he and I ever get to that point?

Veronica nodded in agreement with my comment. I'd never been married, but Veronica had married a terrific guy, and they were over the moon for each other. I'd never seen her so happy as the day she'd married Jerome. No, she actually seemed happier every day since. Surely that was a sign of marrying the perfect person.

"Yes, it is awful," said Sunny. "After they split up and Carlotta quit working at the shop, which is why I got the job, of course..."

"Of course." I silently willed her to continue.

"...Jed would sit in his office and talk to other people on his cell phone. He never shut the door, so I could hear everything. He said some things about Carlotta....well, let's just say, the terms he used weren't flattering. If a customer came in, I'd go over and pull the door closed so they wouldn't overhear him. Because, you know, it's not polite to eavesdrop."

My eyebrows rose. Didn't she realize that's what she was doing every time she listened to Jed? Not that I could judge. I'd actually become quite adept at it since helping to solve two previous murders. It did come in handy. Not that it was a good thing to do under normal circumstances.

Next to me, Veronica glanced past Sunny's shoulder toward the front window, then sighed. "Kimmy is here with Arnie. I'll need to get back to work."

When Sunny turned to watch Kimmy come in, Veronica took the opportunity to whisper to me, "Fill me in on what I missed, okay? This sounds interesting."

"You got it." She was right. Any information having to do with Carlotta piqued my interest, too.

Veronica waved at Kimmy and Arnie and motioned them to follow her into her grooming room. I checked the clock again. My grooming client would be here any second. But I didn't want to miss out on anything Sunny might tell me, for my own curiosity and for Veronica's.

"Has Jed said anything else since Carlotta died?"

Her eyebrows lowered. "Even though they're split up, he still has to take care of the funeral arrangements, since she only had a few family members, who've understandably chosen not to be involved."

"Well, I meant more along the lines of their relationship. Has Jed talked anymore about that?"

She narrowed her eyes in concentration. "The fight over the house was the biggest deal. Jed is living in it now, but wants to sell it. He'd wanted to get rid of it right after they split, but then she died, so now he has her final arrangements to complete first, and the house will have to wait. Also, Carlotta had threatened to get a lawyer and sue Jed because he wanted her to get her own representation for when they went to court over proceeds from the house."

"That sounds complicated."

She tilted her head. "It seemed counterproductive to me for her to get a lawyer to sue him when he wanted her to get one for another reason in the first place." She shrugged. "But what would I know? I've never been married." Her eyes widened as she focused on me. "Wait, didn't I hear something about you and Dr. Chenoweth tying the knot?"

"Nope. All gossip and hearsay. See?" I held out my hand. "No ring."

Her hands settled on her hips. "Then you might want to tell that postal worker, Ricky, to stop telling everyone you're trying to make your honeymoon sparkle. It's no wonder people think you're married, Molly."

"Yeah, I'll be sure to tell him." I gritted my teeth together. I'd told Ricky so many times that it wasn't true that I'd gotten married and that his seeing me holding a book, How to Make Your Honeymoon Sparkle, hadn't meant anything. But he still insisted on spreading the happy news.

Sunny tapped the counter. "Want to know what I think about Jed and Carlotta?"

I waited, hoping she'd say something important, something that would tell me whether or not her boss seemed guilty.

"It is my personal opinion that Jed killed Carlotta."

I jerked. Sunny didn't waste words when she wanted to get a point across. Just as I was ready to reply, the door opened and my client and her cat came in. I waved to them.

There wouldn't be an easy way to continue our conversation now. My client would cause a fuss if she had to wait. And her cat would start hissing. Not a good scenario either way.

"Well, I better get back to work, Sunny. Thanks so much for bringing in the check." And for the information, I added silently. Was Sunny's opinion right? With Jed and Carlotta at such odds when they split up, would it have been frustrating enough for Jed to have murdered his former wife?

Chapter Six

Early the next morning, I met Hank, Jillian, and Evan Lakes at Carrie's Coffees. The four of us tried to meet at least once a month here, but didn't always make it. Thankfully, today worked out, because we wanted to brainstorm about possible murder suspects. Four heads were better than one.

We chose a table near the back of the café, wanting a little privacy, even though there were only a couple of other people around. But I knew that more customers would arrive soon. Carrie's place was super popular and never stayed quiet for long.

With our jobs—me, a cat groomer, Jillian, a librarian, Hank, a veterinarian, and Evan, a photographer—we all came in contact with lots of people, and in my and Hank's case, animals, every day. It was a rare treat to sit down and spend time with just each other and to catch up on what we'd all been doing.

Evan quickly snagged the seat next to Jillian's, leaving Hank and me to sit on the other side of the table, which worked out quite nicely. I couldn't have planned it better. Hank gave me a wink. He must have thought the same thing. He touched my hand beneath the table and gave it a light squeeze.

The door opened, and seven people came in together. It wouldn't be long before more came in, disturbing the quiet. Sometimes in Fabulous Felines, it was a toss-up between who was louder, the cats or their humans. But customers showing up was what paid the bills. And as a small business owner, that was most important.

Carrie, the café owner, stopped by and dropped off some menus, gave us each glasses of water, and headed across the café to take another table's order.

Jillian perused the menu, turning to the different pages. Then she flipped back to page one again, her brow creased, as she seemed intent on making a momentous decision.

Laughing, I pointed to the menu. "Hey, do you think you're fooling anybody?"

She glanced up. "What do you mean?"

"My dear friend, you order the exact same thing every single time. And it's the same thing I bring to you when I visit the library. You never waver from it, or even talk about ordering anything different. I have no doubt what you're going to get here today."

She nodded. "True. But I like to give Carrie and Zelma the impression that I'm carefully considering my options, and that I appreciate their efforts in taking and preparing my order. You know what it's like to have a customer or patron who makes you feel good about what you do for a living. It makes your whole day."

I wholeheartedly agreed. "You're right. And you are thoughtful about things like that."

Evan leaned closer to Jillian. "She's always thoughtful. About everything." The way he gazed at my friend left no doubt as to how he felt about her. Not that any of us had any doubts about it. Still, Jillian's cheeks blazed red, as she made eye contact with him. Then Evan's face turned a dark shade of pink. Those two were adorable.

Hank caught my gaze and rolled his eyes, but he was grinning. He and I were dating, but had fun teasing the other two since their relationship was so shiny and new. I was so happy for Jillian and Evan. I couldn't think of two nicer people. Except maybe, Hank.

Carrie approached and stopped at our table. "Hey all. Good to see you. How is everyone today?"

"We're fine," Jillian answered for all of us. As a head librarian, she was used to being in charge and telling people what they needed to do. When she was in that mode, I usually let her go forward, taking control. It was easier than being on the receiving end of her librarian scowl, or the shushing noise when she wanted me to be quiet. She held up the menu and pointed to the blueberry tarts. "I'll take two of those and a caramel latte, please."

Carrie nodded, then smiled. She had to know that Jillian got that exact same order time after time. But she didn't tease her about it like I did. I guess that was reserved for me, as her best friend.

I ordered the same, except I wanted coffee with cream, while the guys each got jelly donuts and black coffee.

The front door squeaked open, and Trixie came in. Her smile was wide, and she hummed a tune I couldn't quite place. Then, she moved her feet in a kind of happy little tap dance. Since the café was still quiet this early in the day, her actions were noticeable. The few other patrons turned to stare, whispering to each other, and a couple of them laughing out loud.

Jillian turned to me with her eyebrows raised. I shook my head and shrugged, because Trixie wasn't usually the smiley, hummy, tappy kind of girl. While I was glad to see she appeared to be in a good mood, it sure was different than other times I'd been around her. Before, she'd been a little grumpy and bossy, with nervousness thrown into the mix. Not a real pleasing combination.

But the dancing seemed way out of her normal behavior. Maybe she found a new boyfriend. Or won the lottery. Those would both be dance-worthy. I watched her for a few seconds. Well, maybe, if she was a better dancer. But I couldn't really judge anyone on that, since my best dance move was trying not to fall on my backside.

Carrie had turned toward the front entrance as well. We all watched as Trixie danced her way to the order counter, where Zelma, Carrie's assistant, her eyes opened wide, took Trixie's order as they chatted.

"That was…interesting," said Hank.

Carrie nodded. "I thought so too. She sure does look different now."

"What do you mean? She looks the same to me." I studied Trixie again, thinking maybe I'd missed a new haircut or tons more makeup than she normally wore. And I was certain I'd seen her in those red pants and the blue and white top before.

Carrie stuck her order pad and pen back into her apron pocket, something

I'd seen her do before when she wanted to talk with customers. With her being around most everybody in town at one time or another, she would be a good source of news. "Then, I guess you haven't seen her lately?"

I thought about it. "Um, no. It's probably been a few weeks. She doesn't come into Fabulous Felines since she's not a pet owner. And I don't go to the nail salon since I don't get my nails done."

Jillian snickered. "Except for that one time."

I glared at my friend, which only made her laugh harder.

"What one time?" asked Evan, glancing back and forth between us.

Hank's eyebrows rose in interest. "Yeah, I've never seen you with fancy nails before. I always figured it was because you might mess them up when you do cat groomings. So, you used to have them worked on?"

"Worked on?" Jillian giggled. "You make it sound like she hired someone to replace her roofing shingles using ladders and hammers. Do you mean she had her nails *done?*" She held out her hand, showing off her perfectly groomed, filed, and polished pink fingernails.

"How would I know?" Hank clutched at his shirt collar as if suddenly having trouble breathing. "That's not something I normally do."

"I'm glad to hear that." I brushed my elbow against his. After a glance toward Trixie to see that she was still at the order counter, tapping her feet to some silent rhythm, I leaned closer and kept my voice low. "Since Jillian seems to want to embarrass me by telling the story, I might as well get it over with. What happened was, during one of Whitewater Valley's previous murders, I'd suspected a client who'd gone into the salon of possibly murdering the victim." I paused, feeling silly about what happened. It hadn't been one of my finer moments.

Jillian moved her hand in a circle, wanting me to continue. Why did she have to bring it up? Her expression said she was delighted at the turn of the conversation that would put me on the spot.

I frowned at her. "Anyway, I went in there, just to uh, maybe overhear something and..."

"You mean eavesdrop?" asked Evan.

"Yeah, okay. So, I thought I could just hang around, maybe find something out."

"What happened?" asked Hank. "Did you get caught?"

"What happened was *her*." I pointed to Trixie, who was now doing a sort of shuffle, like a dance move out of the seventies.

"What do you mean?" asked Carrie, who now seemed as immersed in my story as the others.

"When I was standing in the shop, hoping to just listen for a bit, Trixie discovered me trying to crouch behind a wall partition and…" I really hated to continue the story. It was embarrassing at best.

"She was trying to hide from Trixie," added Jillian helpfully.

"Yes. That's correct, Jillian." I gave her a narrowed-eye look, which caused her to snort. "Anyway," I went on, "Trixie insisted that if I was there, I had to get my nails done, or leave the salon. I could tell right then and there that I'd have to have the deed done if I had even the slightest chance of overhearing"—I glanced at Evan—"um, eavesdropping on the woman I'd suspected."

"Ah." Hank nodded. "That explains why you had your fingernails worked on, I mean done." He eyed Jillian, and she gave him a nod of approval.

I placed my palms down on the table, just wanting to get the sordid tale out and done with. "So what happened was, I sat in the chair right next to the person I'd hoped to listen to."

Carrie shuffled next to me. "Wasn't that a good thing? What happened after that?"

"Yes, that part was a plus, but Trixie was brand new at the job and…" I let out a low groan, remembering the awfulness that was my first experience in a nail salon. I still couldn't believe I'd gone through that, and had to pay a lot of money for the experience.

"I saw the end result." Jillian tapped the table lightly with her perfect nail. "Believe me, it was horrid. Blindingly bright colors, chipped edges, torn cuticles, and I'm pretty sure there were flags involved." She shivered as if a huge spider had just run across the back of her hand.

"Right." I glanced at her. "I forgot about the flags. At least it was the Indiana State Flag, so it wasn't in bad taste."

Jillian sat up straighter. "While I greatly admire our state flag, in my opinion, it doesn't belong on painted fingernails, which should be a work of art."

I glanced over my shoulder. "Oh, sorry, Carrie. I trampled over whatever you were going to ask earlier about…" I pointed my thumb in Trixie's direction.

"No problem." She smiled. "But I did want to mention that for the last few weeks, she's been coming in here looking totally different. Hair unwashed. Clothes stained and wrinkled. Looked like she'd worn the same ones for a week. She uh…didn't smell great, either. I think that at least a couple of people left the café before ordering, because of her unfortunate stench. I'm glad she got her act together, because smelly people aren't good for business, I'm sorry to say."

"Ick." Jillian wrinkled her nose. "I can't imagine how she would have been able to work on clients in that condition." She peeked over her shoulder. "But she looks fine now."

"Yeah, it's quite a reversal, I can tell you. Glad to see she seems like her old self again. Um, plus the added dance moves."

I gave Trixie another glance. She was indeed still dancing. Now it looked like she was doing the bunny hop. "Do you have any idea why she switched to looking that way, then back to normal?"

Carrie shook her head, then her eyes widened. "You know, come to think of it, the last time I saw her was right before Carlotta was killed. That's when Trixie looked her worst. I thought maybe she'd been sick or something. But she's back to her old self, well, appearance-wise anyway."

"And acting super happy," pointed out Jillian.

Hank nodded. "Yeah, just after Carlotta had been found murdered."

We all turned and stared at Trixie. What was the story there? There had to be one. And I was determined to find out.

Chapter Seven

We'd been slammed, not only with our scheduled kitty clients, but had two other pet parents bring in their cats, insisting today was their day for grooming appointments, even though they weren't due until next week. When that happened, we tried to accommodate them if we could, rather than have the pet parents storm off in a hissy fit. We get enough of those from the furry clients.

Normally, Franklin South wanted me to groom Werner, but since he could see how overrun the waiting area was, he consented to allow Veronica to groom his cat.

Veronica usually had no problem with clients wanting one of us over the other, but Franklin's caustic comments must have rubbed her the wrong way if her facial expression was any indication. But I knew that Veronica, no matter how she was feeling, would give that kitty her best, most gentle, loving grooming appointment.

So when the door opened for what seemed the hundredth time and the person coming in next was Ricky, I took a deep breath and let it out. Checking the time, I grumbled. If we were just now getting our mail, then Ricky was in an abnormally talkative mood, and that was really saying something. The man could talk a blade of grass to death. No really. I'd witnessed it.

"Hey Ricky." I gave a half-hearted wave. Not only was I worn out from the busy day, but I also knew the long-winded account of something I probably didn't give a rat's patootie about was headed my way.

"Hello yourself, Molly. And how are you this fine day?"

"I'm good."

"And how is your handsome husband?" he asked.

A couple of ladies turned my way with surprised expressions, but I shook my head and gave a laugh for their benefit, hoping they'd understand it wasn't true.

"Ricky," I said, "for the twentieth time, I'm not married."

"But you were reading that book in the library a while back. I saw you. About how to make your honeymoon sparkle. Why would you read something like that if you weren't ensconced in wedding bliss? Come on, you're pulling my foot, aren't you?"

I sighed. "No, I'm not pulling your…I'm not pulling anything. It was just a book I'd picked up. By mistake. I'm not married. To Hank or anyone else."

Even though the thought of possibly marrying Hank someday gave me warm fuzzies, we weren't anywhere near that stage.

His face fell. "Oh. Well, that's a shame. Maybe someday though?"

I raised my hands in the 'I don't know' stance. Because if I did anything else, said 'yeah, maybe,' Ricky would run with it and tell others I was engaged. Not that I would mind the reality of that happening either, but it still wouldn't be true.

He dropped his bag noisily on the floor, the loud thump causing a cat waiting in her carrier across the room to arch her back and hiss.

"Goodness." Ricky pointed toward the cat. "That poor thing must have terrible allergies. Did you hear it sneezing?"

I wanted to laugh, but was too tired to manage it. Something rustled next to me, and I jerked. Veronica had appeared, eyes wide, at Ricky's supposed cat allergy diagnosis. How long had she been there, and when had she snuck up on me?

"Hey, Ricky," she said, but her voice came out raspy. I was sure she was as tired as I was, and probably didn't have any remaining energy to listen to our postman for very long.

Veronica slumped partially against me while she braced her hands against the top of the counter. "How can we help you today?"

"I'm so glad you asked."

When he said that, he had a story to tell. What would it be about today? The time the main sewer got clogged down on Main Street, or maybe when his cousin's beard got caught in his harmonica while he played with a marching band?

With reluctance, I leaned against the counter next to Veronica, determined to do my best not to slide down to the floor. Because even that surface looked like an inviting place to nap right now.

As if Jasper and Percival knew my thoughts about naps, they jumped onto the counter, meowed at Ricky, then collapsed together in a tight ball of fur, whiskers, ears, and paws.

"Wow," said Ricky, "your cats sure are lazy. Is that all they do? Sleep?"

Jasper opened one eye, then reached out his paw to smack Ricky's hand.

Ricky's eyes widened, and he rubbed his hand. "Gosh, sorry little fella. I meant no disrespect."

Percival gave a low hiss, causing Ricky to jump. "Good grief, ladies. Another cat just sneezed. I think there's an epidemic of Feline Fluenza running amok in your shop." His eyes narrowed. "Hey, humans can't get Feline Fluenza, right?"

Veronica and I glanced at each other. But laughing still felt like too much use of energy right now.

"No, Ricky." I let out a sigh. "I'm one hundred percent certain that humans can't get Feline Fluenza." I waved my hand. "So what did you want to tell us when you came in?" I didn't have high hopes, but could he possibly know something that might give clues to who killed Carlotta? I forced myself to stand still and wait.

He glanced behind him. The two ladies who'd given us looks about my supposed wedding news had left the shop. "What I heard was this." He framed his hands together as if looking through a viewer lens. "Picture if you will, a woman, her lifespan, and her terrible, horrible, can't-be-believed postal habits."

I rolled my eyes. Couldn't help it. My patience was running out as fast as my energy. "And who might that woman be?"

"Why, Carlotta Sykes, of course."

For the first time in several hours, I felt a spark of energy run through my muscles and veins. This might be interesting if it concerned the recent murder victim. "Okay. Go on."

Veronica sighed, but remained quiet. She, too, would be interested in anything having to do with Carlotta. She nodded her head at Ricky, indicating he should go ahead and speak.

Ricky's smile was huge as he reached back and grabbed his ever-present ponytail. The one that Veronica and I always wondered was like a kid's security blanket for him. Icky but very possible. "Well, for starters, that Carlotta was a real menace."

"Oh?" I asked, as I stood up straighter and propped my forearms on the counter. Percival flipped over onto his back, giving me clear access to his soft, furry tummy. I gladly obliged. When Jasper opened his eyes and saw that his brother was getting attention, Veronica jumped to my rescue, petting Jasper's face and between his ears.

Ricky had let go of his ponytail, but it bobbed up and down as he nodded vigorously. "Yes. You see, Carlotta was what we in the mail community like to call postally irresponsible."

Even though I longed to remind Ricky that there were only three people working in our tiny post office, and that it hardly made it a community, I pressed my lips together and forced myself to stay quiet. Veronica's foot tapped out a quick, irritated beat on the floor, but she too kept quiet.

Ricky crossed his arms over his chest. "That Carlotta," he shook his head, "she was a real armful, that one."

Veronica whispered, "Doesn't he mean handful?"

I shrugged. With Ricky, it was sometimes hard to tell.

Several seconds passed, and Ricky didn't elaborate. Was this how it was going to be? He'd raced in here to tell us something important on a day when I was dragging so bad that even my hair felt tired, and then he just stood and looked at us?

"Listen," said Veronica, "you obviously had something, um, important to tell us today so...." Her eyebrows rose as she stared pointedly at Ricky.

He frowned. "What?" Then he blinked. "Oh, right."

She and I sighed at the same time. I really hoped Ricky's monologue today would be brief. But it wasn't starting out that way.

He leaned closer and stared at us, first Veronica, then me. "Anyway, Carlotta had the bad habit of trying to mail out her letters without putting stamps on them. Can you imagine?"

I could imagine, actually. There'd been times when I'd gotten in a hurry and had forgotten. Thankfully, those times had been when I'd dropped them off at the post office, and Edna Garing, another employee, had teasingly reminded me to put one on.

Veronica huffed out a breath. "Is that all?"

"No. There's more. She…" He glanced behind him again. Was he worried someone else had come in and would overhear? But it was the same cat who'd hissed—sneezed—at him earlier. He focused on us again. "Carlotta is messy."

"What do you mean?"

His face reddened. Was he embarrassed or angry? He leaned partway across the counter and whispered, "She bends her mail. When she puts it in the box. It. Has. Creases."

I assumed Ricky was looking for a huge reaction from us for his proclamation. I side-eyed Veronica, who shrugged. Then, we both let out gasps so loud, Jasper and Percival turned to stare at us. And Jasper hissed.

Ricky pointed to the cat. "I'm telling you. These cats have severe Fluenza. Are you certain I can't catch it from them?"

"Positive." I nodded. "All right, so Carlotta forgets stamps, puts creases in her envelopes…"

He nodded his head hard, making his ponytail land on his shoulder. "Yep, that's about the size of it."

Veronica held out her hand. "That's it? That's the whole big story you wanted to tell us?"

He jerked as if startled. "Well, gee. I thought it was important. And so did you. I mean, you both gasped and everything."

He had us there.

When the door opened again, it was Dodge Zaminski to pick up his cat,

Luther. I gave him a wave as he left, knowing he'd mail in his payment. And that he'd use a stamp. And wouldn't bend the envelope.

"Okay," I looked at my watch, "it's getting late, so…."

"But wait, there was one more tiny thing I wanted to mention."

If it was smaller in significance than Carlotta's mail issues, I wasn't sure I could stand the excitement. "Fine. And what's that?"

Veronica had crouched down below the counter to retrieve her purse. It was time to go home, and her sweet husband would have supper ready for her. Maybe I could see if Hank wanted to grab something to eat with me at the Sandwich Shack.

As Veronica handed me my purse, I caught sight of Ricky, who was glaring at us.

"What?" Veronica blinked. "Oh, right. The other small thing you wanted to tell us. Go ahead. We're listening." Although she was searching for something, probably her keys, in her purse, she didn't seem to be paying attention at all.

His sigh was so loud, Percival and Jasper's fur puffed out. They were tired too, even with the naps, and ready to go home as well.

"Here's the other thing about Carlotta." He placed both palms down on the counter. "I happened to be in the nail salon the day before Carlotta was found brutally murdered, when I went in to leave the mail. She was having a very loud argument with Dalen Sparks, the supply delivery guy. She yelled at him, saying over and over that she wanted him to bring her cat back. Dalen yelled back that he'd see Carlotta dead before giving her back the cat."

Dead? My ears perked up. "That sounds intense." I knew all too well that cats were our family. If Carlotta and Dalen each thought they deserved to keep it, I could envision a rowdy argument happening. If someone tried to take Percival and Jasper away from me, they'd have a serious fight on their hands.

Veronica turned toward me. "Do you suppose it was as simple as that? Maybe Dalen, absolutely furious at Carlotta about his pet, took matters into his hands, so to speak, so he could keep it for himself?"

Ricky appeared not to be listening to us as he muttered, "Why would the supply guy have Carlotta's cat? Had he stolen it? Or maybe he just borrowed it. But why would somebody borrow a cat? To play with? To give catnip to?" With a shake of his head, he looked at us. "Do you suppose those two knew each other well, or something?"

I shook my head, unsure how to answer.

He lifted his shoulders in a shrug. "Then to top it off, I nearly ran into that Sunny person who was standing outside the nail salon window, who by the way, isn't all that sunny. She brushed by me so fast, I dropped my mailbag. On my foot. Then, she had the nerve to hiss at me. Like a cat. It makes me wonder if she'd been spending a lot of time in here with your Fluenza felines."He then gave us a salute. "Well, you ladies have a nice day."

When I looked at Veronica, her mouth was hanging open. Then I realized mine was too. I snapped it closed. Ricky picked up his mailbag and left the shop.

I blinked. "What just happened here?"

"I think Ricky witnessed a possible motive for Carlotta's murder by Dalen Sparks." She glanced down at the counter, then groaned.

"What's wrong?"

"He was here for so long. And left."

"So?"

She waved her hand at the empty counter. "He didn't leave us our mail."

Chapter Eight

My workday ended unexpectedly early when my last client had to have an emergency root canal. The pet-mom, not the cat. I decided my own felines needed to get out and about. They were indoor kitties, but even though they went with me on mobile cat visits and hung out at Fabulous Felines during the day, I tried to get them out on a walk as often as I could. Jasper and Percival both now had on their harnesses.

I needed to get out, too. Someone in this town had ended Carlotta's life, and I was determined to find out who it was. Otherwise, poor Lottie and Florence might be arrested for a crime they didn't commit since the sheriff seemed dead-set on them being guilty. Putting those two older women in jail would be a terrible crime in itself.

Once I had my purse strap over my shoulder and the cats' leashes in my hands, we took off from my shop to take a stroll around the downtown area.

We passed several townspeople, some who smiled and waved, others who were pet parents, stopped to speak to us, and gave love to Percival and Jasper. My cats loved attention, and it didn't seem to matter who gave it to them. They were addicted to having their fur massaged and made no excuses for it.

When we'd walked another block, Carrie was in front of her café, sweeping the sidewalk. I said hello, and she waved back, adding in tiny finger waves for Jasper and Percival as well.

Next, I spotted Sunny, who stood across the street. I waved, but she didn't see me. She glanced at her watch, then looked over her shoulder at the nail salon. Was she waiting for an appointment? Come to think of it, Sunny always did have beautifully manicured nails. With a glance down at my own, I shook my head. Unlike mine.

A car slowed and pulled to the curb beside us. A loud honk startled not only me but my cats. And I'm pretty sure all three of us hissed. I turned, ready to frown at the rude person, when I saw it was the sheriff. I frowned anyway.

"Why did you honk at us? We're not breaking the law."

He glared at my cats. "Maybe it should be illegal. Walking those creatures on leashes? Ridiculous."

I narrowed my eyes at him and bent to pick up both cats who were still puffy from fright. "How can we help you, Sheriff?"

"I want nothing from those two." He pointed out the window.

I doubted my cats would ever want to help him out with anything either. "And from me?"

"Just keep your distance, Molly."

I glanced around. "From what? I'm just walking on the sidewalk. Public space, and all that."

"You know what I mean."

"Actually, I don't. And I have someplace to be so…." I didn't have a destination in mind, but he didn't need to know that. I'd make one up if I had to, just to make him stop bothering us.

"Listen, Molly. Twice now, you've gotten in my way and impeded my investigations into murders."

"There was no impeding. Quite the opposite. I"—with a glance at my cats, I amended what I was going to say—"We, Percival, Jasper, and I, were very helpful in finding not one, but two killers in the past. "

Jasper meowed loudly, as if lending me his affirmation.

"Now cut that you, you varmint." The sheriff's eyes widened.

I tapped my foot against the sidewalk. "Excuse me?"

"Not you." He pointed at my cat. "That creature."

"His name is Jasper. And you know that."

"Whatever. And while we're on the subject of murder, stay away from those two old ladies. They're suspects. Just mind your own business, Molly.

Or else."

I always figured that when a person ended a conversation with "or else," they weren't sure what they might threaten me with. Not that I was in any way threatened by Sheriff King. Just the opposite, in fact. The more he tried to boss me around and told me to stay out of things, the more I wanted to step right in and discover the killer's identity before he or she did it again.

He gunned his motor, startling us again. Percival's claws dug into my arm, as he struggled to get down. I placed both cats back on the sidewalk again, hoping they wouldn't stay upset for long. Kitties had sensitive ears, and loud noises might scare them silly for the rest of the day.

It wasn't the sheriff's fault that he didn't like cats. Everyone was different and had their own preferences. But there was no reason for him to be intentionally rude to them. I mean, I had no fondness for iguanas, but did he see me driving around town, honking my horn and gunning my motor to scare them and make their fur puff out?

I knew my analogy didn't make much sense, but it worked for me, so I was going to hang onto it. At least it gave my irritation a place to land when I thought about Sheriff King's rudeness.

Jasper stayed close beside me as we went on our way, jumping every time a vehicle drove by. Percival walked a little ahead of us, but kept glancing over his shoulder, as if making sure I was still there with him.

"It's okay, guys. Mama's here. You don't have to be afraid."

As we walked beside the large picture window at Paula's Pastries, Paula herself happened to be right inside. She smiled and waved at me. When she peered down through the glass and saw my cats, she motioned us inside.

With a grin, I nodded and entered the pastry shop, the amazing aroma always making me crave whatever the special of the day happened to be. Paula was so kind to not only allow me to bring in Jasper and Percival, but loved having them there, saying they were always well behaved and didn't cause any trouble.

She could only say that because she didn't witness the mayhem they caused at home when they performed their big-time wrestling matches all over the house. But I was grateful they were able to come with me to her shop. They loved going places, and I loved having them with me.

"Nice to see you all, Molly. I have to run out for a few minutes, but Wanda will be glad to take care of you."

"Great, thanks."

When we stepped up to the order counter, Wanda, Paula's assistant, was there to take our order. Well, my order. It was just for me. I'm sure my kitties would love something baked and gooey, but it wasn't on their diets. But I kept treats in my purse for just such occasions.

"What can I get you today?" asked Wanda.

"A cinnamon donut, please."

"Sure. Coming right up." Then she tilted her head toward the back of the shop. "Seems yours aren't the only furry customers this afternoon."

I turned and saw what she meant. Or I guess I should say, who? Florence was seated with Helga and Lottie, and Eleanor was seated at the table in the back corner. The Sphynx cats were wearing matching outfits, as usual. Today they were dressed in little light blue sailor suits with red hats and dark blue booties.

When Lottie spotted me, she turned Eleanor in her lap, helping the cat to wave at me. Not to be outdone, Florence did the same with Helga. Since my cats were sitting on the floor and it wouldn't be convenient to crouch down, pick them up, and have them return the wave, I did it for them.

The ladies giggled, so I figured that had done the trick. The cats and I headed across the café, stopping twice so other customers, who'd reached down to the cats, could pet them. With purrs and waving tails, Jasper and Percival gladly obliged.

When we reached the ladies' table, I glanced around. "Hey, how are you two, um, four, doing today?" Aside from a friendly visit, I wanted to see if they'd heard anything new about Carlotta's murder.

"We're dandy, aren't we, Florence?"

She nodded. "Yes, dandy indeed."

It seemed hard to imagine they wouldn't be even a little bit upset over a body discovered on their properties and having been grilled by Sheriff King. Were they really okay and just giving a polite answer to my question? "May we join you?"

"Of course, dear," said Florence. She pointed, indicating an empty chair. There were times no one could sit with them because they gave two of the seats to their cats. Today, I was fortunate enough not to remain standing to speak with them. Or be forced to sit on the floor, which might not have bothered my cats in the least.

She glanced behind me. "Look who's here, Lottie."

With effort, Lottie finally managed to angle around in her chair, causing Eleanor to give a growl at being pulled a few inches away from the small bowl of cream in front of her on the table. Lottie squinted. "Isn't that Lenny Griffith?"

"Yes, that's right." She pulled her cat tighter against her. "He has some nerve showing his face around town, after…"

I looked in that direction as well. I'd seen the man before, but didn't know him. "Is he a friend of yours?"

Lottie looked at Florence; they gave each other eye blinks, then Florence said, "Not exactly." They went back to eating their pastries and making sure their babies were getting enough cream.

"Hey." Lottie pointed toward the table. "Helga has more cream in her bowl than Eleanor."

"That's because Eleanor is a little piggy and eats too fast."

"What difference does that make?"

Florence closed her eyes for a second. "When your cat eats too fast, it makes it look like there's less in her bowl. But there isn't."

Lottie frowned and looked down. "Yes. There is. I'm staring right at it."

"Remember, when the cats were served, the bowls were identical. I reminded Paula that they had to be equal."

Lottie's lips formed into a pout.

When I looked at Eleanor, she seemed to be pouting as well, as if suddenly finding out she'd been cheated out of her fair share.

I got so caught up in listening to their disagreement, I realized they hadn't really answered my question about Lenny. What did 'not exactly' mean?

I waved my hand to get their attention. "Hey, about that guy Lenny Griffith.

How is it that you know him? You said he's not exactly a friend. And that he had nerve?"

Florence patted Helga on the head and was rewarded with a purr. When Percival heard her, he reached up his paw to pat Helga's leg. She and Eleanor were used to my two being there during their grooming visits, so she leaned over and touched her nose to Percival's.

"So sweet," said Lottie. "A kitty romance."

Florence leaned closer to her friend. "They're all fixed. They can't really have a romance."

"That doesn't matter. It's the feeling of the heart that matters." Lottie placed her hand over her chest. "Oh! They could have a tiny little kitty date. We could dress Jasper and Percival up in little tuxedoes and…"

Uh oh. I knew my boys would never tolerate being dressed. That would only lead to bloodshed, and I had no wish for the ladies to be injured while trying to do something nice. Time to change the subject.

I patted the table lightly, hoping to get their attention without seeming rude. "Listen, I was just curious about that Lenny guy. How do you happen to know him?"

Florence stopped staring at Lottie and focused on me. "Well, dear, he used to be a next-door neighbor of Carlotta. You know, that dead woman?"

Lottie nodded. "Yes, the one who was found between our houses?"

Were their memories that short, or were they still thinking about cat nuptials? "Um, yeah. I remember that."

"That's right," said Lottie, "you were there."

"Yeah, I was."

"Anyway, Lenny had said some rotten things about Carlotta."

"Wow, okay. How did you hear this?"

Lottie gave Florence a look. "We, um… overheard it, I guess."

"Yes. Definitely overheard. While minding our own business and getting our pedicures. We always request seats side by side, don't we, Lottie?"

"That's right. Easier to gossip, I mean, discuss current events when we're sitting next to each other."

I leaned my forearm on the table. "So, when you were… discussing current events, what did you happen to overhear from Lenny?"

Lottie glanced at Florence, then said, "First of all, he stomped over to Carlotta."

"I'd say he did more of a march, she said."

Lottie waved her hand. "All right. As you wish."

I tried to stay patient, but wasn't always successful. The ladies often had a lot to say and took their time saying it. Something tapped my ankle. I glanced down to see Jasper pawing at my leg. "Oh, Sorry."

"For what?" asked Lottie. "Did you do something embarrassing? If you did, I missed it."

I pointed down. "Um, no. I was apologizing to Jasper."

"What did you do to him? Step on his tail?"

"Nothing that drastic, although I'm sure my cats would think so. They ran out of treats, and want more."

"Oh," said Florence. "Well, I think that's drastic, too."

Right then, both Helga and Eleanor meowed at their moms.

"Goodness." Lottie's eyebrows lowered. "What's the matter with our babies?"

Florence squinted at the table. "They finished their cream and want more."

I could see that the ladies were getting as upset as their cats, who were still meowing. If they kept up their caterwauling, Paula might not be so tolerant of allowing our cats into her shop. "Shall I get Wanda?"

"Yes, and please hurry."

I turned, spotted Wanda, who came over, and took the cream order.

"Thank you, Molly," said Lottie, "I was afraid the kitties might get hunger pangs and keel over right here on our laps."

"You're welcome. Glad to help," I said, even though I'd handled the Sphinx sisters enough to know they didn't go without meals, ever. "Okay, getting back to Lenny, you said he stomped, or something. What happened next?"

"While we were sitting there, we had a front row seat, you might say."

"Well said," added Florence.

"Thank you. And he started waving his arms and yelling at Carlotta."

My eyes widened. "Wow."

"Yes, dear, it was a wow moment indeed. Everyone in there was leaning forward, hoping not to miss anything. Although as loud as it got, I don't see how they could have."

"What happened next?"

Lottie started to speak, then sighed with relief as Wanda set two fresh bowls of cream in front of their cats. "Well," she said, "Carlotta reminded Lenny of the fact that they'd been neighbors when they were kids. So, for years and years."

"Interesting," I said. When I first heard they were neighbors, I assumed it was as adults.

"We thought so too," agreed Florence. "And Carlotta said that she hadn't forgotten the thing that Lenny had done a long time ago. That if he didn't do what she wanted, she would tell."

"Tell?"

"That's right?"

I held up my hand. "Tell who, and tell what?"

"If I knew that, dear, it would be a much better story, now wouldn't it?"

She had a point. "Yes, I guess so. And that was all that was said?"

"When Lenny left, Carlotta started crying. But it wasn't like she was sad. More like very angry. Ready to hurt someone."

"She was a mess," said Lottie. "Black rivers running down from her eyes."

I nodded, remembering that Carlotta always wore a ton of mascara. "What happened next?"

"I got a pedicure with pink polish." She tapped her foot on the floor, but when I glanced under the table she was wearing sneakers so I couldn't see her toes.

"And I," said Florence, "got bright green polish. Don't bother looking, you can't see mine either."

I smiled. "Okay."

Lottie eyed Florence. "I've been meaning to ask, why did you get green polish that day when I got pink?"

"Because I wanted to match Helga and Eleanor's outfits."

Lottie's eyes opened wide. "Oh! Why didn't you say something? I would have requested to have green toes, too."

"Our cats were sitting right next to us on those little stools, remember? You could see what they were wearing."

She hung her head. "Yes, you're right. But next time we go, please remind me what color I should ask for."

Florence patted her hand. "Of course. We girls, all four of us, must stick together." The ladies started doting on their cats, giving them head rubs and sweet words. I might as well eat the pastries I ordered. I took a bite. Shoot. In the time I'd listened to the ladies, it had gone cold.

My phone buzzed. It was a text from my uncle Russ, asking if I had time to meet for our weekly chat. I texted him back that I had time, then said, "Ladies and kitties, it was nice to see all of you, but I need to go."

I stood, made sure Jasper and Percival were ready to go, and grabbed my pastry and my purse.

"Ta-ta, Molly."

Lottie and Florence were once again waving their cat's paws at me. I grinned and waved back.

I had a feeling that what the ladies had told me would come in handy later on. I just needed to find out more about the secret between Carlotta and Lenny.

Chapter Nine

I t was a pleasant surprise when Jillian stopped into Fabulous Felines early the following day.

"Hey there." I waved. "I'm always glad to see you, but don't you have to work today?"

She ran her hand through her hair, as if distracted. "Yes, I told Valene I'd be there in a little bit."

I walked around the counter to stand beside her. "So she showed up at work today?"

"Only because I told her she had to."

I glanced around, glad to see that the pet-parents who'd dropped off their cats for grooming had already left the shop. "How did Valene….look?"

Jillian made a tsking noise. "If I hadn't witnessed that fight on the video, I might have been even more shocked at her appearance, but still, she had deep scratches on her face, neck, and arms. Long sleeves and a scarf hide the arms and neck, but the face…"

"Yeah, hard to cover that up unless she wears a full face mask."

"Right, and Valene doesn't play baseball, so she wouldn't have one of those catcher's masks handy. Not that I'd allow her to wear it in the library."

"How is she handling her appearance? I'm sure more than a few people have stared, or asked her what happened."

"The answer to that is that she's not handling it."

"What do you mean?"

Jillian crossed her arms over her chest. "Whenever someone comes to the desk and Valene is supposed to take care of them, instead, she crouches down on all fours behind the counter, makes a pssting sound to get my attention, and waves me over from my desk."

"Hmmm. How's that working out for you?"

"It's not. At all. I really need her there to help me out. I can't do it all myself. At least she's willing to do things where most people won't be able to see her, like doing intake of newly purchased books or computer work. But there are lots of times I need her to take care of the front counter because I'm in the middle of doing something else."

"I understand." I thought of Veronica and how much I relied on her here in Fabulous Felines. I couldn't run it without her. While we did sometimes watch over the shop if the other person took a break or had an appointment, that was never very long at a time.

"I know you do. Thanks." She smiled, then shook her head. "I know I might sound like an ogre, making her come to work, but I literally can't do this job alone, and we don't have any subs right now who can do all that Valene does."

"You don't sound like an ogre. You run the library. That's your job. You're just asking that Valene do her job too."

She nodded. "But I still feel like a meanie."

"You couldn't be a meanie if you tried. Besides, I can't believe you used the word meanie."

"Why not?"

I laughed. "Usually you scold me for using offbeat terms instead of a more, um, proper term."

"Well, all right. You've got me there, I guess. But I still feel mean. I guess mostly because Valene was so despondent."

"Over her appearance?"

"Yes, but more than that, about the cause of the fight. Over a guy."

"From the video, Carlotta really let her have it. I mean, telling her the guy was only flirting with her for books."

"Yeah, Carlotta made her feel terrible, like her feelings didn't matter. I've never seen my assistant that angry before, to fight with another person. Besides, I didn't even know Valene had been seeing anybody."

"Was she really seeing him, though, if he only made contact with her in the library? That doesn't sound like a real relationship to me."

"You've got a point there. But in Valene's mind, at least from what she told me after I confronted her with the video, she was super into the guy. And he was totally into her. She's taking this so very hard. Like her life is over."

"But now that Carlotta is out of the picture...." I raised my eyebrows.

"I don't know if she'll try to reach out to the guy or not. Or if Carlotta's words to her cut so deep, she'll keep believing them and keep falling deeper into despair."

"Do you think the guy really liked Valene as much as she says she liked him?"

"I'm not sure what to think. I want her to be happy. I really do. Let's face it. It's hard enough being a woman in a small town where the pool of good men is dwindling."

I wiggled my eyebrows. "Not that you have anything to worry about."

She glanced down at her manicure, seeming not to want to make eye contact. "What do you mean?"

I lightly pushed her shoulder. "Oh, come on. You and I both know Evan is crazy about you."

"And I'm sure crazy about him, as you know."

I nodded and crossed my arms. "Right. But...?"

"See, he hasn't actually asked me out yet. At least not on an official date."

"Is that all? Listen, some of these good men are also a little shy when it comes to romance."

"Are you speaking from experience?"

"Yep. I am. I'm sure you've noticed that Hank and I are taking it super slow."

A glint came into Jillian's eyes. "Even though you and Hank are married?"

I pointed at her. "Now cut that out. It's bad enough that Ricky has been spreading that rumor around town. Don't you start."

Jillian laughed. "You know I'm teasing you. And that I would never do that."

"I know. I guess on the positive end for Valene, those scratches will heal. I mean, they're not permanent."

"True. It's just frustrating. I wish she'd never gotten into that fight at all. For lots of reasons."

"Wait. Do you think that girl who filmed Valene and Carlotta will post it online?"

Jillian shook her head. "No. She won't."

"How can you be sure? You know how people love to get attention by posting things."

"Because this particular woman is a huge book lover. She reads constantly. I didn't come out and say it, but insinuated she might not be welcome back into the library if I ever saw the video anywhere or heard anybody else talking about it. But…"

"Is there something else that's happened?" I asked.

"While I feel confident that video won't surface online, there were other people here that day. I saw several names of regular patrons who'd checked out books. I'm sure at least some of them witnessed, or heard about, Valene's faux pas."

"You're right. And citizens of Whitewater Valley are quick to spread any kind of juicy happenings."

She nodded. "Yeah. They are. So, there's only so much damage control I can do."

"It will blow over."

She gave me a raised-eyebrow look.

"Uh, eventually. By the way, how upset was she that you made her come in today?" When I heard a rustling beside my feet and spotted Percival, I tapped my fingers on the counter. He jumped up on it and rubbed against my hand.

Jillian ran her hand over Percival's back, causing the cat to let out a booming purr. "Valene sobbed so loud over the phone, my ear is still ringing. I thought about letting her stay home, but those scratches are going to take a while to heal. I can't manage the library alone for that long, and I need her. Besides, she never should have had an all-out catfight in the workplace anyway. Especially not in a library. Shouldn't there be a few places where people behave in an orderly fashion?"

I tried not to smile but couldn't help it. My friend was nothing if not orderly. I patted her arm. "We all know how you like things neat and tidy."

"Hey, what's wrong with that?"

"Absolutely nothing. There are lots of times I wish I was more like you."

"And I feel that way about you, too."

"You do?"

"Yes. You're more open to things than I am. Besides, every cat in the world loves you."

"Not every cat. Once in a while, we get a super moody one who'd rather take a swipe at us than allow us to love on them."

"I'm sure that's the exception, though."

"Thankfully, yes. But about what you said before, about there needing to be at least some places where people behave? You're right." I glanced around the room. "I mean, here in the grooming shop, it happens sometimes, and nobody is surprised. But the library isn't a place where fights should break out."

"Especially not fights where one of the library employees has claw marks."

I shivered, remembering the awful fight from the video the library patron had shown us. I couldn't imagine having to walk around with so many claw marks on my face. At least if it happened to me, I had a good excuse with who my clients were.

"Good thinking on your part, having her come in anyway, since you need her."

She gave me a one-sided grin. "It's what I do."

"True. I can always count on you to be one step ahead of trouble." I rolled my eyes. "Too bad it doesn't always work out that way for me."

Jillian placed her hands on her hips, one of her many librarian poses meant to come across as no-nonsense. It worked. "Listen, Molly, you just need to hang out with your best friend more often. I'll get you straightened out." She winked.

"Thank goodness you're on my side, Jillian. Otherwise, I'd be in more trouble than I usually am."

"You know I'm always here for you. But right now I'm concerned about something else."

"What's that?"

"If Valene was so hung up on this guy, that he would be her one true love, and thought Carlotta was standing in her way of being with him, wouldn't that be a motive for murdering Carlotta?"

"I hate to admit it, but yeah. It would."

Her face fell. "I guess we'd better add her to our suspect list then." She reached into her purse, tugged out a small notebook I'd seen her use before, and reached for a pen that sat on my counter.

"What are you doing?"

"Adding her to my list. Like I said."

"You have an actual written list? I was just giving you a hard time earlier about being organized. I didn't think you'd have a…" I pointed to her notepad.

She jotted down Valene's name, then returned my pen. "Why are you so surprised? You said I'm nothing if not orderly, and you're absolutely right. But it really pains me to think Valene might be the murderer we're searching for."

Chapter Ten

The Sandwich Shack recently added outdoor seating beneath a large awning in front of their shop. When I arrived, Lottie, Florence, and their cats were sitting at a table, this time with the kitties having chairs of their own and bowls of cream in front of them.

With the table next to them vacant, I claimed it, since Uncle Russ would be here soon to meet me. I was hoping he and I could toss around some ideas about who might have killed Carlotta.

Lottie waved exuberantly. "Molly! Hello!" She hiccupped, then grinned.

Had she been drinking this early in the day? It was barely noon.

Florence, with bleary eyes, gave me an exaggerated wink. And she was not normally a winker. I always worried about them unless I was seeing them in one of their driveways for their cats' groomings. At least that way, I knew they were already safely at home.

I sat on the black wrought iron chair, then set my purse on the sidewalk beside my feet. "Hi, Ladies. Um…you didn't drive here today, did you?"

With a flip of her hand, having smacked her nose in the process, Florence said, "Of course not. It's Thursday."

I blinked. Okay, then. At least it was something. "Great. It's nice to see all four of you enjoying some time out."

"Time out?" Lottie scrunched her eyebrows together. "Florence, did you do something to deserve a time out? What transgression did you commit, or how about you two?" She eyed their cats.

I refrained from rolling my eyes, but just barely. "Um, no. By time out, I meant getting away from your homes. You know…. outside?" I tilted my head toward the street.

"Oh…." Lottie gave a slow nod. "I understand now. Why yes, we are enjoying it, aren't we, Eleanor?"

Her cat gave a mew, then went back to slurping her cream. Even though many cats were lactose intolerant and shouldn't have dairy products, I'd never say that to the ladies. Either they'd tell me I didn't know what I was talking about, even though I worked with cats every day, or else Lottie would start shrieking, as she had a tendency to do.

Neither option sounded pleasant to me, so I kept quiet and hoped Helga and Eleanor didn't suffer any tummy repercussions.

Lottie waved at me again, as if she'd forgotten doing it a couple minutes ago. "Molly, might we hope you're meeting a handsome man for lunch today?"

"You know what? As a matter of fact, I am. It's—"

"Oh!" Lottie pressed her hands to her cheeks. "How wonderful. Will there be wedding bells and pregnancies to announce soon?"

"I hope not since he's my uncle."

The ladies let out exaggerated gasps, but that might have had to do with how tipsy they were. At the loud noise, their cats whipped their heads around, wide-eyed as if offended.

"You've met him," I said. "It's my uncle Russ."

Florence nearly deflated in her chair. "Thank goodness. I thought for a minute you were going rogue or something."

I bit my lip so hard against a laugh that my nostrils flared. "Definitely not rogue." When I'd recovered enough not to break out in a snorting laugh, I looked at them. "Are you two holding up all right, under the circumstances?"

With a look of confusion, Lottie tilted her head back and looked up. "Circumstances? I thought that was an awning we were sitting under."

Holy cow, they'd really gotten into their special drinks early today. "Uh, yes, that's an awning. But I meant, how are you holding up with what's going on? You know, Carlotta having been found between your houses?"

"We're fine, dear," said Florence. "Why do you ask?"

My mouth dropped open, and I closed it. Had they forgotten what happened? "Since the sheriff questioned you and thinks you might be suspects in her murder, I thought maybe…"

Lottie's shriek was so loud, people from inside the Sandwich Shack turned to stare.

Rats, should have known better than to state the obvious. "I'm sorry, Lottie. I didn't mean that you were guilty or going to jail or—"

Her shrieks intensified. The door opened, and Lorna Thompson came out. "Are you all right, Lottie? I heard screaming,"

She clutched her throat. "Apparently, I'm going to be hanged from the neck until dead!"

I groaned. "No, that's not it at all. You're fine. I was just asking how you're doing and…" I glanced from Lorna to the ladies. "Right. Never mind."

Lorna's eyes had widened. But after watching Lottie for a few seconds, she must have decided the immediate crisis was over. Plus, she'd been around the women long enough to have seen their often odd behavior. She took out her order pad and pen. "Can I get anyone something to eat or drink?"

"Both, of course," said Florence.

"Okay, great. And what would you like?"

"Two Reuben sandwiches. And refills on the kitties' cream, please."

"Coming right up. Molly, how about you?"

"I'm still waiting on Russ to—"

"Here I am," came Russ's voice from behind me.

I turned and grinned at him, as he bent close to me and kissed my cheek. He sat opposite me and said hello to Florence and Lottie.

The ladies whispered together, then the giggling started.

Russ's eyebrows lowered. "Was it something I said?"

I rolled my eyes. "No, probably the fact that you're handsome."

"Oh?" His face reddened slightly. "Always nice to hear. Especially at my age."

"As if you're old," I said.

Lorna took our orders, then left.

A shuffling came from behind me. Russ was looking at whatever, or whoever, had made the noise, so I turned in my chair too.

It was Ricky.

Just perfect. If he did as normal, he wouldn't simply say hi and move along to deliver his mail. Russ and I would have to wait until he left, whenever that turned out to be, to have a real conversation. Although with the ladies sitting so close, that might have been challenging anyway. Thank goodness my uncle was a good sport. We usually had fun no matter where we ended up or who we spent time with.

"Why hello, all of you," said Ricky. "How nice to see women, a man, and cats all enjoying such a lovely day."

The ladies gave Ricky nods of greeting, but didn't say anything. And Helga and Eleanor didn't bother lifting their milky chins from their cream dishes.

"Molly," said Ricky. "Those old ladies brought their cats. Where are yours? Don't you have like a million of them?"

My eyes widened. "Uh, Ricky, Florence, and Lottie might not appreciate being referred to as…. how you referred to them." I glanced over at the other table, afraid they'd be glaring in our direction, but thankfully, the women both appeared half asleep. "And as for me, Jasper and Percival are back at Fabulous Felines with Veronica."

Ricky's brow furrowed. "Then who are all those other cats?"

"You mean my grooming clients at Fabulous Felines, when people bring them in for me to take care of?"

He smacked his forehead. "Oh, right. That's who they are."

Russ caught my attention and gave a slight head tilt toward Ricky, then grimaced.

Yep, my uncle was right. Ricky was often clueless.

Suddenly, a loud thump came from beside my feet. I jumped and looked down. Why was Ricky's mailbag on the sidewalk beside my purse?

Oh no. He wouldn't….

But deep down, I knew better. Of course, he would. He was Ricky.

He planted himself down in the chair between Russ and me, then placed his elbows on the tabletop. "So, what are you guys having today?"

Apparently, our table for two had morphed into three. And one of us hadn't been invited.

Russ blinked, gave me a slow one-sided smile. I knew that look. Whatever happened today with Ricky would be something we could look back on later and laugh about. I just wish we didn't have to endure it now to enjoy it later.

But I'd spent enough time with my uncle to try to find the positive in situations. Might as well get started on this one.

Right then, Lorna came out with Florence and Lottie's orders, and ours. When Ricky spotted my BLT with a side of chocolate chip cookies, he pointed so close to my food he nearly touched a cookie. "I'll have all of that!"

Lorna raised her eyebrows at the newcomer, wrote down his order, then headed back inside the shop.

Ricky studied our food. "Gosh, that looks good. Too bad I have to wait for mine to come." His sigh was loud and long. Did the man have no shame? No sense of manners or common sense? What was I thinking? Of course he didn't.

His sighs turned to something more like moans, which made my eye twitch. There was no way I could put up with that until Lorna brought Ricky's order. I picked up a cookie and held it out to him.

"Really? For me?" His eyes lit up.

"It's a loan." I pulled it back a couple of inches.

"What do you mean?"

Russ pointed to the cookie in question. "Molly will give you this now, but when you get your order, you'll repay her with one of yours. Make sense?"

"Not really. But we'll give it a try." He snatched the cookie from my fingers, took a huge bite, and licked his lips. "Wow, this is really good. Not as good as Mrs. Kelper's Kelper-doodles, but good just the same."

I raised my eyebrows. "You've tried Kelper-doodles?"

Russ tapped the table to get my attention. "What the heck is a…"

"Well," I explained, "Mrs. Kelper makes these amazing cookies that are similar to snickerdoodles—"

"Only better," said Ricky, who'd snarfed down the cookie and was sniffing around for more.

The man had better back off. I was hungry too, and one cookie was all I was willing to part with. And I was afraid if I held out a second one to him, instead of him grabbing it with his fingers, he'd just take a big bite of it right from my hand.

Russ' eyes lit up. "I love snickerdoodles. Can't imagine anything better than those."

"Ricky is right." I hated to admit it, but Mrs. Kelper did seem to be onto something.

Our postman sat up straighter. "Why thank you Molly." He grabbed his ponytail and gave it a tug, as if giving himself a pat on the back. Strange guy. But even with all his weirdness, I did like him. And I knew Russ did too, which was why he was putting up with the intrusion on our uncle-niece time together today.

Lorna came outside and gave Ricky his meal. He didn't even thank her, just dug right in like Jasper and Percival did when I got out the catnip.

Russ observed Ricky for a few seconds, shrugged, then picked up his own sandwich.

I did the same, realizing how hungry I was, and also that I only had so much time away from the shop and I'd need to get back soon so Veronica could take her own break. She got *hangry* pretty quick when her tummy got empty. I'd learned it the hard way, and liked to keep my assistant happy.

After I'd taken a few bites, I angled around toward Russ. "When I was grooming Mrs. Kelper's cat, Cleo, I noticed the cat was wearing an apron announcing her mom had won."

Russ took another bite, then swallowed. "Won what?"

"Mrs. Kelper apparently won a prize at the fair for her cookies, and—"

"Yeah!" Ricky nodded so fast, his ponytail bobbed against his shoulder. "I know all about that."

"You mean the fair?" I asked. "Did you go to see her win?"

"No. I mean about her prize." He added air quotes to the last word.

Russ leaned forward. "Was there something unusual about her prize?"

"I'll say." Ricky wolfed down a cookie.

It took me a few seconds before it registered. I studied his plate. Wait. That was his second cookie. What happened to the first, since there were now none? He'd eaten them both without reimbursing me for the one I gave him.

Annoyed, I tried to overlook the slight. But I'd really looked forward to that second chocolate chip cookie. I consoled myself with the rest of my sandwich, which was quite good, as always.

When I glanced at Russ, he was staring at me.

"What? Do I have food on my face again?" It was a common occurrence when he and I met for meals together. Actually, anytime I ate, at any given meal.

He pointed his thumb in Ricky's direction. "I was asking Ricky what was so special about Mrs. Kelper's prize." He widened his eyes, wanting me to catch on.

Ricky did seem to know something, or at least acted like he did. Russ was right. Might be worth getting more out of Ricky, even though that meant he'd stick around longer. "Um, Ricky, why don't you fill us in on that?"

He took a bite of his sandwich, set it down, belched – ick! – and then around a mouthful of food, "The prize was a trophy. Another one."

"Were there a lot of them?" asked Russ.

"You betcha, Uncle Russ."

Had Ricky just referred to my uncle as his own? I started to object, but Russ gave me a slight head shake. His nostrils flared as he tried to hold in a laugh.

I decided to play along. It might be the only way to make it through this uncomfortable ordeal. "Okay, how many were there, Ricky?"

"Enough to fill the whole mantle above her fireplace. I know this because, now don't get the wrong idea, she asked me to come into her house."

"Okay." What was he worried about? He'd been in my house and business enough times to deliver packages. At least, when he remembered to bring them.

"Molly." Ricky glanced toward the ladies, who didn't seem to be listening to us. "I wouldn't want it to get out that I was inside a woman's house, if you know what I mean." He waggled his eyebrows.

Eewwww. "I'm pretty sure you're safe on that, Ricky. I haven't heard any kind of rumor like that. Have you, Russ?"

"No," he said quickly. "Nothing of the sort."

"Well that's a relief." Ricky wiped his hand over his brow. "Anyway, I was delivering a package for her. And boy was it a huge box! She asked me to carry it into her living room for her since her arthritis made it hard to carry the box herself." He stared first at me, then Russ. "Don't you want to know what was inside the box?"

The fact that Ricky had stayed around long enough to get his curiosity satisfied didn't escape me. "Yes, I'd like to know."

"It was another trophy. I don't know why the box was so big when the trophy was a little tiny thing. Mrs. Kelper put it on her mantle. She had to scoot a bunch of the others over to make room. Then she said it was one she'd ordered. A first prize one."

Russ's mouth opened slightly. "You mean she ordered *herself* a first place prize?

"That's right," said Ricky. "The funny thing was? She'd ordered it before this year's contest even took place. She must have been certain she'd win. Oh, and she also said something, although I don't think she meant for me to hear it since she was looking down at her cat on the floor, when she said it, but it was that Carlotta had been the favorite to win this year. Apparently the recently-deceased had taken up the noble art of cookie baking and was very good at it. That is, before she died, of course."

He smacked his palm against the table, stood and grabbed his mailbag. "Been really nice catching up with you folks. See ya later." He turned and trotted down the sidewalk, his mailbag nearly knocking over a young woman with a baby in a stroller.

I blinked. "Wow, that was…"

"Right," said Russ. "Do you know what this means?"

I glanced up at him. "What?"

"Mrs. Kelper knew ahead of time she'd win again. Kind of fishy, if you ask me."

"Oh, it's fishy all right. Especially considering Carlotta was who was favored to come in first."

From behind me, the ladies stood, picked up their cats and giggled as they walked by our table. "Bye, Molly. Bye, handsome uncle."

I laughed as they left, always entertained by whatever they did or said. But my smile fell when Lorna came out with the check and placed it on the table. Ricky's meal was on there. And he'd already left.

Without paying for it.

Russ shook his head. "Allow me, Molly. It's what a handsome uncle would do." He handed Lorna his credit card, and gave me a wink.

Chapter Eleven

The following afternoon, I was surprised to see Jed Martin enter the grooming shop, since Sunny had previously been in to pay Regis' bill.

"Hi, Jed. Nice to see you."

"Hey Molly. Have a problem."

"Okay. How can I help?"

He reached into his back pocket and produced a cat leash. Or at least, what used to be one. It was chopped up into several pieces.

My mouth dropped open. "What happened?"

"Carlotta happened."

I jerked. With them separated, and more importantly, Carlotta now dead, it didn't seem a likely scenario.

He held up his hand. "I know what you must be thinking, Molly. But I have no doubt it was her."

It didn't make any sense. "But don't you normally walk Regis on his leash daily? And Carlotta was killed…"

He hung his head. "I feel so bad about the walks. Or I should say the non-walks. Things have been so messy and confusing the last few weeks. I have to admit this is the first time I've even contemplated taking him out for a while."

I did feel sorry for Regis, because I knew he loved to go on mini-excursions. But I could also understand why Jed would feel like his whole life was in a jumble. Unfortunately, family members, including pets, sometimes got temporarily ignored when life turned stressful.

Jed's face reddened. "That's how I knew Carlotta would have had plenty of time to mess up his leash, just to make me mad. Along with the fact that she was furious that her boy toy took away what she thought of as her cat, but it wasn't. As much as she loved felines, she wasn't very popular with them. I can't think of anybody else who would have done that, come into my home, rummage around in my closet, and cut up a leash. It just had to be her."

"I see your point." I reached out and picked up the leash remnants he'd laid on the counter. "I'm so sorry about all this you're going through." While it was true, I felt awful about what happened to Carlotta, I'd never found her to be a kind person. Jed, on the other hand, was a sweet man. It puzzled me how they'd ended up together. Carlotta's only redeeming quality, in my opinion, was that she loved cats. Even if they didn't seem to love her back.

"Thanks for understanding, Molly."

"You're welcome. One thing seems weird to me about this, though."

"What's that?"

"With the way Carlotta always loved cats, why would she have done this to Regis' leash, knowing he'd be upset if he couldn't go out with you for walks?"

Jed ran his hand through his short hair. "Because Regis always preferred me, and Carlotta couldn't tolerate that. She knew I could replace the leash for the cat, but I think she destroyed this one to get under my skin. And it worked. Even though she's dead." A solid ridge of muscle formed along his jaw, as he clenched his teeth.

"So I'm guessing you need a new leash today?"

"Yeah, I do. Hoping you have some in stock. Do you have any blue ones? That's Regis's favorite color."

I smiled as I glanced at Jed's dark blue shirt, knowing he was the one who loved that color since he wore it nearly every time I saw him. "Yes, we have blue. Let me go get one."

"Thanks. That'd be great."

I headed to our back storage room to get the leash. Right after I entered the room, I heard footsteps behind me and turned. It was Veronica.

"Hey," she said, pointing behind her. "Poor Jed is really going through it, isn't he?"

"You heard that, huh?"

"Of course. I don't have a kitty client right now. What else was I going to do but eavesdrop?"

I shook my head slowly. "Have I ever told you that you're incorrigible?"

"Quite often. And thank you." She grinned, then her smile fell. "Honestly, I do hate what that poor man is having to endure right now."

I was glad we wouldn't be overheard back here in the storage area, because Jed might take it wrong. In the interest of keeping feline clients calmer who were waiting for their appointments, we'd had the room encased with extra soundproofing for when a kitty got loud or upset.

Veronica did want to know what was going on, but she liked Jed very much. We all did. He was a genuinely nice guy. And Sunny was fortunate to have found a job working for him at his bookshop. I reached onto a top shelf and pulled down a box of leashes. "I hate it too. He's so nice."

"Yes, he is. Unlike…"

"Yeah, his ex-wife wasn't much fun to be around, was she? I guess it's a good thing for us that she didn't usually come in here." After pushing aside leashes of pink, green, and white, I found one of the navy blue ones. "There. Jed, I mean Regis, should like this one."

Veronica winked. "Yeah, I nearly laughed out loud from around the corner when he said it was the cat's favorite color."

I glanced down at the leash in my hand. "Yeah. Me too. So sweet."

"Very sweet."

I headed back through the shop. When I reached the counter, Jed was standing across the room, staring out of the picture window. His shoulders were sagging, like he was weighted down. But I was sure he felt that way. He'd been dealt such a huge blow.

"Hey Jed." I waved the leash so the tiny bell attached gave a light jingle.

He turned, giving me a sad smile. "Thanks a million, Molly. I hate that I haven't been paying enough attention to Regis. But that's going to change. And right now, starting with his daily walks again."

"That's good to hear. And I'll bet those walks will make you feel a little better too. Getting outside for some exercise always seems to clear my head."

He returned to the counter. "You're probably right. I'd forgotten how much I enjoyed getting outside with Regis. He waves his tail back and forth like it's a flag. And he sniffs everything in sight. He just loves it so much, it makes me happy to watch him."

I nodded. "Yep. It rubs off on us when our fur babies are happy."

Jed reached into his pocket and took out a credit card, unlike how Sunny normally paid his bills by showing up with a check every time.

I told him the amount, then reached for the card he held out. "You know, I could have billed you for the leash. It wouldn't have been any trouble at all."

"True. But I needed to get out of the shop for a bit." His shoulders tensed. " Sunny can handle it for a while."

"And you didn't need to send Sunny with the grooming payment so soon. It could have waited. I know you have lots going on, and I understand."

He held up his hand. "Nope. It was due and needed to be paid. As a fellow small business owner, I get how important it is to have customers pay their bills on time."

"Well, thanks. I appreciate it." I placed the leash and sales receipt in a small plastic bag with the Fabulous Felines logo on the outside, and set it on the counter.

Jed blew out a breath. "Besides, when I sent Sunny over here, the sheriff was on his way over to Second Hand Books, questioning me about Carlotta's murder. I figured Sunny didn't need to hear all that. She's already too involved in my life as it is. I was just relieved no customers were nearby when he showed up. That would have been over the top embarrassing."

I made a face. "Yeah, I've been in that situation before, having been questioned by Sheriff King. It's not enjoyable."

"Exactly. I can think of lots of things that would be more fun." One corner of his mouth rose in a half smile. "Like cleaning Regis' litter box. Or taking out the garbage when it's overflowing."

I laughed, glad that he seemed a little more relaxed than when he'd come in.

"I usually get along with Sunny, and she's a great employee…." He glanced behind him, like he was afraid to be overheard. But we were alone. With the exception of Veronica, who was no doubt still listening.

Jed obviously wanted to say something, but seemed apprehensive. So I waited.

"She…um, you might have noticed she likes to talk. About other people's business."

I glanced down at the counter. "Well, I had noticed that before, yes."

"I suppose she filled you in on my trouble with Carlotta and our fight over getting the proceeds from the sale of our house?"

I nodded. Why deny it? The fact that he asked about Sunny and what she might have said clued me into his already suspecting as much.

"I'm sorry you were dragged into all this, Molly. It's no one's business but mine." He rubbed the back of his neck. "Honestly, if Sunny weren't such a great worker, I wouldn't keep her around. But she is good. And I do need her. Especially since Carlotta and I split and she wasn't there to do the job anymore."

"Don't worry too much, Jed. Yes, Sunny talked a little about your situation, but she didn't go into a lot of detail. And people will understand. You have been through a lot, and people, at least most, won't judge you for it."

He let out a breath. "Thanks. It's good to know I have you on my side."

"Yes I am. And so are lots of other people."

Jed waved and exited the shop.

It was true I was on his side if people began putting all the blame on him for his divorce and all the fights with Carlotta that went along with it. But as I watched Jed pass by the picture window, I wondered if he'd hated his ex-wife enough to have been the one to murder her. Sunny did like to talk, but I couldn't shake the things she'd said about Jed, and how much he'd hated his former wife. And about what a terrible person Carlotta had been.

Veronica stepped up beside me. "I know what you're thinking Molly, and yes, he might be guilty."

"But it's like you said before, he's just the nicest guy."

"Not every killer is a lunatic."

"Point taken."

Chapter Twelve

I had a break in my schedule and was ready to run some errands when I glanced out the Fabulous Felines front window and saw Trixie across the street in front of the Stompin' Boots shoe store. And she was dancing. Again.

What was up with her? Could her now-happy mood really have something to do with Carlotta no longer being around? I knew one person I might be able to speak with about it. Annie Bates owned the nail salon and she was also Trixie's boss. And if Trixie was dancing across the street right now, that meant she wasn't working in the salon. Maybe it would be a good time for me to head over to talk to her boss.

I needed a reason to show up. When I'd gone during a previous murder to find clues, I'd ended up unwillingly on the receiving end of a horrific manicure. And I had no desire to go through that again. I glanced around the front room of my shop. Something on the edge of our front counter caught my eye. Veronica and I had made up some discount coupons for cat grooming, hoping to entice new clients to check out our services for their cats.

She walked out from her grooming room right then. "Oh, hey. I thought you'd already left." She eyed the stack of coupons in my hand. "You're supposed to be taking a break now, Molly."

"I will be."

"Handing out Fabulous Feline discounts looks like work to me." She crossed her arms over her chest.

"Listen." I picked up a small stack of them. "I just now saw Trixie dancing across the street and—"

"Wait, what? I need to see this." She hurried across the floor, then leaned so close to the window glass, her nose pressed against it like my cats did when they saw a squirrel outside.

I joined her, relieved to see Trixie was still over there and not in the salon.

Veronica turned her head toward me. "Why is she dancing?"

"I'm not sure, but while I was in Carrie's Coffees the other day, she did it there too and…"

"Inside the building?"

"Yep."

"That had to be quite the sight."

I laughed. "Believe me, it was, and for all the people in there who saw her."

"I can only imagine." She pointed toward Trixie, who was now doing a hip bump without another person to bump against. She nearly tumbled to the side twice. "But I guess I can now that I'm witnessing it right over there."

After watching Trixie for another couple of minutes, Veronica faced me. "That was weird."

"Yep. I'm shocked, and I've already seen it before."

Her glance fell again to the coupons in my hand. "So you're taking these in order to…"

"I'm thinking since Trixie isn't at the salon right now, I'll go and see if I can talk to Annie about her."

"Ah, and the discount cards are your way in?"

"That's right."

"You're devious." She wiggled her eyebrows. "I like you."

I chuckled. "Okay, I better scram. I don't know how much time I have."

"I'll help you out with that."

"How?"

"I don't have a kitty client for another half hour, and neither do you. How about I keep an eye on twinkle toes over there and give you a ring if it looks like she's headed back in the salon's direction."

"Veronica, I knew I kept you around for a reason. Thank you."

She fluttered her eyelashes. "We all have to be good at something."

With a grin, I headed toward the door, but strident meows floated up from my feet. Jasper and Percival rubbed against my legs, their way of asking me to please come along with me.

"Sorry, guys. I thought you guys were taking a nap. Mama can't take you to the salon. No kitties allowed."

Veronica shook her head. "They should be allowed there, just like some of the other places in town that don't mind."

"I agree." I bent down to give both kitties chin scratches. "But it's the owner's prerogative whether or not to allow pets."

"You could always say they're your emotional support cats."

"I think Florence and Lottie have that market cornered with Helga and Eleanor. Annie allows them to go in all the time."

"But wait, those cats aren't actually support cats, are they?"

"Nope, but that doesn't stop the ladies from doing it." I checked out the window to see that Trixie was now doing an awkward version of a tap dance. "Listen kitties, I need to run, I won't be gone long, okay?"

Jasper meowed, but Percival turned away, giving me a view of his furry back. I'd have to make it up to them later.

Veronica crouched down and picked up both cats, one in each arm. "I'll watch them while you're gone. Maybe we'll even get out some treats."

At the word treats, both cats squirmed to be put on the floor, then they bolted to the counter, where we kept kitty snacks stashed underneath for them.

"Thanks, Veronica, see you all soon." I left the shop, hurrying up the sidewalk, hoping Trixie didn't notice me. I glanced behind me several times, but she wasn't on her way back to work. I wondered what kind of dance she was doing now.

When I reached the nail salon, I stopped outside the door, and squelched a groan that longed to pop out when memory of the terrible manicure experience assaulted my mind. Trixie was nice enough, but kind of strange. And she hadn't known what she was doing when she'd attempted the forced manicure on my poor unsuspecting fingernails. I wasn't sure they'd ever quite recovered.

But when I'd been here last time, Trixie was new, very new, at her job. Maybe I should give her some credit and hope that over time, she'd improved. A lot. At least, for her current clients, I hoped so.

With that in mind, I forced myself to smile. In any event, I knew Trixie wasn't here right now, and with Veronica keeping watch for me, I probably wouldn't run into her.

I opened the door and stepped inside. While Fabulous Felines had the scent of kitty shampoos and soap, the nail salon was more pungent. Veronica and I were exceedingly careful about keeping everything super clean and sanitized. I sneezed at the strong odor of chemicals, causing a couple of nail techs and their clients to look my way.

"Sorry," I said with a wave in front of my nose. "My allergies are acting up."

One customer gave me a nod, as if she understood, and the other client rolled her eyes at me and whispered something to her nail tech.

I shrugged, determined not to worry what someone else thought since I was on a fact-finding mission, and made my way through the salon to Annie's office. Even though I didn't normally come in here, I knew her pretty well, since she brought her cat Kiki to me for grooming.

The door was partially open, but I knocked on it anyway. Annie glanced up from some papers she was looking at, then smiled when she saw me. "Molly, hi. Good to see you."

"Hope it's not a bad time."

"Nope. Just taking a break before my client comes here in a few minutes. What can I do for you?"

I held up the stack of coupons. "Wondered if you, or any of your clients, might like some Fabulous Felines coupons?"

Her eyes lit up. "Wow, thanks. You know I'm always glad to have discounts." She winked.

"Great. Would it be okay to leave some here for clients? And, of course, your nail techs too."

"Sure. We'd really appreciate that."

I glanced toward the open doorway. "Looks like things are busy here.

Going well?"

Her eyes widened. "Oh my, yes. We're super busy."

"Hmmm." I rubbed my chin.

"Is something the matter?"

"No. I just noticed on my way in that Trixie wasn't out there. Does she still work here?"

"Yep, sure does. She's out until later today. I think she had some cancellations. Why did you need to see her?"

"Um, no." I waved my hand. "Just curious. I knew she worked here, is all." I glanced behind me, then back. "I did want to make sure she's okay, though."

Annie tilted her head. "Uh-oh. What have you heard?"

"You see, I heard from someone recently that Trixie had seemed, not herself?"

"Yeah, that was an issue for a bit, that thankfully has been resolved."

"Oh, that's good."

"May I ask if you'd heard anything about her in detail?"

When I'd come into her office, I'd left the door partially open. I pushed it all the way shut. "The person who mentioned it said that Trixie had recently appeared disheveled. And… that some of her clients complained. Uh…apparently, she'd given up bathing for a while."

Annie closed her eyes briefly. "Yeah, it's true. She was going through something emotional and sort of gave up on personal hygiene." The expression she wore reminded me of Jillian's when we'd first heard about Trixie's appearance.

"But she's doing okay now?"

"Seems to be. Of course, I sat her down and told her that if she didn't get her act cleaned up and herself, I'd have no choice but to let her go."

"I'm guessing she didn't take that very well."

"No, she didn't. I'm not sure exactly what was going on with her, but I had noticed recently that she and Carlotta had been at odds. Neither one would tell me what it was exactly…." Her eyebrows drew together.

"Is something wrong?"

"You know, I hadn't realized until now, but Trixie's whole demeanor changed after we found out Carlotta had been murdered."

"Was she upset by the news? I'm sure all of you were, having worked in the same shop together."

"No, that's just it. It was strange. The rest of us are still trying to come to terms with the loss of our co-worker." She shook her head. "But Trixie? She's been happy. Like over the top happy."

That explained the dancing. "You're right. That does sound strange. Even if they weren't getting along well, you'd think she'd still be stunned and upset by Carlotta's murder, right?"

"Exactly."

"I guess it's hard to know how another person might react to a traumatic situation."

"True." She watched me for a second. "Hey, didn't I hear you were there when Carlotta's body was found?"

"Yeah, unfortunately."

"I haven't seen Florence or Lottie since then. We'll have to get them fixed up with another of our nail techs since Carlotta…. Are they doing all right since Carlotta was found between their houses?"

"Yeah, they seem to be."

"Let me guess, they're in denial?"

I smiled. "Maybe a little. As long as they have their cats and each other, they seem fine."

She held up one finger. "And don't forget their beverages of choice."

I blinked. "Wait, they don't bring those in here, too, do they?"

"Yes, they do. I always make sure they haven't driven here, that they have transportation to and from here."

"I do the same, although most times, I do Eleanor's and Helga's groomings in the ladies' driveways. Which is, of course, how I happened to be there when Carlotta was discovered, actually by our cats." I shuddered, remembering all four cats attempting to get too close to the recently deceased body.

She nodded. "Right. I heard about that. How awful that must have been."

"It was." I clasped my hands in front of my waist.

Annie gasped. "Wait. I also heard a client whispering as I went past the other day, that Carlotta was killed with a nail file? Was that true? The sheriff won't tell us anything, so we're kept in the dark. I'd expected to be questioned about her, but he didn't even seem interested."

Yep, that sure sounded like Sheriff King once he'd made up his mind about something. While I probably shouldn't talk about the murder weapon, it sounded as if that tidbit was already floating around town. Maybe talking about it would give me more information about what happened with Carlotta. "Yes, it's true she was stabbed with a nail file." I held up my hand. "I don't think that fact is well known, though."

"Sure, I understand. I won't spread it around. Was just stunned when I heard it. Poor Carlotta. I wonder if she was killed with her own personal nail file? She always carried at least one in her purse."

I lifted my shoulder in a shrug. "I'm not sure." But I remembered how the ladies were quite upset about that particular nail file, as if they knew something about it, or recognized it. But I'd keep that to myself for now. I'd have to speak to Lottie and Florence again to see if they'd tell me what they knew.

Annie stood from her desk chair. "Have you heard if there's going to be a service for Carlotta?"

"I don't know yet. I think there may be an autopsy."

Her face paled. "Right. Because she was murdered."

"I'm afraid so."

"I'd like to go if there's a service. But I don't know any of her family. Except Jed, of course."

"Right. Same here." I wasn't sure if I should repeat what Sunny had told me about Jed taking care of the funeral, so kept quiet. To change the subject, I reached into my bag for the kitty coupons.

Annie's phone on her desk pinged. She glanced down at the screen. "Hey, my client is here, so I need to run. It was nice talking to you, even if the subject matter was sad."

"It's always nice to see you, too, Annie. Do you want me to leave these here with you?"

She motioned for me to follow her out of the office. "Let's give them to Everly, at the receptionist area. I'll have her let people know about them when they arrive for appointments."

"Great. Thanks so much." We walked down the short hallway that led out to the main area.

"No, thank you. I do love a good discount." She winked.

I left the coupons with Everly. Just as I was heading outside, my phone pinged. Veronica had sent an SOS, that she'd had to run to the restroom and had missed when Trixie had left her dancing spot across the street.

I glanced up and almost yelped. Trixie was headed right for me, but was looking down at her phone. I ducked inside the shop next door to hide out, hoping she hadn't noticed me. Boy, that was close.

"Hello, may I help you find something?"

I jumped and turned to see a fiftyish, well-dressed woman standing near the back of the small shop. I glanced around the store at the racks of dresses. Most of them were white. It was then I realized I'd stumbled into Brides Are Us.

Oh no. Hopefully, Ricky wouldn't hear about this and start spreading more rumors about me. The ones I'd heard were bad enough.

"Uh, no, thank you. I'll just be…" I pointed to the door, then scurried out. At least Trixie was nowhere in sight.

Chapter Thirteen

Today's mobile visit was with Dalen's cat. Having learned that Dalen and Carlotta had once been involved, I'd had Veronica contact him for his cat's grooming appointment today. It was a couple days earlier than normal, but I wanted to speak to him alone. Maybe he'd open up to me about his former girlfriend.

Percival and Jasper watched through the front windshield as they perched on the dash. I didn't love it when they did that, would rather them sit on the passenger side seat, but they'd jumped up there after I'd started driving. It seemed smarter to allow them to sit there than to try to reach across and move them when I was in the middle of going through an intersection. Besides, we weren't far from our mobile grooming destination at Dalen Spark's house. Soon, they could go to the back of the van and do their jobs of supervising me to make sure I did a good job for Dalen's cat, Bob.

I smiled as I glanced at the kitties, who were so excited to take a ride in my grooming van as if it was the very first time they'd ever experienced it. They touched their noses against the glass of the windshield and danced in place on the slick surface. Hopefully, they wouldn't slide off. It had happened once before, but their landing was at least soft, the seat cushion or the carpeted flooring absorbing their slight weight.

I turned into Dalen's wide driveway, pulling into the spot he preferred for visitors, a cement space off to the right of the house. It was a large enough area for me to have room to open the back doors and have the steps lowered. I liked it when that worked out. It made it less claustrophobic for me and my furry clients. Plus, pet parents often wanted to hang around and watch the groomings.

"All right, guys. You stay up here for a few minutes while I go and let Dalen know we're here, okay?"

Jasper's high-pitched mew and Percival's eyeblink were both in agreement with my instructions. I could leave them at the shop, or at home, but my two seem happiest when they were with me. I only left them at the shop if I had a pet parent who preferred I not bring them, or a kitty client who didn't like other cats. Thankfully, most were accommodating.

I climbed out of the van and closed the door. For some reason, even though Dalen usually chose the schedule time for Bob's groomings, Dalen never seemed to remember the exact time I'd be showing up. Maybe today, since we'd recently made the schedule change, he'd be ready for me.

I climbed the steps to the front door and grabbed the door knocker, which was shaped like a dragon. I let it drop against the door, listening to the heavy thud that would hopefully alert Dalen to my presence.

Several seconds passed before the door opened. Dalen stood there wearing an old T-shirt and jeans, hair sticking up as if he'd been asleep. His cat, Bob, trotted up to the open doorway, then stepped out onto the welcome mat to rub his face against my pant leg.

Dalen was rubbing his eyes, seeming not quite coherent, so I leaned down and picked up the cat, cuddling him against my chest. "Hi, Bob, are you ready for your grooming appointment today?"

Even though the cat might not realize the significance of the date and time, I hoped my announcing it to him would help Dalen snap out of his reverie and focus on his cat.

"Ugh," he said, then yawned. "Sorry. I guess I fell asleep."

"That's okay." I repositioned the cat in my arms. "Naps happen, right, Bob?"

In response, the cat yawned, causing Dalen to laugh. "Yeah, they do. If you're all set for Bob, you can go ahead with his grooming."

"Yep, we're ready. Want to tag along?"

Dalen didn't always want to come out when Bob was groomed, but this time he nodded. "Sure. If you don't mind seeing my pillow hair."

I laughed and shook my head. "Not a problem. It's what I see every morning in the mirror."

I carried Bob carefully down the steps, with Dalen following us. I handed him his cat when we reached the rear of the van so I could open the doors and lower the steps. As soon as I had the steps down, Jasper and Percival climbed over the front seat to hurry to the back area.

"Hang on, guys." I waved my finger at them. "We need to get Bob in here with us, right?"

I climbed up into the van, then reached down for Bob. Dalen did the handoff, then settled himself on the top step.

I placed the kitty on a towel beside the sink and tested the water to make sure it wasn't too hot. After I placed him in the bath water, I reached for the bottle of shampoo and began lathering Bob's fur. He purred.

I had a few who did that while being bathed, but some only tolerated it. Thankfully, most of my furry clients were so used to their grooming session that they didn't throw hissy fits. At least, not very often. They were cats, after all. On not-so-great days, I felt like throwing hissy fits myself.

From the step, Dalen blew out a long breath.

I glanced over. "Everything okay?"

"I'm just so relieved to have Bob back."

"Had he run away?" I knew what Ricky had said, that Carlotta had taken Dalen's cat, but didn't want to let on that I knew.

"No, see...I don't know if you'd heard it or not, but Carlotta Sykes and I were a thing. At least for a while."

"Oh. Okay." I wanted to ask more, but kept quiet, hoping he'd go on.

He ran his hand through his already-sticking-up hair, making it stand on end even worse. "So, Carlotta was a cat lover." He glanced toward me. "Guessing you already knew that?"

"Yep. I knew she was." Even though it seemed cats hadn't liked her in return.

"We had a messy breakup. I guess I'd neglected to get her to return my house key, because one day I came home from work and Bob was gone."

My eyes widened. "You must have been freaking out. I would have."

"I did. I checked all over the house for him. He wasn't anywhere. I even looked outside, even though he stayed inside all the time and never seemed to want to escape out the door."

"So what happened?"

"During my search, I finally found a note from Carlotta. It was under my covers on my bed, lying on the pillow."

I lowered my eyebrows. "That's weird. So the note..."

"It said she'd taken Bob, because she deserved a cat to love her back, since I didn't seem to want to love her."

"What a sad note."

"It would have been, if she hadn't added the last line—how her main reason was because she hated me so much and knew that taking away Bob would make me suffer. Which it did."

"I'm sorry you and Bob had to go through that. I'm guessing he was scared, too, to be away from his home and from you."

"When I finally got him back, he was terrified. He had a tiny patch of fur that he'd begun to scratch off near his neck. And he'd even lost a little weight, so I'm guessing he was too frightened to even eat."

I patted the cat on the head. "Poor kitty. I bet you're glad to be back home with your dad, huh?"

He meowed and rubbed his cold, wet nose against my wrist.

At Bob's meow, Jasper and Percival must have taken that as their cue to come and help me. They jumped onto a small shelf opposite the sink counter and sat down to watch, their whiskers twitching, and eyes bright.

Dalen pointed to them. "Your cats seem so well adjusted and calm. Are they always that way?"

I glanced at them. "Well, they have their moments when they get the crazies, or are in bad moods and want to wrestle with each other. Overall, though, they are sweet kitties."

"Maybe I should get another cat so Bob can have company when I'm at work?"

"Sure, you can do that. There're always kitties who need homes. Just make sure you do some research on whatever cat you choose. Like if you get it from the shelter, make sure to tell them you have another cat that would need to get accustomed to someone new. They can give you advice on how to introduce them. Or if not, I can always help out too."

"Thanks, Molly. I'll give that some thought. I just love him so much. And I guess I'm extra protective now after him being cat-napped by Carlotta."

"I can understand how you'd feel that way. I'm sure I'd be the same."

"Trust me, you never want to go through what I have."

I shook my head, as I rinsed the shampoo from Bob's fur.

Dalen blew out a frustrated breath loud enough that all three cats turned to stare at him. "I…I can't begin to tell you how relieved I am to have my cat back."

I watched Dalen for a few seconds. He was really having trouble getting past this. Not that I blamed him. It must have been so upsetting. But Dalen seemed to still be obsessed with it.

I grabbed a thick towel and wrapped Bob in it, drying off his fur. "I'm glad you two are back together. He seems relieved, too." I scratched him beneath his chin, causing a loud purr.

Dalen's shoulders relaxed. "I love that sound. What if I'd never heard him do that again? What if…" He held up his hand, as if to stop himself. "No, I have to move on, don't I?"

I wasn't sure if I was expected to reply, so I simply nodded and kept working.

"You're a really good listener, Molly."

"Thanks. I guess I do have the chance to listen to lots of people in my line of work."

"And cats." He pointed to Bob, who was still purring loudly. It must have been the power of persuasion, because Percival and Jasper were now purring too. A feline musical trio.

There was silence for the next couple of minutes while I clipped Bob's claws and checked him for any places on his skin or bumps. Then I looked at his ears, eyes, and teeth.

Dalen had turned a little on the step and stared out toward the neighborhood. His fingers fidgeted against his knees, as if he was nervous or agitated, which went along with his earlier words about Bob having been taken away.

I finished up with Bob's grooming and tied a dark green ribbon around his neck. "There ya go, mister. You look as handsome as ever."

He meowed and blinked his eyes, a sure sign of feline contentment.

"All set, Dalen."

At first, Dalen didn't move, or seem to have heard me. Then, he jerked and turned my way. "Sorry, lost in thought, I guess."

"No problem. Doesn't Bob look handsome?"

Dalen grinned. "Yeah, he really does. Come and see me, buddy." He held out his arms, and I did the kitty handoff. Bob snuggled his head beneath his dad's chin and made biscuits on his chest.

"You do great work, Molly. Thanks so much."

"You're welcome. Want us to bill you as usual?"

"Yeah, that would be great. Thanks."

"No problem. Veronica will send it to you soon." I was ready to clean up the sink and tidy the area before I left, but Dalen hadn't yet walked back to his house.

"Is everything okay?" I asked.

He shook his head slowly, as his eyes narrowed. "Thank goodness Carlotta isn't around anymore to cause trouble and pain for me and Bob. I'm so glad she's dead. She got what she deserved." He turned abruptly and walked back to his front door.

I stared after him for a few seconds before realizing my mouth was hanging open.

I knew he was upset about what Carlotta had done with Bob. But his sentiments were harsher than I'd expected. Had he hated her enough to have stabbed her with that nail file?

Chapter Fourteen

I headed to the post office with a package. My other reason for being there was to pump the postmistress, Edna Garing, for any information she might have heard about Carlotta's murder. Most people in town went in there at some point, if only to purchase stamps, and Edna had a keen interest in what people were up to.

When I entered the post office to mail the package, since I didn't always trust Ricky to pick them up, Edna Garing was standing behind the counter, with a glazed look in her eyes. Was she ill?

As I waited in line behind the only other customer, a man, I couldn't help but overhear the conversation. Or I guess it was better to say, hear his one-sided conversation. Poor Edna looked ready to wilt.

I understood her reaction. There were times, lots of them, when a pet parent would stand at the counter for a very long time talking about nothing in particular before or after their cat's grooming appointment, which put either Veronica or me behind.

We always tried to be polite and cordial, not wanting to upset any of our customers, but at times, that wasn't easy when the next person, or two, might be standing in the waiting area, impatiently wanting to get their cats in for their appointments. And while I hated rushing the first person out the door when they were finished, I also didn't like upsetting the next person in line who'd made their cat's appointment sometimes way in advance.

When the man turned his head slightly to one side, I realized it was Lenny Griffith, the guy the ladies said had an argument with Carlotta in the nail salon recently. They'd mentioned he used to live beside Carlotta when she and Lenny were kids. And that apparently there was some secret between them. Right now, anything to do with Carlotta was of interest. Maybe the secret Florence and Lottie alluded to might turn out to be connected now to her murder.

As Lenny continued to express himself loudly, he waved his hands like a large, excitable goose. Edna's eyes widened. She opened her mouth, but didn't get a chance to speak, as Lenny steamrolled right over her with his quick words. He was very good at talking fast, like he did it on purpose, so the other person couldn't reply or question what he was saying.

Lenny placed his hands on his hips. "I'm sure you'll find this very exciting news, Miss Garing. You see, the qualifications for town council are rigid. Nearly impossible to attain. But I, Lenny Griffith, am beyond a doubt immensely qualified to not only run the best race anyone has ever seen, but I'll win the election, hands down. It's quite exciting, isn't it? You must be so interested in my endeavors. In my zeal to accomplish this lifelong goal."

I shifted the package in my arms, which was starting to get heavy. How long had the man been standing here, and how much longer would he stay?

Edna leaned a little to the side, made eye contact with me, and gave a slight grimace. Did she need me to rescue her from this guy? From what he was saying, it didn't sound anything like post office business. More like a sales call. And those could be lengthy and annoying, depending on the person doing it.

Edna had crossed her arms over her chest. When I noticed her fingernails digging into her opposite arm, it was time to jump in. I dropped the box on the floor hard enough for it to thump. Thankfully, there was nothing in there that was fragile. But the sound didn't make a dent in Lenny's verbosity. He droned on, saying something about needing to curb the crime in Whitewater Valley.

After leaning to the side again to make eye contact with me, Edna raised her eyebrows.

I nodded, acknowledging that I'd give it another try. I moved closer to Lenny, reached up, and tapped him on the shoulder. When he stopped speaking, a pleasant silence filled the small post office. Edna let out a sigh, mouthed thank you to me, then stepped back away from the counter. She stomped first one foot, then the other, against the floor. Had she stood there so long her feet had gone numb?

Lenny whipped around, his eyes wide. "Yes? May I help you?"

I smiled, hoping he wouldn't be too upset. "Um, sorry, just…I was wondering if you'd be finished with your…." I glanced down at his empty hands… "postal business soon. I'm afraid I'm kind of in a rush."

One dark eyebrow rose as he studied me. "And you are…"

"Molly Stewart."

"Never heard of you."

Edna planted her hands on her hips as if ready to defend me. "Molly is our local cat groomer. She owns Fabulous Felines."

He blinked. "That's your actual job? You brush a bunch of cats?"

"Hey," said Edna. "That's not all she does. She also…"

"Thanks." I smiled at Edna to let her know I was okay. I'd faced many people who thought what I did was stupid or useless, and I wasn't in the mood to appease this guy and his antiquated thinking. "Yes, I'm a cat groomer. What do you do Mr.…?" I knew who he was, of course, from the ladies, but didn't want to let Lenny know that.

He stood up straighter and puffed out his chest. "You don't know?"

I shook my head. "Sorry."

"I am none other than Lenny Griffith."

"Um…. Nice to meet you," I glanced away, as if I really didn't care who he was.

"You really haven't heard of me?"

I gave a shrug.

He shook his head, like he couldn't believe anyone, anywhere, would ever not know about his wonderfulness. "I am, as we speak, preparing to run for the esteemed position of councilman of Whitewater Valley."

"Oh. Um, congratulations." It felt weird saying that, like he'd won, even though he apparently hadn't run yet. But what else could I say? He seemed so proud of wanting to do it.

"Thank you. I appreciate that you'll vote for me."

I blinked and mentally reviewed my words. Pretty sure I hadn't agreed to give him my support.

He gave a head nod to Edna, then to me. "Ladies, it's been a pleasure. And remember, don't forget to vote!" He rushed out of the post office, as if his feet were on fire. Was he going to hit every business up and down the block with the same speech?

Edna nearly wilted against the side of the counter. "Thank you so much for rescuing me, Molly."

"You're welcome. How long had he been here?"

"Three and a half days." She rolled her eyes, then laughed. "He'd been here way too long. I didn't have a chance to time it from when he first arrived, but believe me, it seemed like a year."

"I can believe it. He's a talker."

"Yes, he certainly is." She pointed toward my box. "I assume you want to mail that?" She smiled.

"Yes, I do." I picked it up, hefted it to the counter, and tried to set it down without too much of a thump, as I had when trying to get Lenny's attention.

She weighed the box, asked the usual questions about fragility or liquid inside, then gave me the cost to mail. "I'd ask why you didn't have Ricky pick it up, but I think I already know."

"Yeah, it's something that's important, it gets there in this century." I slapped my hand over my mouth, and my eyes widened. I lowered my hand. "Sorry. That sounded awful."

"But unfortunately true." She lifted one shoulder in a shrug. "Ricky's a good guy, I like him."

"Oh, so do I."

"I'm sure you, as a postal customer, have had many, shall we say, interesting encounters with him."

"Yes, you could say that."

She raised one eyebrow. "And working with him is a whole other level."

"I can only imagine. But you're a very patient person. Which, I'm sure, comes in handy."

She laughed. "It does. Although I have my limits, too."

"Doesn't everyone?"

"Yep. Thanks again for helping me get Lenny to stop talking. I wasn't sure how to get myself out of that predicament, aside from just telling him to get out of the post office."

"Was he trying to recruit you or something? Do you have interest in being in the town council?"

"Are you kidding? No way. It was almost like he had some prepared speech and didn't want to stop talking until he'd gotten all his words out. Believe me, there were lots of words even before you came in."

"I'm guessing you might not be the only business he's traipsing around to today, giving his pre-running-for-council speech."

"You're probably right. Better to check through front windows before entering any other establishments today."

I laughed, then my smile fell.

"What's wrong, Molly?"

"What if he comes into Fabulous Felines, too?"

She grinned and waved her hand. "That's easy. Just have the cats hiss at him. Maybe he'll run away."

"We can hope. Either way, I better get back to the shop. I can only imagine what Veronica might say to Lenny if he starts spouting off to her."

The door opened. I turned and held in a groan. It was Ricky.

"Well, howdy there, Molly. What brings you to our humble establishment this fine day?"

I glanced at the box that was still sitting on the counter. Would he take offense to me bringing it in here instead of having him pick it up? "I....well..."

A rustling sound came from behind me. "Ricky," said Edna, "Molly came in for some, uh...."

"Stamps," I called out, a little too loud.

Ricky dropped his mailbag, still mostly full, on the floor, much like he did when he came in to chat with Veronica and me. How many people didn't get their mail delivery today? "You're a silly gosling, Molly."

"I am?"

"I could have brought you some stamps. Saved you having to heft your weight across town to come in here."

Heft my weight? How much did he think I weighed, anyway? I opened my mouth, but had no idea what to say to that.

Edna pointed down at the counter. "Molly wanted to come in to see what stamps we had."

"That's right." I gave him a wide grin. "You know how I love cats, Ricky."

His ponytail bobbed along his shoulder as he nodded. "Yes. I believe I knew that fact before."

"Anyway, I was hoping you guys had some new postage stamps with cats."

Edna glanced down at something beneath her counter. There was an array of stamps placed there beneath a thick pane of clear glass. "Oh, sorry. No cats."

I snapped my fingers. "Shoot. Well, maybe next time, right?"

"Yep," she said.

Ricky tilted his head as he watched me. "You could always ask me about what stamps we have when I'm in your cat house, you know."

Cat house? "Yes, great idea."

"Thank you." He looked behind him, then back. "Hey, that guy who was here just now? I saw him leave. Who was it?"

Edna, who was slumped against the counter, probably exhausted after having to listen to what must have felt like a political rally, waved her hand toward the door. "That was Lenny Griffith."

"Ah." He narrowed his eyes. "I knew I'd seen him before. Didn't know his name, but…"

I stood up straighter, suddenly interested. Did Ricky know something about Lenny? "What were you going to say?"

"Well, probably shouldn't spread this around, but"—he looked at Edna, then me, gave his ponytail a tug, and seemed to make a decision. "I guess it would be all right to tell you ladies."

I wanted to shout, yes, please, tell us! But held my tongue.

He pointed over his shoulder. "That guy, he had some odd bumper stickers."

I deflated. That's all he wanted to talk about? Who cared about that?

"Yeah, I happened to pass his car while I was on the sidewalk and he'd parked and had just walked away."

Edna rolled her eyes. She, more than anyone else, had to be used to Ricky's weird stories.

I, on the other hand, couldn't just stand here and wait. I needed to hurry back to my shop in case Lenny descended on poor Veronica. "What did the bumper stickers say, Ricky?"

"Oh, you know, the usual. Don't forget to vote. Support your local councilman. And then there was another one. Come to think of it, that one looked like somebody had written on a plain piece of paper and used duct tape to put it on the back of the car."

He didn't elaborate on the last one.

"Uh, Ricky? What did that last one on the piece of paper say?" I'd come this far listening to him, I might as well go the distance.

"Oh, That. It didn't make much sense. No sense at all, actually. It said, Nail Techs deserve to die. Isn't that weird?"

My mouth dropped open. "Are you sure that's what is said, Ricky?" He had been known to elaborate before.

"Of course I'm sure. Do you think I normally go around snooping into other people's business while I'm delivering the mail?"

I glanced at Edna, then said, "No, of course not." But what I really thought was that Ricky did that instead of delivering the mail.

I checked my phone for the time. I'd been gone long enough. "I should be going now. Have to get back right away to Fabulous Felines." I gave Edna a meaningful look, assuming she'd pick up on my need to go rescue Veronica from Lenny, if necessary. As I left, I thought about that last bumper sticker. It seemed an obvious jab at Carlotta from Lenny. But had he put it on his own car, or was someone else trying to make it look as if he had?

Chapter FIFteen

Early the next morning, as soon as I got a return text from Veronica that all was quiet on the feline front, I headed to the library for a brief visit. A mystery novel I'd just finished, which was fabulous, was due to be returned. I only had one more day until Jillian would have sent me an angry emoji text about the book being late. Even though I was her best friend, I wouldn't escape her tough head librarian exterior.

I opened the main door to the library, always amazed at the quietness here compared to meowing and purring in Fabulous Felines. Even though I loved coming to the library, I wouldn't trade the kitty noise level of my grooming shop for anything.

When I approached the main desk, I was disappointed not to see Jillian. Not only did I love visiting with her, I always wanted to physically hand her any books I returned to see the look of approval on her face.

In her place behind the desk was Valene. She glanced up. "Oh, hi Molly." She smiled. Well, that was a vast improvement from the way she'd clawed and screamed on the recent video. She still had the scratches on her face and arms, but they were much lighter now, not red and angry-looking from Carlotta's fingernails.

"Hey, Valene." I placed the mystery on the counter between us. "How are you doing?"

She shrugged. "Okay." She looked left, then right. "Guess you heard about my…" She nodded down toward one of her arms.

There was no use denying it. If nothing else, Valene had to know that Jillian and I talked often, and about everything. "Yeah, I heard. I hope you're…."

"I'm doing better, thanks. I guess I should feel ashamed at what happened with Carlotta right where you're standing." She pointed to my feet. "But I don't."

"You don't?" I couldn't imagine taking something like that in stride. I'd want to hide until people forgot about it.

"No. Even though it was a spectacle, and Jillian is still a little mad at me, I think a woman has to do what she has to do. Don't you think so?"

"I…."

She pushed a lock of hair behind her ear. "You see, I made a major decision after what happened between Carlotta and me."

"Okay." I glanced behind me, making sure no one was hovering close by to listen to us.

"I've decided to go after what I want. To pursue what would, without a doubt, make me happy. And that would be Dalen."

I blinked. Dalen Sparks? "But what about….I mean, didn't Carlotta tell you some things about Dalen and her during your, uh…" I pointed down to the apparent fighting spot again.

Valene waved my comment away with her hand. "I no longer consider that a problem."

"You don't?" She'd come a long way from the fight I witnessed on the video and from how Jillian had described Valene's actions when she'd first returned to work.

She shook her head. "See, the way I figure it, Carlotta was trying to get me to back away from Dalen, so she could have him."

I lowered my eyebrows. "Yeah, I guess that might be…."

She stepped closer to the counter. "And you know what else?"

I was afraid to ask, but shook my head.

She tapped her fingernail on the countertop. "I'm convinced that the very reason Carlotta did all of that was to throw me off. To make me think Dalen didn't want me when in fact, the guy is head over heels for me."

My mouth opened, then closed. How could I say anything to that? It didn't seem to be true from what Carlotta had said, but how could I possibly know?

"And," said Valene, with a sly expression, "I also think that Carlotta was jealous of me and Dalen. Of our blossoming love."

Oh boy. This was getting deep. Had Jillian heard all about this yet? I started to reply, but Valene went on.

"You know, Molly, I just have to say it. It's a super good thing that Carlotta was murdered. And in such a ghastly way. It was exactly what she deserved."

I gasped. "You don't really mean that, do you?"

"Of course I do. With her gone, it makes my path to Dalen wide open. Now he and I can experience true love and happiness without that witch causing trouble. I'm thrilled that Whitewater Valley and the whole world no longer have to endure her toxic existence. Thank goodness for sharp nail files, right?" She giggled as if making a joke.

I swallowed hard, shocked at Valene's proclamation, and not sure what to do about it. Valene was proudly telling me she was glad a woman, someone she'd recently had a public altercation with, and who she was in a rivalry for a man's affection for, had recently had the life snuffed out of her. She was so unconcerned about the fact that another person had died. Had Valene hated Carlotta so much and imagined herself in love with Dalen enough, that she'd killed Carlotta to get what she wanted?

"Molly?"

Startled, I jumped and whipped to the left, but relaxed when Jillian walked up beside me. "Oh, hey."

"What's going on?" She studied my face. I could only assume my eyes were still wide and unblinking after what Valene had said.

"I, uh…." I pointed toward Valene, wanting to say what was on my mind, but at the same time not wanting to drag it all up while she was still here.

"What's happened," said Valene, "is that Molly returned a book." She held up the novel, as if her boss wouldn't know what a book might look like.

"That's great." But Jillian's smile was brief. She watched me for a few seconds, then turned to Valene. "I noticed there was a pile of books in the history section that needed to be reshelved."

Valene stood up straighter. "I'm on it." She waved to me, then scurried around the counter and past us, heading across the library.

"Molly? Are you all right?"

I nodded. "Yeah. I think so."

"What in the world just happened? I figured it might have something to do with Valene, so I gave her that task to get her to leave for a bit."

"Have you by any chance spoken to Valene lately?"

"Of course. I mean, she does work here, after all." She pointed toward the shelves of books where Valene had trotted off to.

"No, I mean about Carlotta, and Dalen."

She tilted her head. "Not since I made her come in right after her fight with Carlotta." She huffed out a breath. "I still can't believe she allowed that to happen right here in the library." She focused on me again. "Why do you ask?"

I glanced behind me before saying, "She just admitted she's thrilled that Carlotta was murdered."

"What?" Her eyes bugged out. "I can't believe it."

"It's true. She told me herself, right here. She's ready to go after her man, and now that Carlotta is out of the picture, the way is clear for true love and all that."

Jillian blinked. "Um…. Wow, okay. No, she hadn't shared all that with me."

"Maybe because you're her boss? She might not have wanted to say that in front of you."

"Possibly. But she had to know you'd tell me."

I glanced toward the book aisles. "Maybe that was on purpose."

"What do you mean?"

"If she assumes we'll talk, then you'll find out her thoughts without her going through the possible embarrassment of telling you to your face."

"You might be right about that." She shook her head. "But that's a lot to process, isn't it? And I suppose you noticed how Valene was dressed today?"

I frowned. "I guess not. I was so focused on two things. One, that her scratches had faded, and two…"

"What was two?"

"That I was returning my book a day early, and you weren't here to receive it. It felt like a wasted effort on my part." I gave a mock scowl, which made her laugh.

"Sorry I wasn't here. But I'm so proud of you for bringing back your book before it was due. Great job." She patted me on the shoulder.

I grinned. "But since I didn't pay attention earlier, how was Valene dressed that was so noticeable?"

"To be fair, I probably notice things like that more in library workers than patrons do." She flipped her hair over her shoulder. "You might have noticed that I take great pride in my appearance."

"Yes. I have definitely noticed."

She winked. "Thank you. Anyway, Valene always dressed okay, but it was sort of, I don't know, utilitarian. Sort of for purpose, not for show. Does that make sense?"

I glanced down at my jeans and short-sleeved top. "Like I do?"

"No. You always look cute."

"Just not fixie."

"True. But that's not you."

"Agreed." And I liked it that way.

"Today, Valene had on a skirt just above her knee, a frilly blouse, and medium height black heels."

"Sounds fancy."

"It is. Especially for Valene. But now that you've filled me in on what she said, about getting her man, it makes more sense."

"She's on the prowl and dressing for the part."

"Exactly."

I touched Jillian's arm and leaned closer. I didn't particularly want the older couple passing by us to overhear this next part. "After she said all those things to me, especially about being so glad Carlotta was dead, I had a thought that..."

"That she might have had motive to kill her? Yeah, that thought crossed my mind, too. And it scares me."

"At least you're in a perfect position to keep an eye on her here at work."

Jillian crossed her arms over her chest. "Oh, believe me, I'll be watching her like a cat does a catnip mouse."

I rolled my eyes. "I think you've been spending too much time around me and the cats."

She bumped my shoulder with hers. "Never. But I will be keeping a closer eye on my assistant."

Chapter Sixteen

Hank had invited me to meet him at Carrie's Coffees on our lunch hour, which amazingly happened at the same time today. That was rare. Between his appointments and mine, we were lucky to stop in and give a wave hello every so often. And our conversations lately revolved around the murder. Hank was a smart guy. I depended on his viewpoint to help me figure out who might have ended Carlotta's life.

When I arrived with Percival and Jasper in tow, Hank was standing just inside the café.

"Hey," he said with a smile. The one that always made my knees weak.

"Hey, right back." I nodded down at the cats, who stood on either side of my feet on their leashes. "They thought a visit to the coffee shop sounded like a good idea, too. And they also know how much you like them, so I knew you wouldn't mind."

"Of course I don't mind. How are the cats doing today?" He knelt and gave each one scratches between their ears, earning him purrs. He pointed to Jasper and Percival. "Even though I see lots of cats in my veterinary practice, I never get tired of hearing those purrs."

"I know exactly what you mean." I grinned, glad that not only were Hank and I dating now, but that we had that, and so many other things in common.

"I'd hoped there'd be a free table, but they're all filled up." Hank tilted his head toward the seating area. "And it appears that most of them just got their food, so they won't be leaving anytime soon."

"Rats. I was hoping for the same thing." I checked the clock on the wall right above the order counter. "I'm not sure how long I can wait for one to open up."

"I know. Me too. I guess we could try going instead to—"

A loud psssting noise came from a few tables back. Other customers had turned in that direction to see what it was.

Or rather, who, was making the sound. It was a duet, done by Lottie and Florence. And they were waving us on back.

I smirked. "I think we're being summoned."

Hank peered over my head to the very back corner and sighed. "Yeah, we are."

"Sorry. Are you okay with that? I'd hoped we could sit and talk for a while, but…"

He winked. "Don't worry about it. Like you, I wanted to have some time alone to talk to you. But I know the ladies as well as you do, and I understand how they can be. I'd rather not disappoint Lottie and have her start that shrieking thing she does when she's upset."

"Exactly. Okay. Are we ready?" I gave a gentle tug to Jasper and Percival's leashes, alerting them to our change in direction.

Hank motioned for me to go first, and the cats and I traversed our way through the small maze of customers at tables, several of whom were acquainted with the cats, so we made frequent stops for them to receive the attention they felt they so deserved.

Once at the table, Florence and Lottie each grabbed their respective furless baby, placing them on their laps. Helga wore a frown at having been relocated from her chair, but Eleanor seemed only half awake and hung limply in her mom's arms, so no harm was done. I checked out the kitties' outfits for the day—blue sailor dresses with gold buttons on the front, and tiny blue sailor hats with gold braided trim.

Hank took the empty seat next to Lottie and I sat by Florence, which put Hank and I across the table from each other, so not even sitting together. We made eye contact, gave mutual shrugs, and turned toward the ladies.

I reached over to give Helga a pat, and was rewarded with a nose nuzzle against my fingers. "How are the girls doing?" I asked.

"As for me," said Lottie, "I'm having finger joint pains today, so not great.

Florence, didn't you say you were experiencing a headache?"

She shook her head. "I think Molly was asking about the other girls. You know…." She pointed to first her cat, then to Eleanor.

"Oh, of course." She giggled. "They are quite well. They finished their bowls of cream, as you can see."

I looked down, noticing the two empty bowls that had been shoved to the middle of the table. Hank and I exchanged another glance, both having agreed previously that we wished the ladies wouldn't give their cats so much dairy. But neither one of us wanted to upset the women, so we kept quiet. Hank, however, was diligent in checking out Eleanor and Helga at their regular appointments, careful to question their human moms about possible tummy issues.

I nodded toward Florence's plate. "How's the coffee cake today? As good as usual?"

"Even better. I just love coming here. I'm so glad Carrie doesn't mind that we bring our babies along. I'm not sure I could tolerate any business that kept them out." Her eyes widened as she glanced down. "Oh! I see you have your babies with you, too."

Lottie scrunched down in her seat until I was afraid she might slip to the floor. She peered beneath the table. "Yes, I see them now, too. Excellent. We're all sitting at the kitty table, aren't we? I'll give a big meow to that." Her voice was louder than usual at the last part, causing those around us to chuckle and stare.

Hank's eyes widened, and his nostrils flared. I tried just as hard not to laugh. The ladies didn't always have the same sense of humor as most others around here and could get carried away pretty easily.

Carrie appeared from behind me. "Hello all. Glad to see you and your cats today." She smiled down at Jasper, who was sniffing her shoe. "What can I get you today?"

Hank and I both ordered lattes and coffee cake.

"Coming right up."

I watched as she headed back to the kitchen area. Right before I turned back to my tablemates, the main door opened, and a couple of people stepped in. One of them was Mrs. Kelper.

"Oh look, Florence," said Lottie. "It's that nice, Mrs. Keeper."

"I think that's Kelper," she said.

Lottie frowned. Hmmm. "Are you sure?"

"Very sure."

She shrugged. "Let's say hello." She waved exuberantly at Mrs. Kelper, who didn't seem to notice at first. When she did, she smiled and nodded.

Lottie pouted. "Why isn't she coming over? Hank and Molly joined us after we waved."

It had been the sound like air leaking out of tires that had caught Hank's and my attention when they wanted us to join them, but I wasn't going to mention it.

Finally, Lottie stood and waved both arms over her head as if signaling for help from a desert island.

Hank snorted a laugh, then covered his mouth, as if he'd coughed. I shook my head, barely able to keep from snorting too.

Mrs. Kelper had since moved to the order counter and spoken to Zelma, Carrie's assistant. When she turned to check out the seating area, she must have spotted Lottie's antics because his eyebrows rose to her hairline. With a shrug, she headed our way. Maybe she, like us, knew it might be worse to upset the older women by ignoring their pleas for attention, as well as the fact that all the tables were full.

"Hello, all," she said when she reached us. "I see I should have brought along my cat, too."

"Yes," said Lottie. "Meow!"

Mrs. Kelper jerked, as if startled. "Um, yes, well…."

Hank nodded to Mrs. Kelper. "How have you been?"

Her face lit up. "Thank you for asking, Dr. Chenoweth. I don't know if Molly has told you or not, but I've been having the most exciting time lately."

Was she talking about her Kelper-doodles? I had to admit, they were amazing. The only bad part was, they were so good, and she'd supplied me with so many, I may or may not have overindulged on them. Okay, yes, I definitely did.

Suddenly, Hank stood up. "Please," he said, pointing to his chair, "take my seat."

Lottie frowned. "Then you won't have anywhere to sit, Dr. Chenoweth."

Mrs. Kelper smiled. "Thank you, anyway. I'm not staying. Just came to get a takeout order, so I'll remain standing."

Hank nodded, then retook his seat. I gave him a wink in thanks for being so sweet. It made his face turn pink, which I found adorable.

"What's been going on, Mrs. Kelper?" asked Florence.

She pressed her hands together in front of her waist. "I won the cookie competition again at the county fair!"

Florence and Lottie both took hold of their cats' front paws and made clapping movements. "Excellent," said Florence.

"Thank you." Mrs. Kelper gave a nod.

"How many years in a row has it been?" asked Lottie.

With her eyes crinkled at the corners, she said, "Ten. I'm so pleased."

"You should be," I said. "That's quite an accomplishment."

"You know, Molly, I agree. It really is. I'm quite the baker."

Hank caught my glance and we shared raised eyebrow looks. There was no lack of confidence there.

"I must say," she went on, "that I had the thrill of a lifetime."

Lottie leaned over to Florence and said, "Do you suppose it involved some handsome man?"

Either Mrs. Kelper didn't notice the comment or chose to ignore it. "After last year's win, I had the honor and privilege of having my photo taken with the governor!"

"Wow," I said. "That must have been exciting for you."

"Oh, it truly was. He was so happy for me."

"About…your Kelper-doodles?" Her recipe must be more popular than I realized if it had gotten all the way to the Indiana Statehouse in Indianapolis.

"Why yes, Molly. Of course. He made an appearance at the fair. Didn't you know he'd been here for a visit?"

I squirmed as she watched me intently. "Uh, no. Guess I missed that."

"You really should pay more attention to current events."

Florence and Lottie were nodding in agreement, although I knew for a fact they rarely paid attention to what was going on around them unless it involved their cats, and how they were going to dress them that day.

"Anyway," Mrs. Kelper waved her hand, "I was thrilled to bits when I received an email from the governor!"

"Goodness," said Florence. "How did he even know what your email address was?"

Mrs. Kelper had the good sense to glance away as she said, "I…had sent him a few, uh, several emails in the past."

Lottie's eyes were wide, as if waiting on some great proclamation. "What did the email say?"

Mrs. Kelper let out a breath, seeming relieved she still held her audience's interest. "He congratulated me, again for last year's win, and said he hoped I won again this year."

"And you did. Good for you," said Hank.

She nodded. "I replied to the governor that I'd win again. There was no way I was going to lose after he gave me his endorsement."

Endorsement? Now she made it sound as if she were running for office. Would her Kelper-doodles work as an incentive for people to vote for her? Probably. They really were that tasty.

Helga grumbled as Florence shifted in her chair to see Mrs. Kelper better. "I have a question."

Mrs. Kelper blinked. "Um, all right."

"How did you know you'd win again this year? Weren't there a lot of other people who'd entered?"

At first, Mrs. Kelper's brow furrowed, then she gave a slow smile. "Trust me. I have my ways of getting what I want."

Right then, Carrie called out that Mrs. Kelper's order was ready.

She gave us a wave. "Good to see you all. Have a lovely day. I know I will."

As she walked toward the pickup area, I looked at Hank, whose eyebrows had risen. Was he thinking the same thing that I was? That Mrs. Kelper might have forced the issue to get her main competition out of the way to win the contest? Would the woman have actually killed someone else in order to acquire another first-place honor?

Chapter Seventeen

J ed Martin had phoned a few days ago, telling me he'd found a copy of a book I wanted. I'd been so busy, today was the first chance I'd had to drop by. Aside from getting the book, I was curious about how Regis was getting along with his new leash. But to be honest, I really wanted to keep an eye on Jed since he appeared to have a reason to have possibly killed his ex-wife.

When I arrived at Second Hand Books and stepped inside, there was no one at the front desk to greet me. Usually, either Jed or Sunny was around. Maybe they were in the back doing inventory. Veronica or I always tried to head to the counter when the bell went off on Fabulous Felines' door, but Jed's shop didn't seem to have a bell or chime. Did it used to? I couldn't remember.

It felt off somehow that no one was here to greet customers. Was either Jed or Sunny out of the shop today?

I walked to the counter, ready to wait until one of them came out. There had to be at least one person on the premises since the door had been unlocked.

As I glanced around, I smiled. Jed had the cutest bookshop. Very eclectic in décor and the types of books he carried. I was glad he'd found the one I'd been looking for. Of course, I'd checked with Jillian at the library first, and she hadn't been able to locate a copy. Knowing her, she might take it personally that I asked Jed to help me out when she'd been unsuccessful in acquiring a treasured book. Maybe I'd just keep that bit of information to myself for now.

A door slammed from somewhere in the back. Good. Maybe now one of them would come out and—

"What?" came from someone behind the door on the right. It sounded like Jed. And his voice was loud, something I didn't usually hear.

"That's right!" yelled Sunny.

Why were they yelling? I'd never heard them exchange a cross word before. And to hear Sunny sound like that was a shock. Wasn't she worried about keeping her job?

"Maybe you should find another place to work, Sunny."

I sucked in a breath. Whatever was going on between them must be bad.

"I'm not going anywhere," she said. "You're the one who needs to get into gear and do something."

"Do what?" he asked.

"I think you already know what I'm talking about."

"Sunny, give it a rest, will you?"

"No. I won't. If I can tell you how to do something better than you're doing it, it's my responsibility to do that."

Wow, that sounded like what she'd said to Veronica and me at my shop. But this was to her boss, which seemed riskier of making him upset.

"Listen," he said, "I guess you mean well, but—"

"Jed, you've got to listen to me. Don't you realize how badly things could go if you keep this covered up?"

My eyes widened. Covered up? What had Jed been up to?

There was silence for a few seconds, then Jed said, "I think you're getting involved in something that's none of your business. You work for me. I don't answer to you."

"Well, like it or not, I am involved. You need to come clean about what you've done."

My mouth dropped open. What was so bad that Sunny would be bold enough to talk that way to her boss?

"Sunny." Jed's voice came out like a growl. "You better mind your own business or you might be sorry."

"What's that supposed to mean?"

"Trust me. You don't want to find out."

That sounded like a threat. And Jed was normally so easygoing and good-natured. What had happened, or more importantly, what had he done, that Sunny was so adamant he had to come clean about?

"There are things I know. Things about Carlotta, that—"

"Leave it alone, Sunny. I mean it!"

Footsteps stomped from the back. I glanced around, realizing how this might look if I were caught here listening to their private words. Maybe I should come back later when things weren't so tense.

The door squeaked open quickly, and Jed appeared. At first, his head was down, and he didn't notice me standing here. But after he took a few steps, he stopped suddenly.

"Oh, Molly. I...." He reached up to smooth his hair. When he did that, his hand was shaking. Was that from anger at what Sunny had said to him, or fear that she might tell someone else what he'd apparently done?

I forced a smile. "Hi, Jed. I came in for the book you called about?"

He swallowed, then stood up straighter. "Uh, sure. Yes, I have that right here under the counter." He reached down, then laid the book in front of me. "Is this the one you wanted?" He glanced behind him toward the closed door. Was he nervous about me being here after what was said to Sunny?

"Yes, that's it. Thanks. How much do I owe you?"

He watched me for a minute, eyes narrowed. Then he gave me the total.

"Thanks, Jed. I appreciate you getting this for me. I've looked all over. You must have special leverage that the average person doesn't." I laughed, hoping it would help him to relax.

He shrugged. "Yeah. Guess so."

I paid him, then tucked the book beneath my arm. He hadn't bothered putting it in a sack, but was obviously distracted. And for good reason, from what I'd been able to discern. Maybe I should change the subject. "By the way. How is Regis doing with his new leash?"

A thud came from the back room.

His face paled, then he glanced behind him. "Uh..."

Was Jed upset about whatever was going on back there, or had something happened to his cat? "Is he okay? Did something happen to him?"

He held up his hand. "No, he's just fine. It's…it's going well and he seems glad to be out for walks again." His shoulders relaxed a little as if talking about his furry friend eased the tension.

"Great. Glad to hear it." I was relieved that Jed seemed to be calming down some. I'd never heard him raise his voice to anyone before, and it had been a shock.

The door in the back opened again, and Sunny stepped out. When she spotted me, she stopped and darted a glance toward Jed. Then, she nodded at me. "Hello, Molly. Nice… to see you." She looked behind me to the front door, then back.

"Hi. Just picking up a book that Jed found for me."

She reached up and grasped the locket on her necklace, as if needing something to do with her hands. "Have…have you been here long? I didn't realize anyone else had come in."

Jed turned to stare at me, seeming to hold his breath as if he, too, needed to know the answer.

"Nope," I said. "Had stepped in about two seconds before Jed came out here. Perfect timing, huh?"

They both seemed to deflate with relief. Jed forced a smile. "Yes, perfect timing. Enjoy the book, Molly."

That was my cue to leave. I held it up. "Thanks again. See you later."

After I'd left the shop, I walked a few yards up the sidewalk. Pounding footsteps sounded from behind me. Someone must really be in a hurry. I whipped around, thinking maybe Jed or Sunny had second thoughts and wanted to tell me something, but it was Sheriff King.

Oh. Joy.

I waited until he reached me. Because the sheriff was nothing if not tenacious. If he wanted to talk to me, he'd follow me wherever I went until he said what he wanted. Might as well get it over with now so I could get on with my day.

"Molly!" he shouted, out of breath from what must have been his only exercise for the month.

"Hello." I stuck the book in my purse, then crossed my arms over my chest, waiting as he caught his breath. "How can I help you?"

"What were you doing in that bookstore just now?"

I lowered my eyebrows. "What do you mean?"

"Why were you in there?"

I tapped my purse. "Because I just bought a book." He'd been standing right in front of me when I'd slipped it into my purse, so it shouldn't be a surprise.

He tugged up his pants, then straightened his hat, both of which had gone askew in his quest to track me down. "Now, don't give me that."

"Listen, sheriff, I don't know what to tell you other than I bought a book. Isn't that why most people go in there?"

He shook his head. "You may have bought something, but I know better."

I could see this wasn't going to be as quick a conversation as I'd hoped. "All right. If you have special powers of observation to see inside a building when you're outside, and from down the street, why don't you tell me why I was there?"

"Don't get smart with me, girlie." He crossed his arms over his chest.

I rolled my eyes. I really hated when he called me that. I mirrored his actions and crossed my arms. But I kept quiet.

His bushy eyebrows rose, then lowered. "Fine. I'll say it. You were trying to be an amateur detective." He dropped his arms, then pointed his finger at me.

While I wasn't going to deny I'd hoped to garner some information while in there, I still had the fact of making a purchase as my main reason for going to Second Hand Books. And I certainly wasn't going to tell him what I overheard from Jed and Sunny.

"Sheriff King, as I said, I bought a book. Would you like to see it? It's a really old volume of children's stories about *cats*." My mouth quirked up in a half smile. "Hey, I'd let you borrow it if you wanted to read about all the cats and—"

"No. I don't want to read your stupid book, Molly." He took a step back, as if there was an actual feline in my purse. "You just…. You make sure you're staying on the straight and narrow, young lady."

"Don't I always?"

He glared at me. "I'm keeping my eye on you, woman."

Oh, now it was woman. I might have preferred girlie. No, maybe not. "I'm just living my humble cat grooming life, Sheriff. How can there be anything wrong with that?"

He took another step back but, pointed two fingers of his right hand toward his own eyes, then at mine. "I'm watching you. Stay out of official murder investigations. Got it?" He hitched his pants up again, then pivoted around and stomped past me, going the other direction.

I let out a breath, glad that was all his mini lecture amounted to this time. I glanced at my watch and headed back toward Fabulous Felines. I guess I'd stood in the shop and listened to Jed and Sunny longer than I'd realized, along with being subjected to Sheriff King's rantings. If I didn't hurry, I'd be late for my grooming appointment.

Chapter Eighteen

Even though I'd been in the nail salon previously and had spoken to Annie about Trixie, it hadn't given me all the information I felt I needed. So, I'd taken the frightening plunge and scheduled a manicure appointment with Trixie. Although the thought of her demolishing my nails again made me shudder, it seemed the best way to see for myself what might be going on with the inept nail technician. I had hopes, not high but hopes anyway, that maybe Trixie had improved vastly since our last encounter.

Maybe it wouldn't be so bad.

Time to find out.

I pushed open the salon's main door and stepped inside, assaulted once again by the strong chemical smells from nail products. I sneezed twice, tried to ignore an expression of distaste from a woman sitting nearby having a pedicure, then hurried to the reception desk.

Everly, the receptionist, smiled when she saw me. "Hi Molly. Trixie will be with you shortly."

"Perfect." I smiled, but wondered if it was convincing. Because I sure didn't feel it.

"Also," she said, holding up one finger. "Annie's not in right now, but wanted me to thank you again for bringing in the coupons."

"You're welcome. But I need to thank you, too. You're doing me a favor, after all."

Everly grinned. "You know how Annie loves a good bargain. I think she was grateful mainly for herself and getting a deal on her next grooming appointment for Kiki."

I laughed. "Yeah, that works too."

My laughter died when Trixie sidled up next to me. "Hi Molly. Come on back. I'm ready for you now." She rubbed her hands together as if looking forward to doing something dastardly to my nails. Although, I couldn't imagine it any worse than how they ended up last time.

"Uh, sure." I followed her slowly, hoping somehow I wouldn't have to actually go through with the manicure. But I knew it would happen. I remembered the other time, and how Trixie had grabbed my hands, not letting them go until she'd finished.

No, this was what needed to occur if I wanted to find out more about Trixie and what was going on with her.

"Right over here," she said, waving her hand toward the client chair in her station. "Oh, but you probably remember from last time. By the way, how come it's been so long since your first manicure? Most clients come in often for touch-ups." She frowned down at my hands. "Oh boy. This is going to need more than a touch-up. More like a complete overhaul."

I reluctantly plopped down in the chair, then curled my fingers in toward my palms as if that could protect me from her ministrations. But deep down, I knew better. I just hoped she had some better nail polish colors than last time. They'd been so garish and bright, even my cats had been afraid of them for a while.

Trixie pulled her small table closer, then positioned it between us. She sat in her operator chair opposite me and gave me a wink.

A wink? Was that code for, 'Brace yourself, Molly?'

"Now," she said. "I know how much you loved the colors I used on you last visit, but I'm afraid to say that those shades are no longer available."

"What a shame."

"I know, right? I mean, when I tried to get those again, I was told they no longer made them, nor would they ever, in a million years. What do you suppose they meant by that?"

I held in a sigh, then gave a shrug. What I really wanted to say was, 'what they meant was that the horrendous hues you gave me last time were ugly enough to melt iron.'

"So, since I had to get different colors, I just know you're going to adore what we have for today."

I glanced around at the other clients having their nails done. When Jillian came, she always requested pink, her signature shade. "Don't the customers sometimes request certain colors?" Maybe I could ask for something mild, like light pink, or even cream. Something I wouldn't have to hide in my pants pockets when around other people who might see them.

She shook her head. "Now, Molly, I realize you have your own business and know lots of things about cats. But let's face it, between the two of us, who would you say is the nail professional?"

I clenched my teeth together, knowing there was only one true answer to her question. I hated saying it, but whispered, "You are."

"Right. So let's get on with the fun, okay?"

"Fun, yes. Sure."

It was quiet for a minute before I glanced up at Trixie. She was frowning. I raised my eyebrows in question.

She held out her hand toward me. "I can't do my job if your hands are on your lap."

I looked down. By golly, she was right. Maybe my fingers knew what was coming and had gone into survival instinct mode on their own. I slowly placed them on the table, flinching when Trixie grabbed my left one, leaving the right one alone in the battle for its own protection.

Unfortunately, she didn't have a light touch when filing my nails. I tried to control my facial expression from showing how apprehensive it made me, but on the inside, I was yelping loudly.

Unable to watch the atrocity of what was happening, I looked around the room to distract myself, taking in the other nail techs at their stations. Each one had decorated his or her place with personal photos, cute plaques, and of course, a name plate.

I studied each booth that I could see from where I sat, finally landing on the one I'd hoped to see—Carlotta's. I was a little surprised it was still there, with all of her pictures and decorations, but maybe Annie felt it was too soon to tear it down out of respect for what had happened to Carlotta. And perhaps it was a way for clients and other nail techs to pay their respects, too.

I glanced up at Trixie.

Well, all the nail techs except this one.

"Hey," I said, causing Trixie to jerk, and the nail file she used barely missed scraping across the skin below my thumbnail.

"What?"

I tilted my head in the direction of Carlotta's booth. "I noticed Carlotta's stuff is still up at her station."

Trixie didn't glance in that direction but instead shrugged. "Yeah. So?"

"I just wondered why, since, you know, she died."

She mumbled something I couldn't make out, but kept on working.

"Do you happen to know who might have wanted to kill her? I mean you did work together after all, and—"

Her grip on my finger tightened. I tried to pull away, but she was too strong. "Why do you need to know that, Molly?"

"Uh, just curious, I guess?"

"Maybe you should leave all that to the sheriff, since he's the professional. Just like I am here."

The way she glared at me made me want to run away, but I was trapped. Instead, I nodded and said, "Yes, sure."

If Trixie knew I'd been there when Carlotta's body was discovered, she hadn't let on. But I really hoped she didn't know, since that information might set her off, and my hands would be in more danger than before with her holding a sharp object.

Seeing the nail file in her hand made me think of the actual murder weapon. It could have been any of the workers in here, but my money rested with Trixie as the most likely suspect here.

I was so intent on not making eye contact now, that I wasn't paying attention when Trixie got out the bottles of polish to apply to my nails. Not that it would have mattered since she made it clear that, since she was the professional, she was quite capable of choosing the right shades for me. I kept my gaze averted, looking at other clients, the walls, the floor. Anything but at my nails and the atrocities Trixie might be subjecting them to.

Finally, she released my hand and placed it on a towel on the table.

"There," she said. "Polish is on. We'll let that sit a bit to dry. Don't move."

I nodded, afraid to see what she'd done, yet oddly fascinated at the possible result. I took a deep breath, let it out, and looked at how she'd transformed my nails.

It. Was. Hideous.

I thought it couldn't possibly be worse than last time, but I was wrong. The color was burnt orange with zigzag stripes of bright purple going diagonally across the nails. And at the very tip of each nail was a big yellow eye. An eye!

"Don't you love it?"

Trixie's voice jolted me from staring at my unfortunate fingers enough to lift my gaze to hers. "I honestly have no words to describe it."

She nodded. "Right? I know! And I did the eyes, just for you." She beamed, obviously so proud of the gift she'd given me.

I somewhat assumed the diagonal lines were stripes of some sort. With the orange background, was it supposed to be a tiger?

But that eye…. Did she think I also worked for an optometrist and would be partial to eyeballs? I felt like my own fingers were watching me. Ick. How would I deal with my appendages looking like they were constantly judging me? Or trying to kill me with their dastardly glares?

Trixie tapped her own fingernail on the table in apparent impatience. "I can't believe you haven't figured out the eyes yet. It's from a cat! You know, since you groom them?"

Ah…. now I was beginning to see what she'd done here.

But the eyes at the tips of each nail still gave me the willies. And would do the same for every person who saw them. And possibly some of my furry clients, too. I could imagine a few of them not only hissing at my nails, but taking a swipe at them, as well.

"I…I do see that," I muttered. "Th-thanks so much."

When Trixie finally walked away, I slumped down in the chair. Okay, I'd done the deed. Or, more accurately, had it done to me. I eyed my glimmering fingernails as they eyed me back, already groaning at the thought of Jillian critiquing them. And with the add-on Trixie had done, they were so long now, I'd have to trim them if I had any hopes of completing cat groomings, without poking a cat or myself in the process.

From behind me, a couple of ladies who were having pedicures by a different nail tech began to whisper. But they weren't very good at it, so it came out loud and clear.

"Listen, Bernice, I don't want just everyone to overhear this," said one woman, "but that Trixie? She's a piece of work."

"How do you mean?" asked the other one.

"Well, for starters, she recently was…how should I put this…smelly."

That wasn't news to me, after talking to Florence and Lottie previously.

The other woman gasped. "Why, Greta? What was going on with her?"

"I can only surmise that it's something to do with that Carlotta lady."

I sat up straight in my chair. This could be interesting.

"You mean the one who used to work here? Who was murdered?"

"That's right," said Greta.

A noise like one of them turned in her chair came from behind me. "Tell me. What have you heard?"

"Well, again, I don't want others to overhear…."

I slid down in my chair again, hoping they couldn't see me over the half wall that separated the rows of chairs.

"Go on."

"But apparently, Trixie's job is all she has."

"Okay," said Bernice.

"She lives with her parents and has no boyfriend or any prospects of one."

"What does that have to do with Carlotta?"

"I'm getting to that. See, when Trixie and Carlotta worked here together, Carlotta constantly harassed her."

"How do you know this?" asked Bernice.

"I'm friends with a lady who used to go to Carlotta to have her nails done. She actually witnessed Carlotta being mean to Trixie, to the point she made her cry, right here in the salon."

"That's terrible. But I don't understand why Trixie was smelly."

"It's simple, really. Trixie didn't have anything going for her at home, or with outside interests. All she had was this place. And when that wasn't going well, she just stopped caring."

"And Carlotta tried to ruin her job for her?"

"It sounded that way, according to my friend," said Bernice.

"What all did Carlotta do to her?"

"Carlotta berated Trixie by telling her she wasn't any good as a nail tech and might as well quit."

"Wow, that's harsh. I kind of feel sorry for Trixie."

"Yeah, I kind of do too. From what I'd noticed around here, Carlotta wasn't a nice person."

"Why did Annie keep her around?" asked Greta.

"Because she seemed to perform magic with nails. They were incredible works of art. Even though people didn't like her, some women came to her for the way she did their nails."

"I see."

"Carlotta had also told Trixie that she was so bad at her job, no other salon would ever hire her. And she probably wouldn't ever be any good at any other kind of job either."

"That Carlotta sounded like a witch."

"Yep. I agree. Although…."

"What?" asked Greta.

"Also, from what I've heard, Trixie really is a horrid nail tech. I'd certainly never go to her."

There was silence, and some rustling. Had they turned in their chairs?

"Shhh… not so loud. Someone is sitting in Trixie's chair as we speak."

"Oh! How long has she been there?"

"I don't know. But let's act like we don't see her. No sense upsetting her any more than she might already be, having her nails done by Trixie."

"Good idea. And I'm glad we whispered, so she wouldn't be able to overhear us."

"Exactly," said Greta.

Footsteps tapped in my direction, and Trixie returned. "Okay, Molly, you're all set. Your nails are finished and look great, if I do say so myself."

My smile quivered on my lips as I gave a stiff nod. "Uh, yes. Um, thanks."

"You're so welcome." She held out two pieces of paper. "Here's your bill, that you can pay at the reception area. And here's your appointment for your follow-up nail appointment."

Follow-up? I'd never agreed to that. "Uh...."

She patted me on the shoulder. "So you have a super terrific day, and I'll see you soon!"

As she left, she did a little jig, reminding me of her dancing in Carrie's Coffees and on the street across from Fabulous Felines. At least she was happy. That was good. It was better than what she must have felt when Carlotta had treated her so badly.

I glanced down. But I still didn't like what she'd done to my nails. With a sigh, I got up, paid my steep bill, and left. I seriously doubted I'd come back, but would give the salon ample notice so they could fill my spot with someone else. Even though I didn't like how Trixie did nails, as a small business owner, there was no way I'd leave her hanging with a missed appointment.

Even if she was on my radar as a possible suspect in Carlotta's murder.

Chapter Nineteen

I'd just waved goodbye to my kitty client and her mom when Veronica came into the shop.

"Sorry to be late," she said. "My dentist appointment ran over. I already called and rescheduled my next grooming appointment, but that turned out to be better for Mary Nolan and Wispy today, anyway. The dental patient before me came in late, so that made their whole schedule off kilter." She tapped her shoe on the floor, obviously still vexed at her day falling apart. "But we know about that happening, don't we?"

"Indeed, we do." I sighed. "I always hate when that happens, but it's just a part of dealing with people. But I guess there's not much we can do about it, right?"

She gave a mock scowl. "People, such troublemakers." Then she laughed. "Of course, if it were up to the cats, they'd never be on time so...." She waved her hand.

"You're right about that. They'd be late because they were staring at their empty food dishes."

"Or too busy watching birds through the window."

I held up one finger. "Or the most important..."

"Taking a nap," she said.

"That's right. Catnaps. The be-all, end-all of felines everywhere. To be fair, though, I have to agree with them, Naps are pretty great."

Veronica smiled. "Totally agree." She waved at a couple of cats in their carriers, who I'd already finished grooming and were waiting for their pet parents to pick them up.

Then, she crossed the lobby and came around the counter until she stood next to me. She placed her purse beneath the counter, then glanced down at my hands.

And screamed.

"What in the world happened to you?" She grabbed one of my hands, then gasped. "Why are your fingernails staring at me?" She dropped my hand as if scalded, then wiped her fingers off on the front of her blouse.

"I know." I made a face. "They're horrid. And I didn't have time to trim off the eyes yet. Believe me, I'll be doing that before my next grooming comes in because one of my previous appointments, the cat hissed at my nails the whole time." I pointed toward one of the carriers. "Not that I could fault her for that. They are repulsive."

Veronica glared at my hands, then reached down into her purse for something. She held her nail clippers out to me. "Here. Use these."

I shook my head. "No, I have my own. I can—"

She placed the clippers in my palm, then backed two steps away. "Do it. Now. Please." With another look at my nails, she shuddered.

I had to admit she was right. I might've been able to deal with the nails themselves for a little while before they drove me crazy, and I popped the fake pieces off, but the eyes were extremely creepy. I quickly snipped off the ends of the nails with the clippers, leaving a pile of yellow eyes staring up at us on the counter.

Jasper jumped up beside me, ready for some love. But when he spotted the eyes, he arched his back and smacked the small pile onto the floor.

"Good kitty," said Veronica. She petted his back, and his fur relaxed.

I scratched him beneath the chin. "Sorry, buddy. Mama didn't mean to freak you out."

He closed his eyes in acceptance of my apology, rubbing his face against the back of my hand.

"Now, one more thing." Veronica walked to a small closet off to one side and got our broom and dustpan. Once she'd disposed of the offensive eyeballs, she replaced it and came back. "Listen, Molly. I know you hate getting your nails done, even if they turned out pretty, like mine." She held out her short but neat nails, painted a pretty light blue. "But why did you do that? Those eyes! They made me feel like I'd just watched a scary movie."

"Actually, it was déjà vu, really. I only had my nails done at the nail salon by Trixie because…"

She nodded. "Oh, I get it. You wanted more information on her since she has a motive to have killed Carlotta?"

"Exactly." I checked out my nails, which were still ugly, but no longer causing me to long to wear mittens the rest of the day so I wouldn't have to see them.

"I can see why that's déjà vu after your other trip there when you were ambushed into a manicure."

"Ambushed is right. Trixie wasn't going to take no for an answer last time. This time, I made an appointment with her."

"You're a brave girl, Molly." She patted my shoulder.

"Thank you. I was hoping I'd hear, overhear, eavesdrop if necessary, some information to help me out."

"And?" She moved her hand in a circle. "I need details."

I filled her in on my conversation with Trixie and on what I overheard from the two women seated behind me.

"Wow, it sure does sound like Trixie hated Carlotta."

"I agree."

Her eyebrows lowered when she glanced at our wall clock. "Wait, aren't you meeting your uncle for lunch today? That was today, right?"

I gasped when I saw the time. "Yes, thank you! I need to run. But I'll be back before my next appointment. Sans yellow eyes on my fingers."

"Thank goodness for that!" She waved. "Have fun."

I grabbed my purse, told the kitties I'd see them soon, then speedwalked to Leaning Tower of Pizza, glad it was only a few blocks from Fabulous Felines. I got a couple of strange looks as I passed people, but I waved and hurried on my way. It wouldn't have been the strangest thing townspeople had witnessed me doing, by far.

Once outside of the restaurant, I took a deep breath to calm my racing heart. I opened the door, pleased to see my uncle already seated at a table halfway across the moderately sized restaurant. With the food here being so good and the seating space limited, it was no wonder it was often hard to find a table. Russ waved me over when he saw me.

When I reached him, I bent over to give him a hug before sitting down next to him. "Hey, there."

"Hey, kid. Good to see you." He narrowed his eyes. "Why is your face all red?"

"I sort of um…." I grimaced.

"Ah." He studied me for a few seconds. "Let me guess. You were running late and had to rush."

"Yep." I laughed. "You know me so well." I placed my purse on the empty seat next to me.

"That I do, love." He winked, then pointed toward a glass in front of me. "I went ahead and ordered your usual. That okay?"

"Very okay. Thanks." I took a sip. How thoughtful of Russ to have this ready for me when I got here.

Right then, the waiter brought our food, made sure we didn't need anything else, then left.

"Wow." I pointed to my plate. "You're a magician. What perfect timing."

He waved his hand. "Nah, just got here early because…" His gaze wandered somewhere to his right, but he was holding back a grin.

I tapped his arm to make him look at me again. "Because you knew I'd probably be late and have limited time to spend on my lunch hour?"

"You're a smart girl, Molly."

I laughed. "Takes one to know one. Um, except for the girl part."

"Thanks for that, at least."

I was always glad to spend time with Russ. We ate and chatted about this and that, never landing on anything too serious. There were times when we'd had to have those kinds of discussions, but often, it was fun to just enjoy our time together. Unfortunately, we had to reschedule all too often because one of us had a conflict in our schedule, so today was turning out great already. Thank goodness Veronica had reminded me before it was too late.

I glanced around the room, always appreciative of the lovely hand-painted murals on the walls, making me feel as if I really was in a quaint eatery somewhere in Italy.

"What's happening with suspects for the murder?" he asked.

I held out my hands.

"Not sure what that means, kid."

"I had my nails done so I could talk to Trixie some more. She's high on my list right now."

His eyebrows lowered as he studied my nails. "They're... colorful."

"This is the good version. You should have seen the eyes."

"Do I want to know?"

"Probably not. Anyway, I didn't get very much from Trixie, but two women talking about her behind me made it clear how badly Carlotta had treated her, and how much Trixie hated her."

"That sounds like a possible motive right there."

"I thought so too."

We finished our food. When I was full, I left the rest of my small pepperoni pizza aside, ready for a takeout box. Russ had done the same, although he was very trim and it wouldn't have hurt him to eat the whole thing. But I'd never say anything. In my opinion. He was just about perfect as he was.

Now that all the tables were full and everyone seemed to be enjoying their meals, the room quieted down a little. No one had entered for a while, so when the sun reflected off the glass door, it caught my attention.

The new arrival was Dalen Sparks.

He was more dressed up than normal, his usual attire was either jeans or shorts. He strode purposefully to the counter and asked for the manager. A woman stepped out. "Hello, I'm the manager. How can I help you?"

Dalen stood up straighter, smoothing down the front of his shirt. "I'd like to fill out a job application, please."

The manager glanced behind her, then back. "Well, I can certainly give you one, but we're not hiring right now."

"When will you be?" His voice had a slight edge, as if impatient.

She shrugged. "I really don't have any plans anytime in the near future.

Our staff is small, but it's all we need right now."

"A small staff?" He gave her a hopeful smile. "Then maybe you need some help? I'd be a good man for the job."

"No, I'm sorry. I can't afford another employee right now."

Dalen glanced around the full room of customers. "Really? You seem to be doing pretty well, I'd say."

The door opened again, and a young couple entered. They walked up and stood behind Dalen.

The manager waved at them. "Hi, be right with you."

Dalen glanced over his shoulder, then faced the manager again. "Look, I really need a job, okay? I'm a hard worker, I promise, and...."

"I'm sure you are. I'm so very sorry." She held up her hand. "Believe me, if I had an opening, we could discuss it. But I just don't. Do you want to fill out an application in case there's something in the future?"

I'd had people come in for the same reason and always hated telling them no. Except the time that Ricky asked if he could deliver mail for the cats. When I explained that cats didn't get much mail, expect maybe cat food coupons in their names, he accused me of not wanting to help him further his postal aspirations.

Dalen's shoulders tensed. "No, never mind. I guess even if a person who gets in your way is gone, you still have to clean up the mess they left." He headed toward the door and exited the restaurant.

I looked at the now-closed door and frowned. "Did you hear that part about a person in Dalen's way?"

Russ' eyebrows rose. "Yeah, I sure did."

"Also, why would Dalen come here looking for work? Because he already has a job as a supply delivery guy for the nail salon."

He nodded. "True."

"Do you know him?"

"A little," said Russ. "He comes into the construction site office sometimes with supplies. Not lumber or anything, but things for the office that the receptionist needs sometimes."

"Huh, I didn't realize that."

"Dalen contracts out to do deliveries for a few different places. All over town."

"Then why would he want a job here, in a restaurant? I'd think that would be very different from the work he's used to doing."

He glanced around, then leaned closer. "Yes, it would be way different. But I got this from my receptionist the other day, after Dalen had been in and talking to her."

I nodded. "Go on."

"Since Dalen and Carlotta Sykes had broken up, and from what you'd told me the other day, when they'd had a loud fight in the salon, he was afraid he'd lose the delivery contract with his firm, and that if word got out, his other jobs might dry up too."

"So maybe he's hedging his bets for another job just in case. That sounds like a smart move to me."

"That would be my guess. If he truly does lose his contracting jobs, I'd be glad to hire him on at my construction firm. I happen to know he used to do some of that work in the past." He held up his hand. "That is, if he turns out not to be the murderer."

"Good point."

Chapter Twenty

Mid-morning the next day, I had a little time between grooming appointments. I'd been meaning to visit Evan's photography studio but hadn't had the chance. Several of my clients wanted pet portraits done and had given me pictures of their fur babies, so I left the shop in Veronica's capable hands and walked the short distance to Evan's studio.

Some of the pet parents had said they'd be glad to text or email Evan the pictures, but he said he had a better outcome if he could study an actual photo beforehand to get a feel for how he might photograph the pets.

Percival and Jasper were due for an outing, so I put them in their harnesses and leashes so they could tag along. We had to stop a few times to bat at small stones along the sidewalk or sniff, then hiss, at ladybugs, but we finally got there.

I stepped inside the calming, cool interior, waiting for my eyes to adjust after the bright sunlight outside. The cats, too, blinked a few times, but stayed by my legs.

Evan walked out from a doorway in the back, which I knew to be his darkroom. "Molly? Hey, how are you?" He glanced down. "And you brought two of my favorite cats. Good to see you, guys." He crouched down and petted each cat, causing a duet of rumbling purrs.

My previous visit to the dark room hadn't been a happy one, since that's where Whitewater Valley's second murder victim had been discovered. Jasper and Percival had been with me that day, too, and it had been all I could do to keep them from wanting to check out the body, never a good scenario.

Thankfully, today's visit should be cheerier. "I have some more clients who want pet portraits." I waved the stack of photos, along with a piece of paper with the clients' names, their pets' names, and contact information.

His eyes lit up as he stood. "Hey, thanks! I can always use good news." He held out his hand, taking the stack and glancing through them briefly. "The pet parents got some amazing shots here. Hopefully, I can do as well with a professional photo session."

"I have no doubt you can. I have proof, remember?" The portrait he'd done of Jasper and Percival hung on my living room wall. I smiled every time I saw it. Evan was a very talented photographer, and getting cats to cooperate wasn't always the easiest task.

He placed the photos on a nearby table. "This is great. I have some openings coming up that would work great for pet portraits."

"Perfect." I glanced around the walls of his front room. "I see you have some new photos up." Dogs, rabbits, parakeets, and gerbils filled one entire wall.

"Yes, these were so much fun. I love that pet parents of all kinds of animals want to have their pets' likenesses captured for their homes. When I get a new batch, I try to change them up in here. You'd be surprised how many people drop in just to see if I have their baby's photo on the wall."

I shrugged. "I'm not surprised, given how some of my humans are around their babies. I admit that Jasper and Percival are spoiled." I grinned. "But I have a few parents who are over the top. Not that it's a bad thing. Just different. If the animals are happy, that's all that matters."

"True. You'd know better than anyone, Molly. But, even though I switch the photos out to make room to showcase new ones, there's one I will never move."

"Oh? What's that?"

He waved for me to follow him to the far wall, right next to a back window opening out to luscious green maple trees. It was the portrait he'd done of Percival and Jasper when Jasper was new to our family and the kitties weren't getting along. Evan had used catnip to relax my boys. It was the most beautiful photo I've ever seen.

"Oh, Evan, I knew you'd had this up shortly after you took it, but for you to keep it up….wow."

"Because of you and your cats, Molly, I began a whole new line of my business, those pet portraits." He pointed to the other wall. "I will be forever grateful. To all of you." He smiled down at my cats. "And I'm so glad you guys are getting along now."

"So am I, believe me. Thank you for putting their picture in such a special place ."

He pressed his hand over his chest. "It's my honor. I—"

The main studio door opened so fast that it bumped against the wall behind it. It was Lenny Griffith.

Evan walked across the room toward the entrance. "Hello. I'm Evan Lakes. How can I help you?" His initial startled expression changed into a welcoming smile. I knew that smile. I'd worn it many times. When somebody came in, who I immediately knew would be a person I wouldn't want to deal with.

I had a pretty good idea that Lenny wasn't there for a portrait, but hoped I was wrong.

Lenny's grin was wide, showing off gold crowns on his molars. "Hello there. Hoping you'll do a guy a favor?"

Evan glanced at me. I gave a slight shrug, then Evan said to Lenny. "What might that be, Mr...."

"Lenny Griffith." He stuck out his hand and shook Evan's. He switched his gaze to me. "Oh. We've met."

"Yes, at the post office." Not the most pleasant of experiences.

"You had a large package to mail." His eyebrows drew together as he watched me, to the point I felt uncomfortable.

"That's right."

"And," he tapped his foot, "if I remember correctly, you interrupted me as I was speaking to the postmistress."

"I'm sorry about that." Though at the time I could see Edna needed rescuing. "It was something I needed to be mailed out right away. I'm afraid I was in a hurry, you see, and—"

He held up his hand. "You say that as if my business were unimportant."

My mouth opened slightly, but I pressed it closed. How had his dropping in here gone downhill so quickly?

Evan moved a couple of inches toward me. Was that a show of support? Either way, I was glad for his friendship.

"Mr. Griffith," he said, "perhaps you can tell me why you've come to see me today? Are you in need of a portrait?"

He frowned. "What? No, of course not. Why would I want one of those?"

I watched Evan closely. He blinked, but otherwise there was no outward sign of irritation, which I was certain he felt. I sure did on his behalf. I admired the way he covered up his true feelings. Unfortunately, my expressions went on their own merry way, getting me in trouble, before I even realized I was doing it.

"Because," continued Evan, pointing toward his front door, which sported a sign announcing what kind of business it was, "that's what I do here. I'm a photographer."

Lenny glanced around the room for the first time. "Guess I didn't notice that when I came in."

I rolled my eyes, but was glad Lenny didn't seem to notice. I didn't need yet another reprimand by him since we happened to end up in the same building at the same time.

Evan's foot tapped lightly on the floor, but once again, Lenny seemed oblivious. "Mr. Griffith."

"Call me Lenny." He spread his arms out. "We're all friends here."

But were we? I wasn't feeling any warm fuzzies around the guy.

After giving a small sigh, Evan said, "Lenny, now that you know what my business is, again, how can I help you today?"

Lenny's eyes had a gleam, as if he'd already received what he'd come in for. Confidence oozed out of him, making me want to run away rather than stand and listen to his spiel again as I had in the post office. I had a bad feeling that Evan might be in for a boring, over-informative lecture and that it might be difficult to get rid of Lenny any time soon.

"I'm so glad you asked," said Lenny.

I wanted to leave, since I needed to be back to my shop soon, but a quick check of my watch showed I still had a few minutes. And having previously met Lenny, I wanted to remain as long as I could to support Evan. I'd hate to leave him here alone with the guy, having to endure the drivel he'd spew again about his councilman aspirations.

Lenny opened his arms wide again. I sincerely hoped he was encompassing his environment rather than wanting a hug. "Mr. Lakes, my reason for entering your humble establishment today is twofold."

Evan gave a nod. "All right." I could tell from the way he'd tensed beside me that he wasn't enjoying the visit so far. And I wasn't either.

"You see." Lenny began to pace in front of us. "I've long been in awe of anyone in any kind of public office. It's been my life's dream, no more than that, my mission to someday become a councilman for the fine city of Whitewater Valley."

"That's…nice," said Evan.

I slid a glance toward him, but he was watching Lenny.

"It is nice, isn't it?" he said, with a head tilt. "It's what I've been working toward my whole life. You see, every town needs someone to take care of its inhabitants."

He made us sound like life forms from a distant planet who didn't know how to find food or shelter. I held in a sigh that longed to escape.

"And to lead the way toward wonderful, new, and exciting experiences."

If Lenny's exciting experiences were anything like this talk, I would opt out.

"Our fair city of Whitewater Valley is the future. Its residents are the key to the future. And I am proud to announce that I am the one who holds the key."

Evan raised his hand. "Lenny, while I do appreciate the…talk you've shared with us, I'm still curious about the other part of your two-fold reason for coming in today."

The door to the studio opened, and Florence and Lottie came in, carrying their cats. Did they have an appointment for a photo session?

Lenny glanced behind him, then back, as if whoever had entered couldn't possibly be as important as he was. "Why, it's simple. I came in for campaign donations."

Evan waved to the ladies, then looked directly at Lenny. "I'm sorry. If that's why you're here, then I'm afraid my answer is no."

Lenny appeared to deflate in front of them. "Well, then…I guess I'll just go ask the next business down the block. Thanks for nothing." He stomped out of the studio, leaving all of us, including the cats, staring after him.

Evan let out a breath. "Hello, ladies. Come in to see the proofs of Helga and Eleanor's photo shoot?"

"Yes, we did," said Lottie. "By the way, why do you call it a photo shoot? I mean, shoot? It sounds dangerous, like you might have a weapon."

Chuckling, Evan said, "Not dangerous in the least, I promise. As usual, your girls did an amazing job of having their pictures taken."

"Of course they did," said Florence, cuddling Helga against her chest. "We wouldn't have it any other way, would we, Lottie?"

"No, we wouldn't." She lowered her head and kissed the top of Eleanor's head.

I reached out and laid a hand on each cat's head, making sure not to show favoritism. "It's good to see you all again."

"You too, Molly," said Lottie. "Why was that man here before? The one who wants to run for president."

I nearly choked. If he were president, we'd all be in trouble indeed. "Um, he wants to be councilman for Whitewater Valley."

"Oh, " said Florence. "Then I'm doubly glad we turned him down yesterday."

Evan frowned. "Did he try to get money from you two?"

I happened to know that the ladies were on a fixed income. Even though they had sufficient funds to enjoy eating at restaurants, having their nails done, and having their cats groomed, they didn't splurge on much else. How dare Lenny bother two older women, begging them for money? "So you turned him down?"

"You bet we did," said Lottie. "No way am I giving up our kitty fashion fund for someone like him. I didn't like his demeanor at all."

"Definitely a bad demeanor," agreed Florence.

I was with them there. Not only was Lenny annoying, but he also gave off a vibe of being willing to do whatever it took to achieve his political dream. Even if that meant bothering eighty-year-old citizens out of their meager savings.

Lottie tapped her chin. "Florence, what was it the guy who wants to be president said the other day while we were in the library?"

"You'll need to be more specific. What were the cats wearing?"

"Their white taffeta dresses and black booties."

Florence held up her finger. "Ah, yes. That was Tuesday. We'd thought it odd at the time. It had something to do with church."

I stepped closer. "Church? What did he say?"

She tilted her head for a few seconds as she thought. "It's better to give than receive."

"No Lottie tugged on Florence's arm. "That wasn't it."

"Yes, it was."

"You said it backward."

"If you know so much, then you say it."

Lottie glared at her friend. "All right. I will. He said, 'It's better to receive than give.' Remember? That's why we thought it was odd."

Sighing, Florence nodded. "Yes, you're right. That was it."

"Thank you." Lottie appeared to be preening.

"Wait," said Florence. "There was something else, too. Do you remember what that was?"

"Um, no. I thought I was doing well to remember the one thing."

I patted Lottie's hand, then smiled at Florence. "You're both doing well. Florence, what was the other thing Lenny said?"

"He told whoever he was speaking to that people who go out of their way to help strangers are stupid, and a bunch of losers."

I frowned. Why in the world would anyone say that?

Chapter Twenty-One

Veronica and I were glad the next day was over. It was a whirlwind of fur, kitty shampoo, paws, and meows. I was ready for a break. Jasper and Percival had both been asleep beneath the counter and moved as slowly as sloths to sit beside my feet, their eyes still half closed and both yawning. "Hey, you two, ready to head out?" I put them in their harnesses and attached their leashes.

I glanced up when Veronica came out from her grooming room. "We're headed to the Sandwich Shack for something to eat," I said. "Want to come with us?"

"Aww, thanks. I'd love to, but Jerome is making me some homemade pizza."

"You got a sweetie when you married him. I'm so glad you're happy."

She winked. "Don't I know it. He's a keeper." Then she studied my face.

I reached up to touch my cheek. "What? Am I wearing someone's fur? Or maybe mustard from the sandwich I had for lunch?" I scrubbed at my skin. I probably should check in the mirror before heading out to eat.

She removed my hand from my face. "No, it's not that."

"Then what? You're making me paranoid."

She placed her hands on her hips. "You mentioned my husband and how happy we are."

"Yeah...."

Her eyebrows rose, then wiggled a couple of times.

I should have known what she was up to. I was so tired, my radar was a little slow. "Oh, I get it. You're being a matchmaker again, right?"

She waved away my comment. "I don't need to do that. You already have a boyfriend. And Hank's a keeper, too."

"Yeah, he definitely is. But we're not married, as you know." Although, no thanks to Ricky Notts for spreading that little gem all over town. How long would people keep asking me how my married life was going?

"That's my point. Why not? You're wonderful. We agreed he's a keeper. You both seem to enjoy being together. What are you waiting for?"

"Veronica, we're not nearly ready for that step yet. Just because you got married within a month of meeting your hubs, doesn't mean I can do the same."

She frowned. "I guess. I just want you to be happy, too, Molly."

I smiled. "Don't worry. I am. And if and when that day comes for me, you can stand right next to me as I get married and—"

Her eyes lit up, and she clapped. "Really? Me? Wow, I'm so honored."

I grabbed her hands to silence the clapping. "Calm down. It's not happening any time soon."

"Yes, but when it does, I get to be there." She glanced dreamily at the ceiling. "I'll get to buy a new dress. And get my hair done. Oh, and my nails and makeup, too."

"Of course you get to be there." I shook my head and laughed. "Okay, since you have previous plans with your Mr. Wonderful right now, I'll see you tomorrow."

"Yep," she said, grabbing her purse. "I'd better go too. His Italian dishes wait for no one."

"Have a good night. I'll lock up."

"Don't stay too late, Molly. We had a long day."

"I won't. I promise."

Veronica headed out and closed the door behind her. I tidied up a few things in the front room, then grabbed my purse and the cats' leashes and headed for the door.

When I reached out to set the lock, the door opened. I jumped back. "Oh! Valene, you scared me."

"Sorry, I was sent on a mission from Jillian."

My heart slowed as I nodded. "What's the mission? Is Jillian okay?"

"She wanted me to bring you this." Valene stepped into the salon and closed the door behind her. Then she reached into her large handbag and handed me a book.

"Perfect." I grinned. "I've been looking forward to this. I didn't think I'd get to have this new mystery for quite a while with such a long waiting list."

Valene shrugged. "Guess being her best friend has perks?"

"Yep, guess so. Thanks." I glanced at the intriguing cover of the mystery, looking forward to tonight when I might find some time to start reading it.

"No problem."

It was then that I realized Valene hadn't answered my question about Jillian being okay. "Is something going on with Jillian? I'm a little concerned."

She crossed her arms over her middle. "She keeps asking me questions about why I ended up in a fight in the library with Carlotta. And I keep telling her it had to do with Dalen. I don't know why she doesn't believe me that he and I are…." She shrugged.

"I thought Dalen and Carlotta weren't seeing each other anymore when you were with her in the library."

"They weren't. But Carlotta didn't want to let him go. At least that's what I've heard."

What she'd heard? "Wait, Dalen didn't tell you himself?"

"No, we…. Uh, see, I like him so much. And he comes into the library all the time and flirts with me and…"

I could see where this was going. "He hasn't actually asked you out?"

"No, not yet, but that doesn't mean anything, does it? He's had a lot going on. I think maybe he's waiting for things to calm down before diving into another relationship. With me."

"Okay." I studied her furrowed brow. "Is there more to why Jillian keeps asking you about it?"

"Yeah. See, someone, who I guess must have been in the library that day, tattled to Sheriff King and complained about a loud argument while they were trying to enjoy being in the library."

"Did he come to see you?"

CHAPTER TWENTY-ONE

"Yep."

"At the library?"

"Yep." She held up her hand. "Jillian was out on a break, so she wasn't here when he came in. But, of course, nosy patrons had to tell her when she came back."

Maybe Valene was hoping for her boss not to find out about the sheriff's visit. "Did the sheriff threaten you with anything? About what happened to Carlotta?"

Her eyes widened. "No. He said he knew it wasn't me because it was those ladies who did it, and he's trying to get enough proof to lock them away."

Lock them away?

"He just scolded me for causing a scene in a public place." She pressed her hand over her heart. "Trust me. I was so nervous he'd accuse me. I'm relieved he's looking someplace else. I'm too young to go to prison! And I don't look good in orange jumpsuits! Besides, how would I begin my love story with Dalen if I live in a cage?"

Valene hadn't exactly said she was innocent. And she did have a motive for wanting Carlotta out of the picture because of Dalen. But I wouldn't say what was on my mind right now. I'd keep an eye on her. Still, I wanted to wring the sheriff's neck for not checking into all the possible leads for the murder.

Valene pointed toward the door. "Well, I'd better get back to the library before—"

There was a knock on the door. Who could that be? No one ever knocked, they just entered. Plus, our hours were posted on the outside of the door, so I doubted it would be a client thinking they had an appointment right now. I reached forward and gave the door knob a pull.

Standing out on the sidewalk were Florence and Lottie, along with Helga and Eleanor, of course, who they carried in their arms as if cats were royalty. The ladies rarely came to Fabulous Felines, preferring instead that I simply appear in one of their driveways for their kitties' routine grooming appointments.

My heart sank. I knew it might not be a quick visit. But I made myself smile, because I did love them and didn't want to hurt their feelings. "Hello, ladies. How can I help you?"

"It's actually how we can help that young woman who just came in there." Florence pointed toward the open doorway.

"Valene?"

Lottie clapped Eleanor's paws together in padded applause. "That's it! Very good, Molly."

My eyebrows rose. "Thanks. So...you wanted to see her? She was just leaving, and I was going to close the shop..."

"No, we must see her here and now."

I'd been unfortunately right. That meant, of course, I would be staying as well until the ladies had their say. It would be no use to try to dissuade them. I learned that a long time ago when I first groomed their cats. My life would be easier if I let them come on in and say what they felt they needed to, although I couldn't imagine why it was such an emergency to speak to Valene. Unless they'd gotten her confused with Jillian and wanted to talk about books?

I must have been lost in my own head for too long because everyone, including the cats, now stared at me.

"Molly," said Florence, "Helga doesn't like the sun shining in her eyes, and I've forgotten her sunglasses. Could we please step inside?"

"Of course, sorry." I held the door open wider as they all trooped in.

Lottie and Florence put their cats on the floor. Percival and Jasper, already very familiar with the other two, began sniffing and grooming them. Since I didn't know how long we might be staying, I unhooked my cat's leashes and set them on the counter beside my purse.

Valene looked at the ladies. "You wanted to talk to me? What about?"

"About the most important thing in this world, young lady." Florence stared at her.

"Love," said Lottie, pressing her hands together against her chest.

They wanted to give Valene romantic advice? I'd been on the wrong end of that conversation before. I never knew how to take those two. As far as I knew, neither had ever been married, didn't have current men in their lives, and spent all their time together and with their felines. Not that there was anything wrong with that. It just didn't seem to be conducive to giving advice to another woman about men.

But I couldn't very well stop them once they had in mind to do something. I pointed to the chairs next to the picture window. "Would you all like to sit down?"

Florence nodded. "Thank you, Molly. That would be nice. Do you have anything to eat? We haven't had supper yet."

Yeah, I would've been eating my supper right about now if they hadn't all shown up when they did. My stomach growled, causing all four cats to whip around and stare. "Sorry, kitties. Wasn't trying to insult you. Um, sure, Florence, let me see what I've got."

I went back to our small kitchen area to scrounge around. I came up with several cans of diet soda, some crackers, and a block of cheese that still looked okay. It would have to do. Once I had paper plates and a knife to slice the cheese, I set them on a tray and returned to the main area.

As I set the tray on the counter, Florence was saying to Valene, "You must grab your man, Valene!"

Valene's face paled. "You mean, literally, like really grab him?"

She waved her hand. "It could be taken either way, I think, depending on the circumstances."

"Right," agreed Lottie. "If he's running away from you, you could certainly tackle him. But if he's willing to talk, then use your feminine wiles."

Valene glanced at me, her eyes wide.

I rolled my eyes, then nodded, fully aware of how she must have felt. I grabbed some napkins from beneath the counter, added them to the food, and took the tray to a small table situated between two of the chairs.

Valene looked at me, then motioned toward the clock. "I need to let Jillian know why I'm late getting back."

"Don't worry. I'll send her a text."

Florence's brow scrunched as she glanced down at my food offering. "Good heavens…. That's very…." She whipped around and faced Lottie, sitting in the chair on the other side of the table. They began blinking, ear tapping, and head nods.

Valene mouthed, "What are they doing?"

I leaned closer to her and whispered, "Just their special language. They do this all the time."

"Wow. Weird."

The ladies, still making twitchy movements, didn't seem to notice us. Finally, they stopped their version of sign language and faced me.

"Everything okay?" I asked.

"Well," said Florence, "we decided that if this is all you can afford in the way of food, we need to be giving you much bigger tips after you groom our cats."

I shook my head. "That's not necessary, really. I'm fine. We just don't keep much food here, is all."

Lottie put her hand to one side of her mouth, but her whisper came out loud and proud. "I think Molly needs a man, too. It would help her financial dilemma."

I blew out a breath. This wasn't going well. At all.

"Please have a seat, Molly," Florence pointed to an empty chair. "You can listen too."

I sat, suddenly tired from the busy day, and having to spontaneously entertain three people and two extra cats. Maybe taking a break, even under these circumstances, wouldn't be all bad.

"Good girl, Molly," said Lottie.

I glanced up, glad she hadn't patted me on the head for good measure.

"Now," said Florence to Valene. "We heard about your catfight in the—"

Lottie grabbed Florence's wrist. "Please, not so loud. We do have kitties present. Do you want to give them bad ideas?"

"Ah, yes, you're right. Um, we heard about your altercation…."

"Much better." Lottie nodded.

"…and decided to give you some of our sage advice about trapping a man."

"Trapping?" Valene squeaked out. "I don't think that's how it works."

"Now, Valene, Lottie, and I have years, yes, I'll say it, decades, of experience in the realm of love."

They did? Either they were telling the truth or they had massive imaginations, both of which could be entertaining. Leaning forward, I suddenly had a little more energy to listen.

"You see," Florence waved her hand in a circle in front of Valene. "You're a young, beautiful, desirable woman."

"Um, thanks." Valene's face turned the shade of a ripe tomato.

"And you should use all of your attributes when stalking your prey."

Lottie frowned. "Again, you're giving the cats wrong ideas with the word stalking."

"You're really stifling my creative flow here." Florence glared at her.

"Sorry. Just trying to protect the children." She pointed to the cats. The Sphynx sisters were asleep on the floor.

I watched in fascination as the ladies again did blinks and head tilts. They'd been friends for a long time. How long had it taken them to develop that strange new language?

Suddenly, Florence turned to Valene. "Let us see you walk."

"Walk? What do you mean?"

Lottie turned two fingers downward and moved them across the table.

Valene shot me a look, but I only shrugged. I made a little shooing motion, letting her know to get on with it.

She stood up, frowned, then stomped across the floor to the counter.

"No, no, no!" yelled Florence. "That will never do. You look like an elephant crossing the Serengeti."

Lottie looked worriedly again at their cats, but they were still snoozing. She relaxed. Their babies wouldn't be trumpeting like elephants anytime soon.

Florence shook her head and muttered, "If she ends up going to jail for axing Carlotta Sykes, walking like that will only draw attention to her. Not a good thing."

From across the room, Valene lightened her steps, but moved quickly, as if trying to get away from someone.

With a huffed-out breath, Lottie stood. "I can see you need a visual to understand our point. Watch carefully. This is how it's done." She stood up straight, put her one hand on her hip, and the other held out to the side with her elbow bent slightly. Then, she walked slowly, wiggling her hips side to side. When she got to the counter, she gave a come-hither glance over her shoulder, batting her eyelashes.

My mouth dropped open. Where and when had the lady learned to do that? She moved well for an octogenarian, I had to admit. I wasn't sure I could pull off her swingy gait. But then, I had no desire to, either. Knowing my luck, my feet would get twisted and I'd end up in a bruised heap on the floor.

Valene gasped. "Wow, that was…."

Lottie winked. "I know."

"I knew you could still do it." Florence beamed at Lottie.

I clapped, couldn't help it. A performance like that had to be acknowledged.

Valene and Florence glanced at me, then joined in. When Lottie walked back across to us, she walked slower, as if her impromptu exercise had taken a little wind out of her sails. But her face beamed with satisfaction at her accomplishment.

She sat down beside Valene and patted her on the knee. "See, dear. All it takes is a little change in your movements, actions, and words to get your guy's attention. Right, Florence?"

"Absolutely. Why, men, I've….uh, well, men I've known have fallen into my lair, shall we say, quite quickly, using these techniques and more."

Valene's eyebrows lowered. "I thought all you had to do was be yourself. You know. Be nice. Show interest."

I nodded with Valene's assessment until Florence shook her head. "Oh, Valene. We have so much to teach you."

With a glance at my watch, I knew there'd be no visiting The Sandwich Shack for supper tonight. Dejectedly, I grabbed a piece of cheese and tried to ignore my growling stomach.

An hour later, everyone seemed exhausted from the lectures, demonstrations, and colorful advice. I waved goodbye to Valene, who dragged her feet as she walked up the sidewalk. The ladies gathered their sleepy cats from their spots in one corner of the room and headed toward the door.

Florence watched out the window beside the door. "You know, I really think for the sake of her man, Valene killed Carlotta."

"Of course," said Lottie, "since obviously we didn't do it…. We didn't, Right?"

"No, we did not."

"Maybe Valene can use her new walk when she's in prison for murder?"

Florence rolled her eyes. "Or maybe not such a great idea."

"I hope they won't make her wear orange."

"Orange isn't a good look for anyone, except maybe a carrot. Grab your purse, Lottie, we're overdue for our lemon Slurpies."

Chapter Twenty-Two

At the end of the following workday, I was still dragging my feet. The previous evening's lectures for Valene had worn me out. And I was only an observer. I could only imagine how Valene had felt today. I'd have to catch up with Jillian later to find out.

I'd missed out on food from the Sandwich Shack because of the disruption from the ladies, and was determined I'd get there for dinner tonight. I waved goodbye to Veronica, dropped the kitties off at home, much to their dismay, then headed over to the restaurant.

I texted Hank on the way, thrilled when he gave me a thumbs-up emoji that he could meet me there. When I arrived, the place was about half full. But that would change soon. It was a popular place, and in about a half hour there wouldn't be any seats left. I snagged a table near the front entrance. Not my favorite place to sit, but it was near the wall, so Hank and I at least wouldn't have people sitting on both sides of us.

Music was playing an eighties tune. My foot was tapping the floor before I even realized. But I didn't care. I was glad to have the evening free after last night's unexpected session. I laughed, thinking about the way the ladies gave romance advice to Valene. Was that something they'd done for people before? In the past, they tried to get me to read a certain romance book that apparently was pretty racy. When I declined their offer, they were sure I'd end up a spinster before I was thirty.

Hank walked in the door right then, smiling when he spotted me. "Hey there," he said, bending down to kiss me. "Glad you texted. I had just picked up my phone to give you a call."

I narrowed my eyes, acting like I didn't believe him. "Sure you did."

"No." He sat down next to me. "It's true. Scouts honor."

"You weren't in the scouts."

He gave me a sheepish grin. "Nevertheless."

I laughed. "I believe you. Guess we're on the same wavelength today."

"Yep. Most days, actually. We make a pretty good team, Molly." He took my hand, the warmth from his skin causing me to want to purr.

"Yes, we do."

I thought about the ladies, wanting to help me get my man, like they had Valene. I could only imagine what I'd be in the middle of if I'd taken all their advice. I glanced at Hank. Nope. He and I were taking things slow. Making sure it was right for both of us. And that was just fine with me. Hank was the first guy I'd felt this way about, and I didn't want to mess it up.

Lorna came over to take our order, but she was frowning. She pointed over her shoulder with her thumb. "I wonder what she wants."

We turned to where she pointed. Mrs. Kelper stood next to the half door that led to the kitchen area, leaning over it, like she wanted to see what was going on in there.

We gave Lorna our order, both knowing without needing the menus what we wanted.

Lorna glanced at Mrs. Kelper, then back at us. "Okay. Let me see what's going on over there, then I'll get your order right in."

Hank nodded. "It's fine. We're not in a hurry."

"That's right," I said. "Do what you need to." I knew all too well how things could come up at work, usually at the worst possible moment.

"Thanks, you two." She hurried back toward the counter area.

I gave Hank's hand a squeeze before letting go. "I wonder what that's about."

"I don't know. But I'm guessing since we have front row seats, we're about to find out."

He was right. What a great opportunity to possibly find out something interesting. My chair squeaked as I turned it a little to the side.

He smirked. "Are you doing what I think you are?"

"What? You said front row seats, right? If there's going to be a show, I don't want to miss it."

He snickered.

"Hey, are you making fun of me?" I narrowed my eyes.

"Nope. Wouldn't dare. I love everything about you."

My face grew warm. "Right back at you, doc."

A loud thud came from the front, like a foot stomp. I jumped at the noise and angled around a little more in order to see better. What was going on?

Lorna, with a frown, was now standing in front of Mrs. Kelper, who had her hands firmly planted on her apron-covered hips. It was the same one she'd worn when I'd done Cleo's grooming, where they'd matched—white with red trim.

At first, the women must have been whispering, because as close as Hank and I were sitting, I couldn't hear them. And believe me, I tried. I tried reading lips, but I wasn't very good at it. Normally, when I attempted that, I came up with supposed conversations that were either scary, ridiculous, or laughable. It also wouldn't do me much good to lip-read since Lorna was partially turned away from me.

Hank poked my shoulder. "I can't hear them. What are they saying?"

"I don't know. I can't quite…" I cupped my hands behind my ears, hoping to zero in on the two women, but still couldn't hear their words. Then, I leaned forward so far in my chair, I would have tipped over if Hank hadn't reached out and grasped my arm to tug me back upright. I peered at him over my shoulder. "Thanks."

He shrugged. "It's what I do."

"Keep me from falling over?"

"Among other things. The list is long when it comes to you, Molly."

I couldn't deny it. He was right. If I went too long without doing something clumsy, I'd wonder what was wrong with me. And so would those who spent any amount of time around me.

Hank's intake of breath was loud as he looked past me.

"What happened?"

He pointed toward the front, and I turned that way again. The women were now nearly nose to nose, with narrowed eyes and tensed shoulders, like feuding wrestlers, ready for a takedown. If they had been cats, there would have been hissing. And their claws would make an appearance.

"It's getting intense over there," I pointed out. "Should we intervene?"

He watched them for a few seconds. "Let's wait and see. So far, there's no bloodshed."

My mouth fell open. "Do you think there will be?"

"Let's hope not. Maybe it's something small." He held up his thumb and forefinger an inch apart. "A tiny dispute."

As I viewed the women, I shook my head. Mrs. Kelper's arms were waving around as if she was experiencing spasms, and Lorna's face had turned red from what I'd guess to be embarrassment. "Does that really look tiny to you?"

His eyebrows drew together. "Not really. Wishful thinking, I guess. It seems to be getting worse."

The restaurant door opened, and two couples entered. Mrs. Kelper and Lorna were positioned to the left of the order counter, so the customers could still walk up there if they wanted to. But the newcomers whispered and pointed toward the women, as if not sure what to do. I didn't blame them. What a spectacle to find in an eating establishment. It didn't make for an inviting environment for a relaxing meal.

Anna, Lorna's assistant, appeared in the order counter window. She bit her lip as she watched her employer and Mrs. Kelper in an obvious altercation, but finally gave a nod to the customers and motioned them closer to take their orders.

Afterward, the couples found a table not far from us and sat down. Like me, they might be wondering if they'd get their food any time soon, if at all.

Anna waved frantically to get Lorna's attention, but her boss was too consumed to notice her, since her eyes were totally focused on Mrs. Kelper.

With a few more people in the room, Mrs. Kelper must have been having trouble hearing Lorna's responses because her voice got louder. Either that, or she was madder than she'd been a little while ago and had lost any filter she'd had when she'd first come in.

Hank and I had been watching the scene from the start, but now that it was more audible, other customers turned to stare along with us. How embarrassing for Lorna that she was faced with having to deal with this in her place of business.

Suddenly, Lorna took a step back. "Listen. You're causing a ruckus in my place of business and—"

"You think this is a ruckus? I'll show you differently."

"Mrs. Kelper, the answer is no. Not sure how I can say it any plainer."

She gave a foot stomp. And was probably the one who'd performed the first one, too. "But it's not fair. You have to help me."

"No, actually, I don't."

I didn't fault Lorna one bit. It was her business to do with as she pleased. And being confronted like this, practically commanded to do what the other woman wanted, was so very unfair.

Mrs. Kelper waved her arm, indicating the room. "You own an eating establishment. The perfect place where I could make money from selling my Kelper-doodles."

Hank leaned toward me and whispered, "I really hope Kelper-doodles aren't some kind of dog. Why would she want to sell them in here?"

I shook my head, not wanting to miss anything. I'd fill him in later about my weird experience with the lady and her cookies.

The door opened again. Two twentysomething women stepped in and glanced around. When they saw the commotion at the front, they waited by the door before edging around the other women and reaching the order counter.

Anna, her eyes wide and hands fidgety, tried again to get Lorna's attention, but failed. She took the new order, then darted away, presumably to fix all the food herself since her boss was otherwise occupied.

Lorna reached out her hand, as if to touch her adversary's shoulder, maybe to calm her down, but Mrs. Kelper gasped loudly. She whipped around and her eyes widened as if just now noticing the other people in the room. "Did you all see that? You're witnesses. She tried to hit me!"

Lorna's mouth dropped open. "What? No. I didn't. I really…" Her gaze found mine, her expression pleading.

I pointed to my chest and raised my eyebrows. When Lorna gave a nod, I stood up.

Hank shifted behind me. "Molly? Where are you going?"

"Lorna needs me for support."

"I'm coming too." His chair scraped against the floor as he stood as well. He clasped my hand in his and we walked the short distance to the front. I was calmer this way. So glad to have Hank beside me.

When I stood behind Lorna, she turned and gave me a grateful smile. Mrs. Kelper, however, didn't even seem to notice the addition of two new people to their conversation. She pointed to her apron. "I'm a baker. That's who I am. I bake the world's best cookies and named them after myself."

Beside me, Hank nodded, presumably having figured out the mystery of the Kelper-doodle name.

"Mrs. Kelper," said Lorna, her voice sounding tired, "I'm sorry I can't help you but—"

"Oh, but you can. I know you can. Don't you want to have available for your customers the product of a first-place award-winning cookie baker?" She stood up straighter and had a daring look in her eyes.

This was going south, and fast. Did Mrs. Kelper really believe she'd get the desired results by haranguing Lorna and accusing her of trying to hit her?

The door opened again, and a family of five entered. Poor Anna. Would she ever get all her work done? Since we arrived, I hadn't seen anybody get their food. Including us. She leaned over the counter again to look at Lorna, but when she still couldn't get her attention, she heaved a huge sigh and retreated again to the depths of the kitchen area. Normally, Lorna fixed most of the food for the customers, and Anna assisted as needed. Did she even have experience fixing complete meals? And every time the door opened again, the meal orders stacked up even more.

Mrs. Kelper let out a loud moan and placed the back of her hand against her forehead as if burdened. "I worked so very hard to be a champion baker. You should be jumping up and down at my offer to sell my cookies in your restaurant. If I hadn't won that cookie contest, first place, may I remind you, I would have just died, right there on the spot."

I cringed at the word died, as I did every time anyone said it, including myself. It was an unfortunate reminder of what happened to Carlotta.

Mrs. Kelper leaned closer to Lorna and poked the front of her shoulder. It was the first actual physical contact between them, which sometimes meant a situation was escalating. "Now you listen and you listen good. I went through a lot to win that contest. A. Lot. And no one is going to take it away from me, or tie my hands when it comes to selling my award-winning product. So, here's what's going to happen. Either you start selling my Kelper-doodles and I mean today, or...." She placed her hands on her hips and allowed the threat to simmer in the small space between them.

"Or what?" Lorna mirrored the other woman by placing her hands on her own hips.

"Or I'll go all over town, telling everyone who will listen not to visit your restaurant ever again."

Lorna's eyes widened as if she'd received a shock. "You wouldn't dare."

"Oh, wouldn't I? I'll tell them your food is no good. Even better, I'll say it gave me and everyone in here food poisoning. How does that sound?"

Lorna's eyes were still huge when she turned to look at me. I patted her arm and gave her an encouraging smile, hoping she'd take comfort in my and Hank's presence behind her.

She turned back toward Mrs. Kelper. "I don't believe you'd do that."

"Really? Do you think Carlotta Sykes thought she wouldn't be murdered? Believe me, if she had hung around, I would have had serious competition for that first-place honor. But she died before the contest. A win-win for me."

A shock coursed through me. Was that a confession of murder? Hank grabbed my hand again and held it tight. Murmuring came from behind us, as others stood and openly gaped at the two women. One whole table got up, walked past us, and left. Was it because they hadn't got their food, or because a possible murderess was in their midst?

Chapter Twenty-Three

The next day, I received a text from Jillian requesting emergency blueberry tarts. Since I didn't have to start work for an hour, and Veronica was there early to do a grooming of her own, I picked up the requested food and headed to the library.

When I reached the main doors, Sunny stepped out. Two things surprised me, one that she was holding a stack of books—because, why have so many from the library when you work at a bookstore—and two, that she'd obviously been crying.

"Hey," I said. "What's wrong?"

She sniffled, glanced down at her purse hanging from a shoulder strap, then placed the books on a nearby cement ledge before claiming a tissue from her purse pocket. "Oh, Molly, it's just terrible."

I glanced around, making sure no one was nearby to overhear, then stepped closer. "What's terrible?"

"It's Jed."

"Oh no. Is he ill? Or hurt?" I hadn't heard anything like that, but the day on the gossip train was still young.

"No, it's not that. It's….he's…." She snuffled into her tissue again, before stuffing it into her pocket.

I watched her for a few seconds, wanting to give her time to settle down before I asked anything else. "Is it something to do with your job?"

She nodded. "Unfortunately. You see, I'm not at all sure I can continue my employment with Jed anymore."

My heart sank. Jed really depended on Sunny at the bookshop, since he and

Carlotta had split. "I don't want you to tell me anything confidential… but if you need to talk about something, I can listen."

"Jed used to be such a nice man. I loved working for him."

"But now?"

"He's changed. I….he makes me nervous now."

I couldn't imagine that. However, I didn't see him every day like she did. But I still wanted to hear her reasons for thinking so. "How so?"

"Just now, in the library, he yelled at me. For no reason. I didn't even know he'd be in there."

I glanced at the main doors. "He yelled? In the library?" I was sure that wouldn't have thrilled Jillian. Yelling was nearly a capital offense in there.

Sunny wrapped her arms around her middle. "And also, yesterday at work, I was doing a book order for one of our regular customers, and Jed stormed into the back office. He started shouting."

I thought back to when I'd overheard their argument recently in Second Hand Books. I'd assumed that was a one-time thing since Jed was normally so kind and nice. But now I wondered if I'd been wrong. "What was he mad about?"

"That's just it. He didn't really say. Wasn't specific. How am I supposed to try to fix a problem if he doesn't tell me what it is?"

"Yeah, that's hard, I'm sure. Did anything else happen?"

Her arms lowered to her sides, and she studied me. "What do you mean?"

"I don't know. Like… were there threats of any kind?"

She glanced down at her shoes, then shrugged. A single tear ran down her cheek.

"Sunny? What else happened?" I hadn't expected a yes to my question, but it had seemed the next logical step. Was this way bigger than I'd originally thought?

"He…he didn't actually hurt me, but…"

My antennae rose. What was going on here? "But…"

"He sort of bunched up his fist." Her fingers curled into her palms as if demonstrating.

"But he didn't hit you, right?"

She glanced down. "No, he didn't. But I was scared. I thought he was going to. My heart was beating so fast."

I reached out and rubbed her shoulder. "I'm so sorry. That must have been scary and confusing."

"It was." Her gaze rose to meet mine. "Now, can you see why I said I'm not sure if I can work there?"

I nodded. "I do see that. But...are you sure, I mean, do you think it was just an off day? Did he apologize?"

"He did say he was sorry. And that was good. But...I just don't know."

To divert her attention, I pointed toward her stack of books. "You must be an avid reader, like me, right?"

"I love to read. That's one reason I was so excited to work in Jed's shop in the first place, being surrounded by all those different books all day long. It was a dream come true."

I smiled, thinking of all the cats I got to see every day in my shop. "Yeah, being surrounded by what you love makes it not seem so much like work."

Sunny eyed the stack of reading material. "You might be wondering why I get so many from the library."

I glanced at the books. "What do you mean?"

"Since I do work in a bookstore."

"Well, it did cross my mind. But I didn't want to ask."

"I got a lot this time because I read them so fast, plus...I need some distractions while I decide what to do about my job."

I nodded, encouraging her to go on.

"But also, even with my employee discount and Jed's marked down prices in the Second Hand Books, I still can't afford them very often."

I remembered those days. Being younger, having more bills to pay than money to pay them. "It sounds like you need to keep your job? At least until you find another one, maybe. Unless, you feel like you're in danger, then, of course, you shouldn't stay."

Sunny frowned. "I...I guess I don't feel in danger exactly. He did apologize after all."

Even though Jed appeared to be off lately, I'd always liked him and wanted to give him the benefit of the doubt. "Is it possible he's got something going on outside of work that's causing him extra stress? He did just lose his ex-wife, after all. Not that taking it out on you is okay, not at all. But sometimes people's stress level shows up after the fact."

"Maybe." She shrugged. "But you're right about one thing. I should keep my job as long as I can. At least until I find something else."

"I think that's a good plan. Keep an eye on him, and if things do seem to be getting worse, you can always leave, right? You need to take care of yourself, Sunny."

"Thanks, Molly." She smiled. "Talking to you really did help."

"I'm glad."

She picked up the books and gave me a nod. "I'll see you around."

"Yep, see you."

I glanced down at the sack in my hand, hoping the pastries hadn't gotten cold while I'd stood out here with Sunny. I hurried to the door.

It was quiet, as usual, when I stepped inside, but more so this early. A few people were sitting at tables reading or perusing books on shelves, but most of them looked a little sleepy. Just like I felt.

Because of the quiet, when I gave the pastry bag a little shake, Jillian was able to hear it, whipping around to face me, a huge grin on her face.

"Thank you, Molly. You're an angel."

I handed her the sack. "So you've told me on previous pastry runs."

She reached into the bag, took out a tart, and took a huge bite. "Simply scrumptious."

"Did you intend to do that? Have both words start with the same letter?"

"Of course. I *adore alliteration*. See what I did there?"

I laughed. "You're one literary librarian."

Her eyes widened. "Hey, you did it. Yay!" She glanced toward the sack. "Want a pastry?"

I waved my hand. "No, all for you."

"But you deserve one as a reward for picking them up."

"Who's to say I didn't already have one while in the pastry shop?"

She winked. "Ah, my resourceful friend. I knew I liked you."

"Good thing you do, or you might not get any more pastries."

She narrowed her eyes at me, but was giggling.

I let her finish her pastry and wipe off her hands before I said, "Hey, on my way in here, I saw Sunny right outside."

Jillian let out a sigh. "Yes, it was pretty tense in here for a little while."

I pointed toward the door. "She was crying while standing out there."

"I hate to hear that. She didn't cry while in here. She was more mad than anything. I tried to calm her down, but she just wanted to get her books and leave. Not that I blamed her. I would have been upset too."

I nodded. "She talked to me for a bit. I think she felt a little better by the time she left."

"That's good." Jillian shook her head. "I'd never seen Jed like that before. He was really wound up. Seemed to have a quick temper today."

"Did it upset any of your other patrons?"

"A couple of women came out from behind bookshelves to see what was going on, but the argument was quick, so no one left because of it. Except for Jed. You must have just missed him. He left shortly before Sunny did."

"That's going to make their next day at work together interesting, to say the least."

"Yeah, I thought of that too. I know that Valene and I had a few rough moments when she came in after her fight with Carlotta, but we're back on good terms now."

"I'm so glad to hear that. I know you value her working here."

"I do."

I leaned against the front of the counter. "What was the argument about between Jed and Sunny? She didn't really say exactly, just that he yelled."

"I couldn't get any specifics. It happened quickly in aisle seven, then Jed stormed out."

"Wow, that's awful. And I believe you and Sunny, but it's still hard to imagine with Jed."

"And it was even worse because he left with a book."

"Okay. Isn't that what library patrons usually do?"

She tapped the counter with her finger. "Molly, he didn't stop to get it checked out. He's running around out there with illegally obtained reading material."

I wanted to laugh at her serious expression, but knew she wasn't joking.

She frowned in the direction of the entrance. "Normally, I would have followed him out to sternly remind him he needed to follow proper protocol."

"But you didn't?"

"No. His face was red. He was obviously angry. I figured that this time, and this time only, I'd allow him to take the book with him, but wait a couple of days and give him a call."

"You've got a caring heart, Jillian." I said it partly in jest, but knew she might not get the joke. That was okay, our senses of humor weren't the same, but we were best friends in spite of that.

"Thank you."

I needed something to get her mind off her current situation. A smile crept across my face.

She pointed at me. "What's that for? Did something funny happen that I don't know about? Please tell me. After the rocky start here this morning with Jed and Sunny, I could use a laugh."

"Then you're going to love this."

Her eyebrows rose as she waited.

I held out my hand. "All right, so I was getting ready to leave work last night when Valene showed up."

"Oh, that's right. You'd texted me that she was with you and the ladies? But she hasn't come in yet, so I don't know what happened."

"Florence and Lottie popped in right after Valene showed up with the book—thanks, by the way."

She nodded. "No problem. A special delivery is the least I can arrange when you make emergency pastry runs. What did the ladies want, anyway? About what? Their cats? What the cats were wearing?"

"For once, it wasn't about Helga and Eleanor. Those two..." I laughed. "They saw Valene stop into Fabulous Felines and wanted to talk to her."

"Really?

"The ladies decided Valene needed help getting her man."

CHAPTER TWENTY-THREE

Jillian's mouth dropped open. "What? Her man?"

"Yeah, since she has a thing for Dalen. And now that Carlotta is out of the picture, they thought she needed advice on love and *you know*." I wiggled my eyebrows.

Her eyes widened. "Um, they talked about…"

"Not in specific terms. But they gave her some come-hither advice."

Jillian spurted out a laugh. "I can imagine what they said. Those two are a riot."

"They even made Valene walk across the floor to see how she did it, then critiqued her."

"You're kidding. I can't believe I missed it."

"Nope, and it gets better. Lottie then showed her how to walk to attract her guy, swinging her hips and giving a meaningful glance over her shoulder. It was priceless."

"I wish I'd been there! But thanks for telling me. That does improve my mood."

I gave her a slight bow. "Glad to be of service. It truly would have been more fun with you there, though. I didn't have anyone to make eye contact and raise eyebrows with. That's half the joy."

"If they do something like that again, be sure to video it for me."

"You got it. Wish I would have thought of that at the time. Speaking of videos, any repercussions from the one of Valene and Carlotta in here?"

"Not that I'm aware. Thank goodness. I guess the woman who took the video knew I was serious when I said she'd better not put it online or show anyone, or she'd be out on her keester and no more library books."

"Did you actually say the word keester to her?"

Jillian smirked. "No. But I wanted to. Thought I'd save that just for when I told you."

Chapter Twenty-Four

As I passed by the window at Paula's Pastries, I spotted Trixie sitting inside, talking on her phone. Her face was red, and her other hand was clenched in her lap. If I could somehow get in there without her noticing, maybe I could listen to her half of the conversation.

I ordered some food at the takeout counter and headed across the room.

As I approached her, I eyed the table next to her. Trixie's back was turned toward me, so I reached the table and sat down.

But I didn't want her to see me gawking at her in case she turned back around, so I kept my back to her, not wanting to act like I was trying to listen. Even though I was. I pulled out my own phone and scrolled through, trying to act uninterested in whatever she was doing.

When Trixie let out a loud gasp, I jumped in my seat. Did she notice? A quick check over my shoulder showed she wasn't looking in my direction. Good. I didn't want her to focus on me. But what had made her so upset?

I heard a loud crack, like maybe knuckles rapping hard on the table. She let out a sound somewhere between a groan and a moan. "I was getting desperate," she said into her phone. "I don't know what would've happened if I had lost my job."

Silence.

"Did I tell you the latest?" she asked. "Mom said if I don't move out soon, they'll toss me out in the street, naked and starving."

My eyes widened. Wow, that sounded harsh. I wondered if her mom was serious or joking while trying to prove her point.

"Yes, Mom did say that," Trixie continued. "You know how she has always treated us, ever since we were kids. Not showing any compassion. Only doing what she wanted. I'm not sure she even wanted to have kids in the first place. I always got the feeling she felt like she was stuck with us."

It sounded like Trixie was possibly talking to a sibling, though I'd never met any of her family before. It didn't sound like a happy, cheerful home life.

She made a shuffling noise in her chair. "Of course, I want to keep working at the nail salon. As you know, creating nail art is my passion."

I rolled my eyes, not at her being passionate about something, instead because of how my nails had turned out when she'd done them. However, people were passionate about different things. Lots of times, I'd gotten teased or even scorned for loving cats so much. So who was I to judge about something another person loved to do?

"I told you," she hissed, "it was because of that witch, Carlotta."

Carlotta? Witch? I sat up straighter in my seat. Now we were getting somewhere.

"She said the most terrible things about me." Trixie's voice was raspy. Was she starting to cry? "Hurtful, mortifying words. I can't begin to tell you some of what she called me."

I hated that for Trixie. Nobody should have to put up with verbal abuse of any kind. No matter how the other person felt about them.

"Well," said Trixie, "I think now that Carlotta is good and dead, I'll be able to get more clients. I'm really hoping to snag a bunch of hers." She paused. "Who? Oh, those two weird old ladies? Ha! Yeah, I'd even take them on, even though they both probably have that icky old person smell. But there's no way I'm touching those cats of theirs. Never. Can you just imagine all the possible diseases those things might be carrying? Even if I wore gloves, those cats are not welcome in my chairs."

First of all, the words 'good and dead' sounded ominous. While it was true Carlotta had made Trixie miserable, being glad that she was dead seemed out of line. And the way Trixie talked about Florence and Lottie and their cats made me angry. They were sweet women. Yes, they were a handful and kept everybody on their toes, but I counted them as friends. And of course, I adored Helga and Eleanor as well. Plus, I knew for a fact the cats were healthy and well cared for. Trixie had no right saying those things about them.

I hated it when people who were older than me got a bad rap because of their age. As if they could control that. Plus, I always found their stories fascinating. And nobody had more interesting tales to tell than Lottie and Florence.

"Listen," said Trixie, "If I can get Carlotta's clients, I'll surely make enough extra money to be able to move out of our parents' house. I can't wait."

Paula approached carrying a small take-out bag, gave me a smile, then walked past me.

"Hey," said Trixie. "My food is here. Gotta go. I'll let you know how it all goes."

A chair scraped on the floor, then Trixie, still looking at her phone, sauntered past me again, with the pastry bag in her other hand. She didn't glance over at me, so I didn't think she ever noticed me. That was good.

Paula came up from behind me. "Hi Molly. Here's your order. Sorry for your wait."

"It's not a problem. Thanks." I smiled. On my way out of the shop, I waved at Wanda, who was standing behind the order counter, then headed outside.

It was a gorgeous sunny morning. On days like today, I almost wish I could groom my feline client out of doors. But of course, that wouldn't work well since they were mostly indoor kitties. Later today, though, I did have some mobile visits, so at least the back of my van would be open to the fresh air.

As I walked along, I spotted Trixie standing in front of Evan's studio. She was talking to a man, her pastry bag shaking up and down as she demonstratively waved her arms. As I got closer, I realized the guy was Dalen. They would, of course, know each other because Dalen delivered items to the salon. But why did Trixie look so upset?

I'd have to pass by them to get to Fabulous Felines unless I chose to use the sidewalk across the street. But if I walked closer to them, I might be able to hear their conversation. And if they saw me on the sidewalk close to my business, it shouldn't seem out of the ordinary. I tried to keep my pace slow so I'd have a better chance of not missing anything important.

Trixie had stopped waving her arms, probably to the great relief of her poor, smashed pastries in the sack. But she now had her index finger poking Dalen right in the center of his chest.

What was she doing? My footsteps tapped on the sidewalk, but she and Dalen still hadn't noticed my approach.

I couldn't hear her words. They were mumbled. But Dalen's reaction was a different story. He shook his head quickly, back and forth, with his arms out to his sides. Whatever Trixie told him wasn't words he wanted to hear. But now I could see Trixie's reddened face and clenched jaw. She was mad. But about what?

When Dalen took a step backward, Trixie only moved in closer. She was so much in his personal space that if it were me, I'd have to tell her to move. From my viewpoint behind Dalen, I could see that his muscles were tensed and his shoulders bunched up as if wanting to cover his ears from her voice. Whatever she was telling him must have been bad. Did it have to do with her trying to get Carlotta's clients? Not that Dalen would have any say in the matter, that would be up to Annie, but maybe he'd voiced his opinion about it.

When it was obvious I wasn't going to hear their conversation, I headed toward them, not being careful to keep my footsteps silent. I reached them, having to step out onto the street to get around them. I stopped, as if just having noticed them.

"Oh hey," I said. "How are you guys doing?"

Trixie's face was still red, and her eyes narrowed. Was that because I'd interrupted her berating of Dalen or just at me in general? Dalen, however, seemed to deflate with relief, glad for a chance to possibly escape whatever was going on.

Trixie glanced at her hand, then dropped it to her side. "We were, um, just…" She shrugged.

"Yeah," said Dalen. "Just… catching up."

If that was his version of catching up with someone, then count me out. The tension between them crackled.

Trixie studied me for a second. "What are you doing here, Molly? This is a private conversation."

That's simple. I do work on this block. And you do happen to be standing in a very public spot." I pointed ahead of me where I could make out my Fabulous Felines sign farther up the sidewalk.

Dalen glanced behind him, appearing desperate to escape. Trixie glared at him, then said, "Don't forget what I told you." He didn't reply, but did take one step backward.

With a beleaguered sigh, Trixie said, "I guess I should be getting to the salon. Lots of clients need my unique ministrations today."

I bit my lip. She hit the proverbial nail on the head at the word unique.

She turned on her heel and practically marched across the street, then took a right turn and headed the other direction.

Dalen shook his head. "That girl…"

I lowered my eyebrows. "Is everything all right?" I knew, of course, that it wasn't, but didn't want to appear overly nosy.

"No, it's not. She's…" He rubbed the back of his neck, then glanced across the street. Was he making sure Trixie wouldn't be able to hear him? "She has made it abundantly clear that she expects me to tell all my customers, no matter the type of business it is, that she's the best nail technician in Whitewater Valley and that they should all go to her."

My mouth dropped open. "That seems like a lot to ask of you. Or of anyone. Besides, I'm guessing some of the businesses you deliver to might not have people working there or their customers, who would even be in the market to have their nails done."

"Yeah, I'd feel silly doing that. Especially to places like the tool and dye shop and the automotive parts store. I doubt many of those guys would have any interest. And a couple of them might even toss me out on my ear for suggesting it."

I crossed my arms over my chest. "Why would Trixie think you'd even want to?"

He glanced across the street again. "She has some weird notion that I owe her this, somehow."

I shook my head. "That doesn't make any sense."

"No, it doesn't. From her warped way of thinking, because Carlotta and I were once involved, I would now want Carlotta's former clients to have the best of the best. As if I would want to do some sort of tribute to Carlotta. Trixie's words."

Good grief, now that Carlotta was dead, Trixie sure had taken advantage of the absence of what had sounded like a super negative verbal barrage from Carlotta. I couldn't blame Trixie for feeling relieved over that being done. But she was going way over the edge with how she was going about it.

"Besides," he said, looking at something over my shoulder, "with the way things ended up between Carlotta and me, the very last thing I'd want to do is give her a tribute. She was an awful woman, and I have to say it, the world is better off without her." His fingers curled into his palm at his side. Then he seemed to remember I was standing here. "Uh, sorry, Molly. Whatever Trixie has going on shouldn't be something that takes up your time."

As Dalen stalked off down the sidewalk in the opposite direction from where Trixie had gone, I stared after him. Did Trixie think she had some sort of hold over Dalen? It was obvious that he had no intention of ever doing anything to honor his former love interest.

The door next to me squeaked open. Evan stood in his studio doorway. "Hi Molly. Did you want to see me about something? Sorry if you knocked. I was in the darkroom."

I blinked, still trying to process what I'd seen and heard. "Although I always love seeing you, I didn't need anything particular right now."

Evan stepped outside, and his eyebrows lowered. "Are you all right? You look, I don't know, bothered? Concerned?"

"Both of those, actually."

He touched my elbow lightly. "Can I do anything to help?"

"No, but thanks. It was just something I was witness to." I pointed downward.

"Right here? What happened? I didn't hear any loud noises while in my darkroom."

"Definitely not loud. No, it was Trixie and Dalen. She.... Apparently, she told Dalen he needed to tell everyone and their brother that they needed to go see her for their nail appointments."

"Really? Not to sound mean, but why? I mean, it sounded like you had a bad experience with her before, and Jillian told me once there's no way she'd even let Trixie near her nails."

"She told him that since Carlotta is dead, he should want to do it as a way to honor her, since they were once an item."

His eyebrows drew together. "But I thought he and Carlotta had a terrible argument in the nail salon."

"Yep, they did. I think Trixie is so full of glee that her mean co-worker is dead, she wants everybody else to rejoice along with her. She even used the word witch when describing Carlotta."

He grimaced. "Ouch. Well, I guess she could have used a word a lot worse, but still."

"Yeah, I agree." Then I remembered seeing Trixie earlier. "Also, Trixie sat behind me in Paula's Pastries. She was on the phone, I think maybe with a family member, and said that her mom had threatened to toss her out of the house naked and starving if she didn't move out soon."

"Must be a close family, huh?" he joked.

"Right. I can see maybe parents wanting their grown children to leave the nest, but that sounded cruel. Trixie told whoever was on the phone that now that Carlotta was gone, she'd be taking all her clients so that now Trixie would have enough to finally move out. She wasn't at all sorry that Carlotta had been murdered. And was, in fact, overjoyed."

Evan shook his head. "Not a lot of love was lost there."

"No, I'm afraid not." I pointed in the direction of Fabulous Felines. "Well, I should get to the shop."

He glanced down at the bag in my hand with longing.

I knew that look from Jillian before. And to be honest, I'd seen it in my mirror when I was hungry. "Hey, would you like a pastry?"

His gaze snapped up to meet mine, and his cheeks reddened as if he'd been caught doing something illegal. "Uh…"

"Please," I said, holding out the sack.

"I don't want to take yours, Molly. I didn't mean to…."

CHAPTER TWENTY-FOUR

I smiled. "I bought plenty for me and Veronica. Please, take one. I insist."

He grinned. "Well, if you insist."

I opened the bag wider. Evan reached in and gingerly plucked the pastry sitting closest to the top. "Thanks. This is great."

"You're welcome."

"Has anyone ever told you that you're a good egg, Molly?"

I laughed. "Now you sound like Veronica. Enjoy the pastry, and thanks for listening." I waved as I left, wanting to tell Veronica what had just happened with Trixie and Dalen. I also knew I'd get a scolding because our pastries had gotten cold. But knowing Veronica and her nose for news, she'd get over the pastry faux pas when I filled her in on the latest happenings.

Chapter Twenty-Five

The next day, before my first grooming client was due, I dropped into Hank's veterinary office. He started seeing patients very early every day. Andrea, his receptionist, smiled when I walked inside.

"Hey there," she said. "Good to see you. Hank is almost done working on a rabbit's foot and will be out soon."

"I hope that means he's having good luck?"

Her brow furrowed for a few seconds. "Oh, rabbit's foot. I get it!" She grinned. "Guess I've been so busy, I didn't think about it."

I waved my hand. "I know what you mean. Some days just take over. And your schedule is way different by the end of the day than how you planned it."

"You're exactly right. We've been slammed." She pointed to a rather large stack of paperwork on her desk. "I'm guessing you have that happen too?"

"All the time. Then, other days are lighter, like today, so I can slip over and see Hank." I glanced behind her and down the hall, hoping to spot him. But he must have still been working on the bunny.

She rolled her shoulders, as if they were stiff. "I know he'll be glad to see you, even though he's been busy. He might be ready to see a face not covered in fur."

I laughed. "Don't be too quick to say that. I'm sure I have lots of cat hair on me from my grooming clients. Even though I wear an apron, it's inevitable. It goes everywhere and sticks to everything. Kind of like when you get static cling."

"And not just the fur, right? When I got home the other night, I had a doggie treat stuck in the cuff of my pants. I'm not sure how it got in there. But some poor dog went without his treat yesterday."

"Were you saving it for a snack?"

She wrinkled her nose. "No way. Those things smell like…. Well, let's just say I don't always understand why dogs even like them."

I had to agree, at least with the stinky canned food Jasper and Percival wolfed down every day. But I was glad they liked it. Full kitties were happy kitties.

Footsteps came from behind me, and Hank appeared. "Hey, there. Good to see you." He gave me a light hug. It might have been a little more involved, but Andrea was watching us closely, giving me a wink. I was sure my face had turned pink, since I wasn't usually one for public displays of affection, or much of anything else.

She kept watching us. Good grief. Maybe I should see if I knew anyone for Andrea so she'd have her own boyfriend to pay attention to her.

I tried to ignore her as I smiled at Hank. "Thought I'd take the chance you had time off when I did, but Andrea's been telling me about your hectic day."

He rubbed his hand through his hair, leaving a small clump of what I assumed to be white rabbit fur stuck to his head. "Hectic is right. Cats and dogs everywhere."

"And, apparently, a rabbit's foot?" I reached up and grabbed the bunny fur.

When he saw it, he chuckled, took it from my fingers, and tossed it in the trash. "Yeah, poor thing got clipped by a car in their driveway. His human's car. An accident, of course, but it happens, unfortunately. He didn't realize the rabbit had hopped out the front door when he was leaving." Hank glanced behind him. "Oh, here they come now."

A thirty-something man carried a large white rabbit in his arms, its hind foot in a tiny bandage. The bunny was nuzzled against his or her dad's chest, eyes nearly shut, half asleep.

"Thanks, Doc," said the dad. "I appreciate you squeezing us in." His eyes were red, and worry lines marred his brow.

Hank petted the rabbit's back, but the bunny was so sleepy, it didn't respond. Probably had been given something to calm it while having treatment done. "No problem at all. She's going to be fine, so I don't want you to worry."

The dad let out a breath. "Okay, I'll try."

Andrea waved at the man. "I'll send you a bill so you don't have to worry about that today, okay?"

"Thanks a lot," he said, cuddling the bunny closer. If it had been a cat, I would've heard a purr.

I rushed toward the door to hold it open for him, because the bunny was taking up both arms. "Do you have a way home? Need someone to drive you?" I was worried he might not be able to drive like that.

"My wife is waiting out in our car. But thank you. I appreciate the offer." He nodded and left.

Just as I walked back over to stand beside Hank, the door opened again. It was an older woman with a huge St. Bernard on a leash. The lady was so tiny, she could have ridden the dog like a pony.

"We're here," she announced, sounding out of breath. "I hope we're not late. Sometimes Hoover doesn't like to come inside from playing with the squirrels in the yard, and I have to give him a firm talking to."

I held in a snort, picturing her standing in front of an animal who, on all fours, was nearly as tall as she was. And her, shaking her finger at his large head, trying to make him listen to her.

"You're right on time," said Andrea.

"Thank you, Andrea." She and Hoover walked toward us. "Hello, Doctor Chenoweth."

"Good to see you and Hoover today, Mrs. Griffith."

I blinked. Her last name was Griffith? Could she be related to Lenny?

I glanced at Hank, who was looking back at me. He shrugged. "Sorry, Molly. I'd hoped…" He let his words drop off, probably not wanting Mrs. Griffith to know we'd wanted to spend a little time together.

I waved my hand. "It was my fault. I should have called first." Even though Hank never minded me dropping in. "But, I'll see you later, I guess?"

"Yeah." The corners of his mouth turned down.

Mrs. Griffith, who was ready to walk past us, stopped in her tracks, causing

Hoover to let out a surprised whine. "You two are a couple, aren't you?"

My face heated. "Um, yes. We are."

"Wait," she said, "I've seen you before. Molly, right?"

I nodded.

"You groom cats."

"Yes, I do." She was obviously a dog person. I never knew when people learned who I was whether they'd be for cats, or not.

"She owns Fabulous Felines," said Andrea. "A few blocks from here."

Mrs. Griffith nodded. "Yes, you take care of my neighbor, Opal Hyatt's, cat."

I smiled. "That's right. I love it when she and Fern come in."

"They seem to love you, too." She smiled, then tilted her head. "But you aren't working today?"

"I am, I just…." I clasped my hands together in front of my waist. "There was a little time in my schedule, so I thought I'd stop by."

She nodded. "To see your boyfriend?"

"That's right, she did," said Hank, taking my hand in his.

"You two are too sweet." Her eyes crinkled at the corners.

I grinned. "Thank you." Hank and I shared a glance, making my heart beat faster even though we now had an audience of two. Three, if I counted Hoover. But he'd lain down on the floor and now looked bored.

Mrs. Griffith pressed her hand, not holding the dog's leash, over her heart. "My husband and I have been together for what seems like one hundred years. In a good way." She chuckled. "So I always like to see happy couples." She glanced at Hank and gave a sharp nod. "Well, you need to see Hoover, and you also want to spend a little bit of time with your girl. Why don't you bring her back with us while you do Hoover's exam?"

Hank and I eyed each other. He shrugged. "I don't mind if you don't, Molly."

"I don't mind at all. Thank you, Mrs. Griffith. That's very nice of you."

"I'm never one to stand in the way of love." She coaxed Hoover to stand, then waved her arm for us to follow her. "Let's go then."

"Wait," said Hank, "you don't know what room to go to."

"Then yell it right out," she called over her shoulder.

"Second one on the left." Hank hurried to keep up with her. I followed behind more slowly, giving them a chance to get settled in the room first. The spaces weren't very large, and Hoover would take up the same area as a human.

I stood in the doorway until Hank waved me in. Then I stood in one corner to give him room to work, while Mrs. Griffith held Hoover's huge paw. The dog looked at her with big, sad eyes, but seemed comforted that his mom was with him.

Hank checked the dog's eyes, ears, and mouth, much as I did to my feline grooming clients. Then, he checked the paw in Mrs. Griffith's hand and his other ones. When Hank lifted Hoover's tail, the dog gave a low bark.

Mrs. Griffith patted his paw. "Now, now. You're okay. The doctor is just being thorough, which we appreciate, don't we, Hoover?"

Hoover gave a nose snort. I wasn't exactly sure what that meant, but I chose to think it was in agreement with his mom.

As Hank continued to check over the dog, I faced Mrs. Griffith. "Are you by any chance related to Lenny Griffith?"

Her brow furrowed. "You bet I am. Unfortunately. It's by marriage, though. My husband is his uncle."

"Oh, Okay." Maybe bringing up Lenny's name hadn't been such a great idea after all. I was ready to let it drop, but she leaned closer.

"You know, now that you bring him up, there are a few things I need to get off my chest."

Hank looked at me, then at her. "Go ahead," he said. "Molly and I are both great listeners."

I nodded. "Please, go ahead." It wasn't the visit with Hank I'd hoped for, but I did like seeing him with the pets he cared for. It was one of the many things we had in common. Even the pet hair we were covered in.

She patted Hoover's paw again. "It all came back to me when that Carlotta Sykes was killed."

I stood up straighter. I hadn't expected much to come out of asking her if they were related. But this could be good. Hank and I looked at each other before he went back to checking Hoover.

Hank smoothed his hand over Hoover's back, then felt around his belly. "What do you mean?"

She glanced at him, then back at me. "It was something I'd temporarily forgotten because it happened so long ago, but when Lenny was little, my brother-in-law's family lived next door to Carlotta's."

I thought back to the ladies telling me the same thing. I nodded, hoping she'd go on.

Mrs. Griffith ran her hand over Hoover's head and nose as Hank gave Hoover an injection. The dog closed his eyes for a second, but gave a sigh when his mom kept petting him. "You see, the church Lenny's family went to had a fledgling missions program. It had only been up and running for a year, and the couple from their church who wanted to travel abroad to minister to people there had finally gotten enough donations from the church to leave on their trip."

"That's wonderful," I said. "I've always admired people willing to uproot their lives to help others." I was such a homebody, it seemed especially brave to me.

She snorted, startling the dog. "Well, it would have been wonderful."

Hank gave Hoover some head pats, earning him a nose nuzzle from the dog. "Did something happen to the couple?"

"No, but something sure did happen to their funds. Or should I say, someone happened."

I bit my lip. I could see where this might be going.

Mrs. Griffith gave Hoover a kiss on his head. "You're such a good boy, sitting still for your shot."

Hank nodded. "A very good boy. Here you go, Hoover." He held out a handful of treats. When Hoover caught a whiff of them, his head whipped around and his tail thumped against the top of the counter.

I patted Hoover's side. "Good job, Hoover."

With a sad shake of her head, Mrs. Griffith went on. "When Lenny was just eleven, he snuck into the church office one Sunday and stole the money. He'd told his dad that he needed to use the restroom and left the sanctuary."

"I bet he got in a ton of trouble for that," I said.

She tapped her foot on the floor. "No, he didn't."

"How was he able to get the money?" asked Hank. "Wasn't it in a safe, or something?"

I ran my fingers through Hoover's soft fur. "I wondered the same thing. Wouldn't a church have a safe for their offering money that they got every Sunday?"

With a long sigh, Mrs. Griffith said, "There was a safe, yes, but the lock had been damaged shortly before that when someone had broken into the office over a previous weekend. They hadn't had time to have a locksmith repair it, or the funds to buy a new safe yet, so it sat unlocked. That wasn't common knowledge at the time, so…" She flipped her hand.

I watched Hoover as he finished eating his treats. "Do you think Lenny had anything to do with the break-in?"

"I've always thought so, but it was never proven who'd done it."

Hank's eyes widened. "But he was only eleven years old. That's so young."

"I know," she said. "But he was a rascal of the first order. Always in trouble. Always acting like a bully. He was big for his age, and some of the smaller kids were afraid of him."

I watched as Hank assisted Hoover off the exam counter. "So when the money disappeared, the missionaries didn't get to take their trip."

"That's right. It was heartbreaking for them, the church that'd raised the money for them, and mostly for the families whom they were hoping to help overseas."

"What happened to Lenny after he stole the money?" asked Hank.

"That's just it. Nothing happened. Nobody found out it was him."

I jerked. "Wait….did Carlotta find out?"

She nodded. "That's right. Her family didn't attend church, but Carlotta was out riding her bike that Sunday morning and witnessed him taking the money from the safe while she happened to be parked outside the church office window. Everyone else was inside the sanctuary, and she had the parking lot to herself."

"Wow." Hank patted Hoover, who was now leaning against his leg, the pain from the shot apparently forgiven. "And she kept his secret?"

"She did. Until right before she was killed. When they were little, she told him she'd seen him take the money, but that if he wouldn't bully her, she'd keep it quiet. It went okay between them until she contacted him recently."

"What did she say?" I asked.

"Carlotta said she needed a large sum of money for court expenses because of her ex-husband's greed in their dispute over who should get their house. Right now, Lenny is also begging people for money for campaign funds so he can run for councilman."

I nodded. "Yeah, I've been in a couple of places where he was asking for money."

"So have I," said Hank. "It wasn't the most comfortable situation."

Mrs. Griffith gritted her teeth together. "He's making a real pest of himself, I'm afraid. And my husband is embarrassed to be related to him the way people are talking about Lenny behind his back."

"But if Lenny doesn't have any money to give Carlotta…." I looked first at her, then at Hank.

"Then he'd be up a creek, so to speak. And because Carlotta knew what Lenny was trying to accomplish by being on the council, and she had this awful secret about him, well, you can guess the rest."

"She was blackmailing him," said Hank.

"Trying to. Until she was stabbed and left for dead between those two older ladies' houses."

"Do you think Lenny had anything to do with her murder?" I crossed my arms over my middle, alarmed at everything she'd told us.

"Not sure. I think it's a very real possibility. My husband, even though he doesn't like Lenny, doesn't want to believe he would've gone that far. I keep my opinion to myself, but I've been keeping an eye on my nephew."

Now that I've heard Mrs. Griffith's story about Lenny, I'd be keeping a closer eye on him, too.

Chapter Twenty-Six

My late afternoon appointment was to see Helga and Eleanor again. And of course, their moms, Florence and Lottie. I was concerned about them, since Sheriff King had already decided they were guilty, and he was now trying to locate proof to tie them to the murder. I was glad I got to see them today to check on them. Plus, they always had news to tell me. Maybe today's would be useful, and not about which of their cats looked more attractive in their newest outfit.

Percival and Jasper were having way too much fun trying to catch a fly that had gotten into my van. I hadn't realized until we left that it was in there, but I didn't think trying to dislodge it while I was driving was wise.

Besides, it kept the kitties occupied for a little bit.

As usual, when I pulled in front of the ladies' houses, I waited for the all clear to know whose driveway to park in. Today, it was Florence. Once parked and with the stairs at the back of the van open, I approached the ladies, was told Helga would go first, and I grabbed both furless babies and carried them to the van. I placed Eleanor on a blanket-covered shelf, and sat Helga next to the sink.

After the ladies were seated in their lawn chairs with their beverages of choice, some concoction of hot pink today, I undressed Helga and placed her in the bath water. The girls had been wearing yellow dresses today with white daisies, very cute, as usual. Next, I reached for the shampoo bottle.

"So what's going on these days?" I asked. "Anything newsworthy?"

The women glanced at each other, winked a few times, then Florence gave Lottie a sharp head nod.

"Well, now that you ask," said Florence, holding her glass close to her lips, "we've heard quite the interesting tidbit." She took a drink, which left pink smeared across her mouth like too-bright lipstick.

"Oh indeed," added Lottie. "It's juicy."

I smoothed shampoo onto Helga's skin. She closed her eyes and gave a purr. I loved that these kitties liked having their baths. It soothed their skin, especially the special brand I used for them. "Sounds interesting. Care to share?"

Lottie took a slurp of her drink, then hiccupped.

Florence gave her a stern look. "Aren't you going to excuse yourself?"

"Whatever for? I'm just enjoying my refreshment."

She pointed at Lottie's mouth. "That noise you just made. It sounded like a sonic boom."

Her mouth dropped open, and she checked behind her. "What boom? I didn't hear a boom."

This conversation would get us nowhere. I waved my shampoo-laden hand to get their attention. "So, what was the interesting thing you two heard?"

Lottie's brows scrunched in concentration, then she sat up straight. "Oh, that's right. We were in Carrie's Coffees. The kitties had really wanted to go there. They do have their favorite places, after all."

"That Trixie person was in there, " added Florence.

My interest was piqued since I'd been keeping an eye on her lately. "What did Trixie do? Was there more dancing?"

Helga looked at me over her shoulder. Probably miffed because I'd stopped rubbing my hand across her skin while I talked to her human.

"Dancing? Did we know about dancing?" asked Lottie.

Florence placed her finger on her temple. "I don't remember. You'd think I'd remember something like that."

I covered Helga's face as I rinsed the shampoo from her body. "It's okay. Don't worry about that. What did she do?"

"It was more what she said, wasn't it, Lottie?"

She'd been about to take a drink, and nodded her head so hard, her chin dipped into her glass. She wiped her chin with her sleeve, then took a sip. "Indeed. More what she said."

A minute went by when the ladies were slurping their drinks, while I dried off Helga. Finally, I turned to the ladies again. "Um, what was said?"

Lottie's brow furrowed. "By who?"

"By…Trixie?" When Helga started to squirm a little, I scratched her chin, and she relaxed.

"Oh, of course. It was quite startling."

"Yes, very startling," said Florence.

I blew out a sigh and checked Helga's ears and eyes. "What might Trixie's words have been?"

Lottie shifted in her seat. "Trixie said, loud and proud for the whole place to hear that now that Carlotta had been murdered, and had gotten what she deserved, Trixie could now have a good life and wouldn't be tormented by that…. What was the word she used for Carlotta?"

"I believe it was witch," said Florence.

"Are you sure? I was thinking of a rhyming word that started with a different letter."

"You could be right. But congratulations on getting the rest of what she said right. You nailed her words."

"Thank you." Lottie grinned, showing off pink-stained teeth.

I held Helga close to my chest as I trimmed the small tips of her claws. "She actually said Carlotta had gotten what she deserved?"

"Indeed, she did," said Lottie. "Oh," she held up her hand, thankfully not the one holding the glass. "After she spoke, she laughed."

Florence looked at her. "It was more of a cackle."

"I was thinking guffaw."

I checked Helga's skin closely, making sure there weren't any scratches or bumps. "Either way, she seemed happy that Carlotta was dead?"

Lottie nodded. "Overjoyed."

"Jubilant," added Florence.

"Wow."

"Exactly our thoughts," said Florence.

CHAPTER TWENTY-SIX

"Did she say or do anything else?"

Lottie's eyebrows lowered. "You know, now that you mention it. There might have been dancing."

"Really?" I held Helga close, giving her a cuddle against my chest.

"Yes. I hadn't thought about it before, but she did this thing."

"What sort of thing?"

Lottie peered into her nearly empty glass as if hoping it might refill itself. "At the time, I thought she was having some sort of spasm, flipping her arms around and gyrating."

"I thought it was a shimmy," said Florence.

I shook my head. This was harder than usual to get information out of the ladies, and it was never easy. "So she might have been dancing?"

Florence furrowed her brow. "Yes, looking back, I think it's a possibility."

"But she wasn't very good at it," said Lottie.

"No, that girl needs lessons."

Lottie's face brightened. "Maybe we could teach her! We did help that poor Valene learn how to walk to catch a man. Surely we could teach Trixie how not to dance like a chipmunk attempting the cha-cha."

I sputtered a laugh, that came out to fast and way too loud.

Lottie's eyebrows drew together. "Bless you. Oh dear, I hope there's nothing catching."

Florence looked inside her cup. "Doesn't matter. Whatever is in our drinks will kill off any germs."

Lottie smiled. "You're right. No need to worry, then."

"Speaking of Trixie," I said, as I redressed Helga. "Did she say anything else?"

The ladies looked at each other. Finally, Lottie held up one finger, thankfully not with the hand that held her glass. "There was one other thing."

"Oh? What was that?"

"She said now that the stumbling block had been removed from her place of work, she could finally get on with her life and be happy."

My mouth dropped open. That sure sounded like a confession to me. I placed Helga on a nearby shelf next to Jasper and Percival. They snuggled up next to her, getting ready to take a group nap.

When I picked up Eleanor, she sighed and hung like a limp dishrag over my arm. But she never complained during her grooming. She and her sister tolerated the frequent bathings that Sphinx cats required quite well.

"Oh!" Lottie leaned forward, spilling a few drops of her drink on the driveway.

Florence had jumped at her friend's exclamation. "What on earth is wrong with you? You scared me to death!"

"Sorry. But I just had a vivid memory that I think needs to be shared with Molly."

I couldn't imagine much juicer words than what they'd just disclosed, but I was up for whatever else they might know. "What's that?"

"It's been a little while, I mean before Carlotta's remains were found back there, obviously." She pointed in the direction of their houses.

I refilled the sink, then bathed Eleanor. "Why was that obvious?"

"If you'll let me finish, then we'll both know, dear."

"Right. Sorry." Once I'd dried her off and checked her over, I wrapped her in a towel.

"Anyway, I have a memory of Trixie talking to someone. I don't know who because she was behind me at the supermarket, and I couldn't turn around quickly enough to see who she was speaking to."

"All right," I said. Then I cringed, wondering if I'd get scolded for speaking again. I redressed Eleanor and placed her on the shelf beside her sister.

Lottie must not have noticed me speaking out a turn again, because she continued. "Trixie said that her life would be so much better, perfect, in fact, if one thing happened."

I waited as I stepped to the shelf of the four snoozing cats and gave them all head rubs. The purrs reached the one-hundredth decibel level.

"That one thing was this. If Carlotta were dead, then all of Trixie's problems in life would be over, and she could truly live."

"Well said." Florence set her glass down and clapped. "You got all the words right."

"Thank you." She beamed. "Especially since I'd forgotten the entire incident until now."

Florence tapped her temple. "We've still got it."

"You bet we do." She winked.

I straightened the grooming area, putting used towels in a small laundry hamper and cleaning the surface around the sink. "Thanks for filling me in on that."

Lottie glanced up at me. "We figure, the more you know, the quicker you can get us off the hot seat for Carlotta's murder. Not that we're super worried." She peered down into her cup. "Why is this empty?"

"Because you drank it all," Florence pointed out.

"But I don't remember doing it."

"Still counts, though. Your glass is empty, so you get to refill both our glasses from the pitcher. That's the deal."

Lottie mumbled, "But it's all the way over in the garage."

"Sorry, I didn't make the rules."

"Yes you did."

"Okay. But you still must get the pitcher."

Lottie set her glass on the driveway next to her chair, got up slowly, then ambled her way to a table in the garage. She came back out, staring at the pitcher, as if it were the most precious thing on earth, then, thankfully, without stumbling or falling since she wasn't watching where she was going, set the pitcher between their chairs and sat back down.

Florence picked up her glass and held it out. "Aren't you going to refill my drink?"

She shook her head. "Yours can wait. Mine is empty."

Florence guzzled what was left of hers and held out her cup again. "So is mine."

With a mean stare, Lottie grabbed the pitcher, refilled both glasses, then set the pitcher back down with a thunk.

I picked up Helga and Eleanor, placed them near the opening of the van, and climbed down the ladder. Once I had them, one beneath each of my arms, I headed toward the ladies. "I'm glad to help figure out who killed

Carlotta, since as we all know, it wasn't either of you."

"That's right." Florence clinked her glass against Lottie's. "But we do have a theory as to why Trixie went off the deep end and killed Carlotta."

"What's that?" I was almost afraid to hear.

"She worked in a nail salon, right?"

I nodded.

"They have tons of chemicals that she's breathing in all the time."

"True." Where was Florence going with this?

"We think"—she tilted her head toward Lottie as if I wouldn't know who she was talking about—"that Trixie got an overload of dangerous chemicals, that went to her brain and she went all toxic crazy."

I wasn't so sure about their conclusions of Trixie going toxic crazy, but their other revelation, about Trixie announcing her life would be better now that Carlotta was dead, might be useful. I handed each lady her sleepy cat and took a step back.

"And," Florence went on, "she was so high from them that she took a nail file and stabbed Carlotta completely to death."

Lottie gasped. "I'd nearly forgotten about the nail file."

"Me too."

I frowned, remembering the way the ladies were freaked out when they saw the murder weapon and how they'd whispered about it the day the kitties had discovered Carlotta not far from where we stood. "By the way. What's the deal with this nail file business? It's not the first time you two have mentioned it."

The women looked at each other, gave some winks, then Florence turned to face me. "When we saw that nail file sticking out of Carlotta's neck..."

Lottie moaned.

"...at first, we thought it was one of ours. They give them out at the salon for regular customers."

"And we're about as regular as they get," added Lottie.

There was nothing regular about these two. "So you both had one like it?"

"Yes," said Florence. "Well, I had one but somehow," she glared at Lottie, "it ended up ground to a metal pulp in the garbage disposal. Lottie had one, but misplaced it."

My eyes widened. "Did you ever find it, Lottie?"

She waved her hand. "Yes, I found it in a place I must have put it so I could find it later, but then I couldn't find it."

"Where was that?" I asked.

" In my nail kit."

I wanted to shake my head, but refrained. "I'm glad you found it." At least it wasn't the actual murder weapon, just a look-alike. But how many of those nail files were floating around town? It could have belonged to anyone.

Chapter Twenty-Seven

s soon as I stepped into Fabulous Felines, I realized I'd forgotten my phone. I let out a groan, startling Jasper and Percival, who stood next to me in their harnesses and leashes. "Sorry, guys, Mama has to go back to the house."

Veronica walked in from the back area. "Leaving so soon?"

"Yep. Phone. Must have left it at home."

She rolled her eyes. "I hate that. Sometimes I think mine should be strapped to my wrist. Want me to keep an eye on your littles?" She pointed to the cats.

"Yes, if you don't mind."

"I never mind these two." She grinned as she came around to the front of the counter, leaned over, and wiggled her fingers at the cats. They came running, closing their eyes and rubbing against her legs.

"Thanks," I said. "I won't be gone long."

"Sorry to say, your first one canceled anyway. Chipped toenail."

"The cat? Oh no, tell her to bring Tootie in when she can today. I'll take care of it so the cat's claw doesn't get caught in anything."

"No, it was Mrs. Redmond's nail. Said she's headed to nail salon for an emergency pedicure today."

I placed my hands on my hips. "I see where her kitty rates. Let the grooming go by the wayside so her own toenails can be pretty. Sorry, probably sounded catty, didn't it?"

She winked. "No problem here. I like catty." The cats were both now lying on their sides, exposing their tummies for more pets. Veronica obliged.

"All right. I still won't be gone long. When I get back, I have some other things to do here anyway."

"See ya." She waved. Then she glanced down. "Anybody up for some treats?"

Both cats flipped over onto their paws and gave warbly meows.

"I'll take that as a yes," she told them.

I closed the door behind me as I stepped outside, grateful for such a great assistant to be my right hand, or paw, as it were, in the cat grooming business. Veronica was the best.

When I reached home, I parked in the drive, not bothering to open the garage door. I would be in and out, so would just hop up the steps to the front door.

Once inside, it was quiet. Too quiet. I was so used to either having the cats come home with me, or meet me at the door if they were already there. But I'd be back with them in just a few minutes.

Now, where was that phone?

I normally kept it on the table in the hall leading to the garage. I was halfway down the hall toward the back of the house when my doorbell meowed. I jumped, not expecting anyone to show up. And yes, I'd purchased that feline sound for my doorbell specifically from the installation company. The electrician had thought it was ridiculous, but had humored me since he was getting paid anyway.

When I got to the door and opened it, I jerked in surprise. "Uh, hey Trixie." What did she want? It wasn't like I'd missed an appointment with her. I'd called and cancelled the other one she'd given me in plenty of time for her to put another client in that spot. But why else would she come to my house?

She scowled. "I need to talk to you."

"I'm only home for a minute, then I have to..."

She stepped into the foyer, forcing me to back up. What was she doing?

Whoa. She was way too close here. I held up my hands between us, hoping she'd get the drift that she had crossed a line. "Not sure what's going on, but..."

She closed the door behind her, giving off weird signals. My back stiffened.

I felt as if I needed to protect my home from an interloper.

Trixie crossed her arms over her chest. "There's something I need to say, and I need to do it now."

I thought about the reason I'd come back home, to get my phone. Too bad I didn't already have it with me. I'd love to call a friend for backup right about now. Without my phone in my hand, I instead jingled my keys, anxiety giving me extra tension and a bad case of the fidgets.

She glared down at my hand. "Do you have to do that right now?"

My mouth opened, then closed. I wasn't sure what to say to that. It was so odd to hear her be forceful and rude. Finally, I stuck them in my pocket and put my hands on my hips. Might as well look confident, even if I didn't feel it. She'd caught me off guard, showing up at my house unexpectedly. "Why are you here? Shouldn't you be at the salon right now?"

"I had a lady come in for some emergency nail repair, but I told her to sit and wait and that I'd be right with her. Imagine how mad she'll be when she realizes I left the building." She snickered.

That had to be Mrs. Redmond. Now I was doubly annoyed that she'd stood me up for her cat's appointment to get her own toenail smoothed down, then she was in turn stood up by Trixie so she could come and bother me. Now to find out why. "All right, Trixie, I don't know what's going on, but I'm in a hurry, so why don't you just tell me what's on your mind?"

"Fine." She tapped her toe on the wood floor, the sound echoing through the quiet hallway. "A few people have told me, well, let's say I'd heard some people say, that you've been asking questions about me around town."

I forced myself not to grimace. I hated that she'd heard about it, but couldn't be too surprised. Especially since I had gone to speak to Annie that day and had asked about Trixie.

"You need to stop," she said. "It's affecting my work schedule."

"How so?" I drummed my fingers on my thigh. Since I couldn't jingle my keys, my tension needed an outlet.

Trixie narrowed her eyes. "Clients are coming in, asking me questions. It's embarrassing."

"What kind of questions?" I could imagine what type of question, but wanted to hear it straight from her.

She shrugged, then glanced away, as if not wanting to answer. Finally, she focused again on me. "I went through a bad time….I had trouble, um….well I just didn't feel like fixing myself up for a while, okay?"

"Uh, yeah, okay." Of course, I knew about her showing up to work disheveled and smelly, but I wouldn't mention that. I pointed to her blouse. "But you look fine today."

A tiny smile tugged up the corners of her mouth. "That's because things are looking up for me."

Since I knew she meant Carlotta's murder, I didn't have it in me to congratulate her on her good fortune. I waited for her to say more.

"But," she pointed right at my face, "you still need to stop talking about me."

I didn't answer. There was no way I'd promise to stop keeping tabs on her, since I was starting to think more and more that she might have been the one to stab Carlotta with that nail file. The weapon itself seemed to point right to Trixie, since she would have had access to plenty of those where she worked.

"And another thing," she said. Her smile was replaced by downturned lips and a furrowed brow. "People have also said you made fun of my dancing."

I bit my lip. Now I did have the urge to laugh, remembering her awkward attempts. It wouldn't have been so noticeable if she hadn't done it inside businesses and out on the street, where everyone and their cat could see her. I was pretty sure my cats found her moves humorous when she'd danced across the street from Fabulous Felines that day. I know I had.

I reached up to push some hair away from my face. Trixie's eyes widened. "What?" I asked.

She grabbed my hand. I tried to tug it away, but the little nail technician was stronger than she looked. "What have you done to your nails?" she screeched. If my cats had been here, they'd be running in place from the loud noise right now.

"Uh…." I glanced down at them, way different than they'd been after she'd given me quite possibly the ugliest manicure in history. The eyes, of course, had gone by the wayside as soon as Veronica had seen them the same day they'd been applied.

But after that, I'd filed them all down and used polish remover to get rid of the garish colors she'd used. There were still smudges of the hideous shade in tiny cracks in the nails, but it was much better than before. I pulled harder at my hand, finally getting her to loosen her grasp. I rubbed my fingers, hoping to get some sensation back into them soon. Why had she held it like a vise grip?

"I spent so much time on your nails, Molly! I agonized over them. Put my entire being into painting them." She waved her hands around. "And you've destroyed my beautiful work."

Even though I'd hated what she'd done to them, it wouldn't do me any good to mention that right now.

"How dare you decimate the expression of my art?"

Of course, the beauty was in the eye of the beholder. I inwardly groaned. Why had I thought of eyes? But no one I'd never seen had worn anything close to what I'd had, nor would they want to. Sure, there might be people out there who wanted their fingernails to look back at them—I shuddered—but I wasn't one of them.

"Tell me, Molly. Why did you cut off the eyes I painted?"

I had to give a plausible reason, hopefully without making her madder than she was. "My cats were afraid of them. There was lots of hissing."

Her eyebrows drew together. "But those were tiger eyes. Tigers are felines. Your cats should have known that and admired them. Loved them even."

I shrugged, not wanting to say anything else about the hideous nails that might make her mad, like actually using the word hideous.

When Trixie's face reddened and her eyes narrowed, I knew my ploy of blaming my cats for me cutting off the nails hadn't worked. I stuck my hands back in my pockets, in case she decided to grab them again.

Trixie took a step forward, reducing the space between us again. I glanced over my shoulder, really wishing I had my phone right now. When I turned back in her direction, her face was too near mine. I let out a startled squeak.

"You better stay out of my business, Molly. I'm finally happy. Now I have a job without that witch to mess it up for me, and I'm not going to let you ruin what I've worked so hard for. A life without Carlotta to make me miserable." As she spoke, she poked my shoulder with her razor-sharp nails. "You better watch your step. You have no idea what I'm capable of. And believe me, you don't want to find out." She bared her teeth like a feral ferret. I was thankful she didn't growl at me, or worse.

She turned on her heel, stomped to the door, and stormed out of my house. I ran to the screen door and peered out. She was jogging down the sidewalk. I shuddered. What had just happened?

I'd never seen Trixie act this way, or appear so angry. She'd been anxious and even bossy when trying to get me to hold still so she could do my nails, but this was a whole other level. Those nails of hers resembled ten tiny weapons.

They sure hadn't looked so scary when I had been in the nail salon. If I had seen those, as sharp as cats' claws, I wouldn't have been able to have mine done at all, even though I was there to spy on Trixie. As it was, it had taken all my gumption to force myself to sit in Trixie's client chair.

I took a deep breath to calm my racing heart, then hurried to find my phone, which was where I figured it would be, on the table close to the garage entrance.

When I returned to Fabulous Felines, Veronica was standing behind the desk with a smile on her face. But when she looked up at me, the corners of her mouth turned down. "What's wrong?"

I blinked. "What do you mean?"

"You look…" She waved her hand up and down my body, then pointed toward my face. "You're pale. And your pupils look like you've been sniffing catnip. Is that why you were gone longer than you said you'd be?"

I glanced at my watch. Sure enough, I'd been gone much longer than I realized. Then, I set my phone and keys on the counter. "You will never believe who came to my house."

"You mean just now? While you stopped in?"

"Yep."

When I didn't say anymore for a few seconds, she huffed out a breath.

"Don't keep a woman in suspense, Molly. Who was it?"

"Trixie Torbeck."

Her mouth dropped open. "At your house? Why?"

"At first, she said people had told her I'd been asking around about her lately, which, technically, is true."

"Okay, and…." She moved her hand in a circle.

"She also didn't like that I'd critiqued her dancing skills." Although, I wasn't any kind of vision on the dance floor myself. But at least I tried to keep those so-called skills confined to my living room. And only danced in front of Jasper and Percival.

Veronica let out a snort. "You weren't the only one. I saw them through the window too, remember."

"Yeah, and a whole lot of people in Carrie's Coffees and probably other businesses she entered and boogied in."

"Was that the whole reason?"

"No, well, then she grabbed my hand."

"Grabbed?"

"Yep. She's a strong little thing." I wiggled my fingers. A couple of them still tingled.

"Why did she do that?"

"She noticed my nails were no longer staring at her."

"Thank you, again, for cutting off those eyes. They gave me the willies."

"Same here. And you're welcome. So then, she said I'd be sorry if I didn't stop checking around about her with people. She got close. I mean, actually, in my face."

With a gasp, Veronica widened her eyes. "Wow, were you…."

"I was scared, yeah. But hopefully she didn't notice. But when she said I had no idea what she was capable of and I better watch out, I nearly wilted. Thank goodness she stormed out right after that."

She patted her chest. "Goodness, my heart is racing, and I wasn't even there."

"I'm glad you weren't. It was awful."

"So what are you going to do?"

"Do?"

She crossed her arms over her chest. "I know you, Molly. You're planning something."

I nodded. "Yeah, I am. I'm not sure exactly what, yet, but I want to get some of us together and discuss what to do next. I really think Trixie is the one who killed Carlotta."

"Listening to what just happened to you, I have to agree."

"Are you free tonight to have supper someplace and talk it over with some of our friends?"

"Sorry, doll, but Jerome and I have tickets to a movie he's been dying to see, and it's the last showing."

"That's okay. I can fill you in later."

"Thanks," She smiled. "You know I have your back, sister."

"Yeah, I know."

"It's why you love me."

I laughed. "Of course."

Chapter Twenty-Eight

That evening, I was able to get Hank, Jillian, and Evan all together at Leaning Tower of Pizza for a discussion of what to do next in nabbing Carlotta's killer.

Hank had picked me up, and when we got there, Jillian and Evan were already seated. Jillian waved her arm in the air, motioning us over. She and Evan were seated so close together, there wasn't even daylight between them. They were adorable.

Hank glanced over at them, then back at me. He grabbed my hand, then winked, giving me a warm, fuzzy feeling all the way down to my toes. We walked across the restaurant, nodding and saying hi to several people we knew. When we reached the table, I was glad Jillian had gotten one in the back corner, a little bit away from other tables. What we had to discuss would be a sensitive topic, so no need for everyone to know our business.

I'd suggested we could meet at my house to have the talk, but Evan had his heart set on eating here. His big, imploring eyes had won me over, so here we were. Not that I was complaining. I loved their food too, and it would be tastier than what I might throw together at home.

The waiter approached, but before we could order, Hank touched my arm. "Hey, look, Russ is here."

I leaned past Hank to see the front order counter. "Looks like he's ordering takeout. Let me go get him. Maybe he can join us."

Everyone nodded yes, as Hank slid out of the booth so I could go see Russ. When I reached him, he smiled and hugged me. "How's it going, kid?" he asked.

"I was hoping to catch you before you ordered takeout." I glanced at the woman behind the order counter, who was speaking to someone on the phone.

"You did? Are you here alone? I'd be glad to join you."

I pointed across the room. "I'm actually here with Hank, Jillian, and Evan."

He shook his head. "Sounds like a double date. I don't want to intrude."

"You're not. We're actually on a mission. We'd love to have your input."

He grinned. "Well, in that case…" He pointed out our table to the waitress. She was still on the phone, but gave us the thumbs up. When we reached the others, they'd all moved around the semi-circular bench to make room for both of us.

Once we'd all ordered, I called our impromptu meeting to order. Nothing formal, just, "Hey, thanks, guys, for being here."

Jillian leaned forward against the table, so she could see me better, since Evan was sitting between us. "Okay, Molly," she said, "I'm intrigued. What's the latest on finding Carlotta's killer?"

Russ' eyebrows rose. "Ah, so that's the discussion. I'd meant to call you today, Molly, to ask that very thing, but got caught up at work."

"Yes," I said, "there are lots of people I've kept my eye on, but after what happened this morning, I really think it's Trixie Torbeck."

Evan's mouth dropped open. "Wow. I mean, I knew she had motive, but she seemed sort of mousey-like sometimes."

"Yeah, that's true, but if you'd heard the way she spoke to me this morning and the way she, well, yes, I'll say it threatened me, you'd wonder about her too."

Hank's eyebrows lowered. "You didn't tell me about this morning. Should I be worried?"

"It turned out okay." I patted his arm. "It actually happened so fast, I didn't have much time to do more than react." I described the scene to them, every person there with unblinking eyes and rapt attention.

"You mean," said Jillian, "she stalked you to your house?"

"Um…" It hadn't occurred to me at the time that she might have followed me there. But then, why else would she have come to my house right at that moment, when I'd normally be at Fabulous Felines and she'd be at the nail salon?

"Jillian is right," said Russ. "I think that's exactly what she did."

I blew out a slow breath. "Yeah, I think you're both right. Just hadn't realized it at the time. She barreled her way in and just started talking, then talking turned to threats at the end."

Evan nodded. "And don't people sometimes change the things they'd normally do and say when they feel like they're backed into a corner?"

"Definitely," I said. "That's exactly how she acted. I even had the thought at the time that she was like a feral ferret."

Jillian let out a laugh so loud, people at surrounding tables turned to stare. Her face reddened. "Oops. Too loud."

Evan winked at her. "Nope, totally adorable."

I giggled, which made Jillian's face even redder, then forced myself to settle down so my friend wouldn't have more attention on her.

I placed both palms flat on the table. "Okay, here's what I'm thinking. Since I'm ninety-nine percent sure Trixie is the one who—"

"You have doubts?" asked Russ.

"Not much. There are several other possible people, but honestly, the dangerous vibe I got from her this morning nearly wiped me out. I'd never seen her like that. And yes, I still think she acted like a ferret."

Chuckling came from around the table, as the waiter brought our food. Once we were all settled with our meals, I continued. "Aside from how she acted toward me, there's also the murder weapon."

"That's right," agreed Jillian. "Trixie had perfect access to that where she worked. I'm sure lots of us, me included, carry one in our purses, but…"

"I personally don't carry a purse," said Evan, his eyes twinkling.

Jillian elbowed him, but smiled. "True, but lots of us do. Still, I can only imagine how many nail files there'd be just sitting around the salon."

"It still doesn't explain why she was found between the ladies' houses," said Russ.

I nodded. "Yeah, that was weird. But it doesn't make sense, no matter who might have killed her and left her there. I guess we may never know that answer to that."

"So," said Hank, "knowing you as I do, Molly, I know you've got an idea brewing in the cute little head of yours."

I grinned. "Why, thank you for the cute remark, and yes, you're right." I took a few bites of pizza, then sipped my drink.

"What's your plan?" asked Hank, pausing to make a yummy noise over his food.

"I think, if you're all agreeable and available, it should be a group effort."

"I'm all for that," said Hank. "You've been through bad experiences twice now when cornered by murderers who had you in their sights as their next victim."

My skin felt chilled, thinking about those times, and how grateful I still was that everything had turned out all right. "Yeah, exactly why I'm hoping you all can help me out by confronting Trixie. With all of us there, I figure we'll all be safer."

"What about Sheriff King?" asked Hank.

I shook my head. "He won't consider any suspects except Florence and Lottie."

"That's awful," said Jillian. "Those two are a delight. I can't imagine them ever harming anyone. I mean the way they mother those cats would be enough to tell you what kind of people they are."

"I agree," I said. "They may be daft and love their adult beverages a little too much, but they have good intentions. Plus, the sheriff doesn't want me to check into anything. He thinks I should keep out of it and let him go after who he wants."

Russ bumped my shoulder with his. "I'm so glad you didn't listen when he wanted to put me behind bars for something I didn't do. Thank you, love. And on Lottie and Florence's behalf, thank you for looking out for them, too."

I leaned over and kissed his cheek. "You're welcome."

While we were enjoying our meal, someone appeared beside our table. I glanced up, expecting the waiter to offer drink refills or maybe check to see how we were doing. But I was wrong. And disappointed.

It was Sheriff King.

He stood there with his arms crossed over his chest. "So. What's all this?"

We glanced at each other. Finally, Russ said, "Hello to you, too, Sheriff. We're eating dinner."

"I've never seen you all—or even a few of you—together without something going on."

"What's going on," said Evan, "is that the Leaning Tower of Pizza has the best food in town."

The sheriff waved away his comment as if it were trash.

I tilted my head. "Sheriff King, if you don't think much of their food, then why are you here?"

He opened his mouth, then closed it. Setting his hands on his hips, he focused right on me. "Now listen here, Missy."

Jillian snorted a laugh at his pet name for me, earning her his glare in return.

"What do you need?" I asked him. "We are kind of in the middle of something."

"Aha! I knew it." He stuck out his chest as if he'd won something.

"Knew what?" asked Hank. "That we're eating dinner together as a group? Last I knew that wasn't illegal."

The sheriff pointed his stubby finger in Hank's direction. "Don't you start, Mr. Dog Person."

Dog person? I huffed out a breath. Why did the sheriff hate animals so much?

"And you, Molly. Miss Cat Lady."

"Why do you say that like it's a bad thing?" I asked. "I happen to be proud of taking care of cats."

"You people…." He shook his head. "Let me just say for the record, that none of you better be doing any kind of checking up on people in this town."

"Why would we do that?" I asked.

"You know why."

I leaned forward on the table. "Sheriff, isn't it true that you've made up your mind that Florence Makes and Lottie Campbell are guilty of Carlotta

CHAPTER TWENTY-EIGHT

Sykes's murder?"

His face reddened. "That's none of your concern."

"But I was there the day her body was found. For Pete's sake, I'm the one who called you."

"And a good thing you did your civic duty to tell me what you found. Otherwise, where would this investigation be?"

A voice from across the room called out Sheriff King's name.

He glanced over his shoulder and back at us, but didn't move.

Russ pointed toward the front counter. "That lady over there. She's holding a sack and calling your name. I wonder what she has for you. Could it be.... food from here?"

He grumbled something not very nice, then turned and left.

I shook my head. Why wouldn't our town's sheriff ever open his mind to checking out all the possibilities when a murder occurred instead of blaming whoever happened to be standing the closest?

We all watched as the sheriff paid for his meal, glanced our way one more time, then slunk out of the restaurant.

Evan rubbed his hands together. "Now that he's left us alone, what's the plan, Molly?"

"I was thinking if we could all meet at Fabulous Felines tonight, then go to the nail salon at seven p.m. Trixie will be working late and will be the only one there by then."

Jillian's eyebrows lowered. "How do you know all that?"

"I happen to know a certain nail salon owner who loves free cat grooming sessions."

"Ah, and you bribed her with that for information about Trixie's schedule."

I gave her a mock scowl. "Bribe is such a negative word. But yes, of course, that's what happened."

A laugh went around the table.

Russ held up his hand. "Not that I approve of bribery"—he glanced at me—"but I have to say, Molly's track record of finding killers is very good. I'm going to trust you with this, kid, and I'm behind you all the way."

"Thanks, Russ. It's not that I love sneaking around and spying on people either, but…"

"But," said Hank, "you do what you have to for the people you care about."

I nodded. "That's it exactly."

Evan smiled. "As a recipient of Molly's help in a previous murder in town, where the sheriff hounded me, so sure I'd done the deed, I for one would like to toast Molly."

When they all lifted their glasses in my direction, my heart warmed. These people were all my family, whether by blood or through friendship. And I treasured them all.

To avoid any further focus on me, I smiled at them all, then said, "All right, if everyone is on board, let's plan to meet at Fabulous Felines tomorrow night at seven. Sound good?"

Every head nodded as we finished our meals.

What in the world would I do without my friends to back me up when I confronted Trixie? Thankfully, I wouldn't have to find out.

Chapter Twenty-Nine

I had some time during the lunch hour, so I used it to head to Jed's bookshop. I'd received a text from him that the leash I'd sold him was defective. I had a sudden vision of poor Regis getting wrapped up in it or choked, and we couldn't have that! I grabbed another one, blue of course, and headed to the bookshop. Jasper and Percival, ready to stretch their tiny legs, were only too happy to make the short journey with me.

Another reason to take them was to compare their leashes and harnesses to the ones I'd sold Jed. They were identical. Maybe I could figure out what went wrong with Regis's before I returned it to the manufacturer.

Jed hadn't been in the best mood lately, so hopefully, hand delivering a new leash and harness set, along with my cats, who, I had no doubt, would do their best to cheer Jed up, would put him in a better frame of mind.

When we arrived at the bookstore, I peeked inside the front window. I didn't see Jed. Maybe he was in the back somewhere. Surely a lot of his time was spent unloading book orders and packing books up to send to buyers as well.

I opened the door, which squeaked, causing both cats to jump. "It's okay, guys, just a door. Nothing scary. We won't be here long. Remember, I need to get back to work to make some kitties even more beautiful."

Jasper sat down on his haunches and gazed up at me. The slow blink he gave was a sure sign he approved of my plan. Percival gave my ankle a head bump, then sat down next to Jasper and began grooming his brother's ears.

Usually, someone came to the front when their door opened. Except for the other day when I came in and overheard Jed and Sunny arguing. Were they having another disagreement? After what Sunny had told me at the library about Jed, it didn't seem like they'd have a long working relationship together.

Maybe they hadn't heard the door? I glanced at my watch. There wasn't too much time before I had to be back at work. Should I leave the leash with a note for Jed and then just go?

I rummaged in my purse for a pen and a small piece of paper when I heard footsteps. I glanced up and smiled. "Hi, Sunny. I thought maybe no one was here."

She smiled. "Sorry about that. Jed isn't here, but he told me he'd asked you to drop by with a new leash for Regis. The defective one is in the back. Let me go get it for you."

"Sure. Is Jed okay? He just texted me earlier today."

"He had to go to the dentist. Emergency visit because he broke a tooth. A molar, I think."

"Ouch." I pressed my hand against my own cheek in sympathy, having had that same thing happen before.

"Yeah, I know. Awful." She frowned. "Okay, I'll be right back with the leash."

She turned and went into the back room on the right. When she came back out, I wanted to see how things were going between her and Jed after what she'd told me at the library. Maybe it was better that Jed wasn't here right now. Even though I hated the reason he had to be away.

Jasper strained at his leash, reaching out his paw toward a nearby bookshelf. Oh great. My cats were already bored?

With a sigh, I walked a few steps toward the shelves, which were located closer to the main counter. Why did cats' curiosity always pop out at the wrong times? What was I thinking? They were always curious and would want to check out everything in the shop.

Percival, unable to stand that his brother was sniffing something interesting that he wasn't, sidled up next to the other cat and stuck his nose between two books sitting on the bottom shelf.

"All right, you guys," I said, "try not to knock anything over, okay? We don't want to upset Jed any more than he already has been lately."

Footsteps came from the back. "You've got that right, Molly. Jed sure has been hard to be around."

My face heated. I hadn't meant for that to be out loud. Darn my habit of saying whatever was on my mind to my cats. "Uh…. Sorry. I didn't mean…" I shrugged.

She held up her hand. "It's okay. Don't worry on my behalf." She walked around the counter and past me. Where was she going? I glanced down at both of her hands. And where was the leash? Had she gotten back there and spaced why she'd gone?

I heard a small thunking sound. What was it? When I whirled around, Sunny's hand was on the door lock. What was going on?

Sunny removed her hand from the door lock but leaned with her back against the door, her arms now crossed over her chest.

"Sunny? Is something wrong?"

She grinned. "Nope. Everything is perfect."

I shook my head slowly. Had I missed something? Maybe she was happy because things had improved with Jed. And that would be a good thing. Or she was still upset with him, but glad he wasn't here right now. But neither one explained why she'd locked the door.

I pointed toward the doorknob. "I need to leave here soon. They're expecting me back at work and—"

She shook her head. "Don't think so."

"Um, what?

"You're not leaving."

"Is this a joke?" I gave a nervous laugh. "I really do need to get back to Fabulous Felines."

"That is the dumbest name for a business I've ever heard."

I jerked. What was wrong with Sunny? What happened to the tearful girl who'd poured her heart out to me about Jed while we stood on the library steps? "I'm not sure what's going on here."

She shrugged. "Then let me fill you in. First of all, Jed didn't send you a text."

"Yes, he did. It's right here on my phone. I'll show you." I reached into the outer pocket of my purse but came up empty. Where was my….

Sunny reached into her left pocket and tugged out a phone. Mine. "Looking for this?"

"Hey, how did you…"

"Guess I never told you I'm a pretty good pickpocket. Gee, sorry, that little fact must have slipped my mind. Growing up, I learned lots of tricks to help me get things I wanted. I had also swiped Jed's phone earlier and sent you the text, pretending to be him."

Was she serious? This was way different than the way she came across before, all business, and telling people better ways to do things. But I didn't have time for her games. I held out my hand. "Whatever. I'd like it back now, please."

She shook her head. "Not going to happen."

I huffed out a breath. "Look, Sunny. Not sure what's going on here, but it needs to stop. Right now. I brought over the leash for Jed and…"

"Like I said, he didn't text you. I did."

My hand landed on my hip. "Why would you do that?"

"Sending you a message about a cat in need was the one way I could think of to get you here."

"All right. Since you're being so weird about it, I'll play along. Why did you want me here so bad?"

"There are a few things we need to clear up, Molly."

Something brushed against my ankle. Percival was pawing at me. His eyes were huge. Jasper gave a tiny, almost silent mew and pressed his side against my leg. They could sense something was off. Too bad they couldn't explain to me what was actually going on. I stared at Sunny. "If you have something you feel you need to get off your chest, then by all means, say it. Then, I need to go."

Wanting to get closer to the door, I took a step backward, hoping she wouldn't notice. If she'd turned the lock on the door, couldn't I just as easily unlock it to let myself and my cats out? I had the advantage of having the exit close behind me, so maybe I could grab the cats, unlock the door, and get out of here.

"Don't even try it, Molly. You'd need the key to open it. And, of course, I'm not going to give it to you." She patted her front pants pocket.

I stood up straighter, trying to look braver than I felt. This was getting way off track, and I still didn't know the reason why. "Just go ahead and tell me what's going on, will you? You're not making much sense, and I'm really worried about you."

"Don't worry about me. I'm fine. What's done is done." She brushed off her hands like she'd taken out the trash.

My eyebrows lowered. "I don't follow."

"You're not very bright, are you?"

I opened my mouth to retort, but she moved closer to me.

"Okay, I'll spell it out for you. You've been barking up the wrong tree this whole time."

At the word barking, both cats puffed up beside me. They'd heard the word before and knew it went with the loud, scary noise they'd heard once from a person who'd brought their untrained German Shepherd into the grooming salon recently.

"And just what did I get wrong?" I asked.

"I did it." She pointed her thumb toward her chest. "I killed Carlotta."

My heart lurched in my chest. Time seemed to stand still. No, that couldn't be true. Trixie had killed Carlotta. I had it all figured out, didn't I? But I stared at her, with her knowing smirk and self-satisfied expression. Had I really heard her right? Surely she didn't mean…. "But you didn't…."

She laughed. "Yep, it's true. And proud of it. I should have done it a long time ago, but didn't have the best opportunity until now."

I shook my head. "But, why? Why would you have done that? I didn't realize you even knew her."

She waved her hand. "Trust me. We go way back. All the way back to the same father, in fact."

I gasped. "Carlotta was your sister?"

"Half-sister. And a terrible one at that."

I glanced over my shoulder and back, desperately hoping a customer would want to come into the bookstore right about now. "Listen, I'm sorry you've obviously been through something… terrible and… felt the need to, um…"

"Molly, you're not getting it, are you? You, and your annoying fluffballs are not leaving this shop. At least not breathing."

Percival puffed up to twice his normal size and let out a loud, spine-tingling hiss. Jasper's sound was more of a growl, low and menacing.

Sunny glared at my cats. "It will be a pleasure to silence those two. Worthless furballs."

My heart raced. I was frightened. But no one, and I mean no one, talked about my babies that way. And I wouldn't let anyone, even this apparently crazy woman in front of us, do anything too harm, even one whisker on my kitties.

A sound came from outside the door. Wait. Was someone trying to get in? But footsteps followed, as whoever it was had left.

I let out a long breath, feeling deflated. While I could and would fight with everything I had to save Jasper, Percival, and myself, it sure would be a whole lot easier if someone were here to give me backup. But without my phone, it was impossible to let anyone know what was going on. Veronica was the only one who knew where I'd been headed, and she wouldn't be expecting me back quite yet.

Maybe if she tried to call or text me and couldn't get through, she'd get worried and contact one of our friends to see what was going on. I knew she had a full schedule and couldn't simply leave the shop to come here and check on me. But she might get hold of Jillian or Hank.

Sunny was watching me with eyes that I could only describe as glittery. Like she was very much looking forward to doing something to me and my cats that might put us out of commission for good.

As if knowing my thoughts, both cats let out howls.

She covered her ears. "Make them stop! Right now. Or you'll all be sorry."

I bent down and clasped both cats around their tummies, as I picked them up. Not an easy task since they weren't kittens anymore, but it was the only way to calm them down. Percival climbed onto my shoulder and perched there. At least he hadn't perched on top of my head like he'd done a couple of times before when he was frightened, so it could be worse. Jasper clutched to my chest, rubbing my arm that was wrapped around him with his nose.

When it was quiet again, Sunny lowered her hands. "Glad I won't have to listen to terrible noises like that for much longer. It's bad enough that Jed's cat comes in here sometimes, and I have to put up with him hanging around and purring." She made a face. "Now that has got to be the worst sound ever."

Wanting to put on a brave front, I said, "I happen to think the purr is the gentlest noise there is. Purrs have been shown to be beneficial to people. Lowering their blood pressure and helping with pain."

"You're full of it, Molly. I knew you were one of those cat people, but, honestly, making up terrible lies about them too."

"It's not a lie. They really…"

She stomped her foot, causing both cats to dig their claws into me. I winced, but didn't move, not wanting to alarm them further.

"Stop talking about the stupid cats!" She yelled. "I'm sick of them."

I still had a tiny hope that someone would show up here. Even though they wouldn't be able to open the door since it was locked, maybe just the fact that a person might try the doorknob or look in the window would force Sunny to change her awful plan for me and the cats.

But until that happened, I had to buy us some time. Sunny obviously had a story to tell, if Carlotta really had been her half-sister. Maybe she'd be mad enough about her relationship with Carlotta that she'd talk about it.

"Hey," I said. "You said Carlotta was a bad sister. What did that mean?"

"What do you care?"

I shrugged, forgetting Percival was still perched on my shoulder. He mumbled something catty and shifted a little, so his whiskers were tickling my face. I wrinkled my nose, hoping I wouldn't sneeze. At this point, anything might set Sunny off again.

She glanced at her watch. "I guess I have a while yet before Jed comes back from his appointment. If he even comes back. I personally hate going to the dentist for anything and nearly wilt when I have anything more than a cleaning."

At least she'd stopped talking about doing something bad to me and the cats. That was progress. I was getting tired of standing so stiffly, with one cat stuck to my chest and another on my shoulder. "Um, hey, would it be okay if I sat down?"

"No. You don't get to move. I will, however, give you the fascinating story of growing up with the worst sister ever to live on this planet."

I took a deep breath and let it out, willing myself to relax. If I couldn't move, maybe I could at least be slightly calmer.

"Now," she said, "it all goes back to when Dad married Carlotta's mom. That was before I was born, and my stepmom already had Carlotta, who was a baby. I came along eight years later. You'd think that Carlotta might have been excited to have a baby sister, but that wasn't what happened." She looked at me expectantly.

"What happened?"

"Carlotta decided she wanted to be an only child again. She was never nice to me, and I remember that as a toddler, she used to pinch me and tease me all the time. Then when we got older, she always demanded the best of whatever we had. The better bedroom. We always had to watch whatever TV show she liked."

I started to shrug again, then thought better of it. "That doesn't sound like anything life-altering."

"I'm not finished yet, am I?"

The cats pressed even closer to me, even though I hadn't thought it was possible. Pretty soon, they'd both be sitting inside my shirt.

"Anyway," said Sunny, "it got worse as we got older. Carlotta started telling our parents lies about me. That I'd done all these awful things to her. Ruined her stuff in her room. Tore up her school supplies. Which, of course, I hadn't. Because I'm a nice person."

I bit my lip. Since when did nice people kill their sisters and threaten to kill someone standing in front of them who happened to be wearing two cats?

"Carlotta left home at age eighteen. I was still little. She never came back home. Just went on her merry way and disappeared. When I got old enough to leave home and go out on my own too, I decided to find her. That woman owed me. Big time. Not only had she mistreated me when I was a kid, she also got the money from our parents to use for finding a home, and buying a car. Things got tight for them by the time I got old enough to be out on my own, so I got nothing. And it's all her fault. She ruined any chance I had of a good life."

When I tried to reach up and readjust Percival, who was slipping from my shoulder, I couldn't feel my arm. Great. It had gone to sleep.

Sunny turned to one side and began to pace in front of us. Jasper flipped over in my arms so he could watch her. At least his claws weren't stuck into my shirt any longer.

"So," she said, "once I was old enough to go out on my own, even though I wasn't given a dime to help me out, I decided to track down my dear sister. It took a while, but I'm savvy on the computer, and finally found out she worked at a nail salon here in Whitewater Valley." She glanced at me like she wanted my approval.

"That was…very resourceful of you," I said.

"Thank you. I thought so as well. As you must have figured out by now, I successfully found her."

I nodded, figuring it was expected of me. But I wiggled my left arm, trying to get some feeling back into it. Why had Percival slid partway down my shoulder? Then I heard it. Kitty snores. Right in my ear.

With a sigh, I squeeze my hand into a fist, trying to get sensation back in my arm.

"Hey," said Sunny. "What's the deal? You planning to punch me or something?"

"What? No! Of course not. It's just that…well, he"—I tilted my head toward Percival—"has fallen asleep and my arm is also asleep and I can't feel anything, so…"

She held up her hand, stopping me. "Do what you need to so I can finish my story. I don't have all day since Jed might come back here after his appointment, and you need to be gone by then. And when I say gone, I don't mean back to your stupid shop, if you get my drift."

Chapter Thirty

Sunny's drift about me being gone had been acknowledged quite clearly. No way I could misinterpret her meaning.

I set Jasper on the floor, then grabbed Percival from my shoulder with my opposite hand. A prickling feeling darted back into my numb arm. I grabbed a chair placed next to the front window and tugged it back to where I'd been standing, and sat. Then I coaxed both sleepy cats to me and placed them on my lap.

Sunny crossed her arms. "Are you finally done?"

"Yes, all done. Um, sorry."

She huffed out a breath. "Now, where was I?" She pressed her finger against her lips.

"You found out that Carlotta worked at the salon."

"Right. Thank you. So anyway, when I discovered where she lived, I moved here. I had to take a rundown apartment and this crappy job"—she waved her arm indicating the room where we stood—"and decided to confront her."

"Did you know Jed was her ex-husband when you took the job?"

"Of course. Social media is wonderful for finding things out about people. Carlotta had a few posts about splitting up with Jed, but she hadn't deleted earlier posts about her and Jed having this bookshop. A picture of the two of them made it super easy to track it down. The first time I saw the outside of the building, there was a help wanted sign out front. It was my lucky day."

I frowned. "So you just moved here, took the job, then went over and killed her?"

"Of course not. I went to see her first. To see if she'd give me some money. She did owe me, after all."

I didn't reply, just shifted the cats on my lap to get a little more comfortable. Not that anything about this experience was meant for my comfort in Sunny's viewpoint.

"And do you know what she said when I told her I wanted money?"

I shook my head, but had a pretty good idea.

"She. Said. No. Can you imagine? After all she'd put me through. All the pinching, teasing, lying, then leaving me alone with our despicable, cheap parents, and never contacting me again. I was livid when she said no. I mean, that was the least she owed me. Right?" She stared at me.

"Uh, right."

She nodded, seeming satisfied that I saw it from her point of view. "I tried several times, but she always refused. Then, the final time I tried, she said she knew I was working for her ex, and that he and I deserved each other. But she wasn't going to tell him who I was, since she didn't want to even speak to him. She told me she hated me, never had wanted me around in the first place, and had left town to get away from me. From me! Can you believe it?"

Since she didn't eye me that time for a response, I didn't give one.

Sunny slashed her hand through the air. "I'd had it with her. No more messing around. I was stuck living in this awful town because I didn't have enough money to move somewhere else, and there was no way I was going to put up with her for one minute longer. I knew that the only thing I could do to make her go away forever was for her to stop breathing. So I made that happen. Then left her in the dirt. Where she deserved."

I couldn't take it anymore, I had to know. "Why did you kill her between the ladies' houses?"

"I thought maybe I could lure Carlotta there in the middle of the night, then the women would get blamed. Those two old bats," she waved her hand. "I never liked them. And their cats were weird. They didn't even have any fur."

"Sphynx cats actually do have fur, it's just super short and so fine you can hardly see it."

"Do I look like I care?"

"Uh, no."

"Anyway, those women came in here one day, whining about how we didn't have some book with a guy on the front holding some lady. They didn't know the title. How was I supposed to find it without a title? They got upset, and one of them started making this awful shrieking noise, kind of like your awful cats do. They wouldn't leave me alone about that stupid book. And every time they saw me anywhere in town, they followed me, haranguing me about when the store would get it in. It nearly drove me mad!"

I was certain Sunny was already crazy before she met the ladies. But she must have been talking about Lottie. She did have a habit of shrieking when she got upset. I thought back to the ladies trying to get me to read a certain bodice-ripper romance a while back, and how they'd found it at the library. Maybe it was the same book? Anyway, romance wasn't my genre. I liked mysteries. Which might be why I seemed sort of successful in tracking down killers.

Until today. Would I get out of this mess with myself and my fur babies intact?

Suddenly, Sunny stopped and faced me, giving me a hideous glare that made a shiver race across my shoulders. Now I could see the real woman, not the practical, no-nonsense bookshop worker. This person had a vendetta. And I, apparently, was in her way.

I took a breath to calm myself, but it didn't do a lot of good. I took another and let it out. "Sunny, why did you want me to come here today?" I could have used the word lure but she was already mad enough.

"Because you're always in the middle of everything, aren't you? Butting in, showing up everywhere in town."

I frowned. "If you mean going to different businesses and restaurants, then yeah, I guess I do. But what's wrong with that? I'm trying to support local businesses."

"You're also close to those two old hags. I've seen you spending time with them."

"They're my friends. I like them."

She shook her head. "I don't see how that's possible. They're so weird."

Yeah, but so are you.

"You're always sticking your nose in where it doesn't belong."

I held in what I wanted to say, that she had just described herself.

"And, from things I'd gleaned from listening to other people, you think you're some kind of sleuth when a person dies. Even Sheriff King has said so. I heard him tell you one day to leave stuff alone."

"Maybe I feel like he needs a little help?" I tried to be diplomatic and still get my message across that he wasn't doing his job. That once he decided someone was guilty, he stopped looking at anyone else. He'd done it twice before, and I couldn't bring myself to trust him this time. Not when Florence and Lottie were innocent.

"Why couldn't you mind your own business and stay out of things? It was going so well once Carlotta was out of the way. I was going to see if I could somehow get money from her estate since we were related." She tilted her head. "You know, I could still try that. Once you and your mongrels"—she pointed to Jasper and Percival, who were now staring at her, tails twitching and bodies tense—"are out of the picture, I'll be free to do what I want."

"Why would you think that? There are other people who are helping me find who killed your sister."

"Half-sister."

I sighed. "Anyway, several of my friends want to find the identity of, well, you, as much as I do." I wouldn't add that we all thought Trixie was the culprit. Why give the real murderer more ammunition to blame someone besides herself?

"Where are these people? I don't see them." She placed her hand above her eyes and scanned the room.

I really wish they were with me too. But I had no way to contact any of them since Miss Pickpocket had stolen my phone.

Sunny let out a dramatic sigh. "This has all gone on long enough. It's entirely possible Jed will come back here soon, and I can't risk him seeing you here. Alive or…. Time for you three to go bye-bye." She took a couple of steps toward us.

My cats both pressed down hard on my legs with their paws. What were they…

In tandem, they sprang into the air side by side, each landing on opposite shoulders of the woman in front of us. She screamed and waved her hands at them, trying to break free.

I jumped up, glad my arm was no longer numb, and ran toward them. As soon as I reached out to grabbed her upper arms, first Percival, and Jasper leaped to the floor. What were they doing? I needed their assistance right now. But I didn't have time to keep track of them.

Sunny dug her nails into the underside of my arms. I tried to do the same to her, but my nails were too short. Those could have done a lot of damage. Oh, the irony that I'd recently clipped them off, and thinking the woman who'd put them there had been the killer.

My skin burned where Sunny clawed at me, but I didn't let go of her. I pressed down harder into her skin. Her foot brushed against mine. Was she trying to kick me as well? A growl came from below, then a second one. Sunny shoved me back, and I stumbled, landing on the floor next to the chair. My jaw dropped open. The cats were attacking her shoes. But why? They were doing more good sitting on her shoulders.

I pushed up from the floor and hurried toward them. Then it became clear. They had untied her shoelaces with their teeth. Smart kitties!

Sunny screeched, "Get away from me, you hideous creatures!" She tried to kick them, but now that their job of untying laces was accomplished, each cat sat squarely on a shoe, front legs wrapped around Sunny's ankles.

I knew how tightly those paws could hold on, as the cats often did that to me while we were playing at home. But this was no playtime. Jasper and Percival were helping me. And they wouldn't stop.

While the cats had her feet occupied, I grabbed her lower arms this time, hoping to avoid being clawed again.

"You can't do this!" she yelled. "I'm going to get what's coming to me!"

"Yeah, you sure will. But it's not what you're thinking." Even though my words came out brave, inside I was quaking. Sunny was strong. And mean. And determined. Would Jasper, Percival, and I be able to totally subdue her somehow until I could find a phone and call somebody?

I gasped when the doorknob rattled. Somebody was out there. "Hey!" I yelled. "Help! We're in here!"

"Stop that," hissed Sunny. "No one is going to help you." She tipped her chin up, then, in one quick motion, banged her forehead into mine. Stars, mingled with dark blotches, blurred my vision. I sank to the floor like a bag of cement.

I felt pawing at my face, then whiskers from either side of my cheeks. Both cats had come to check on me. That meant no one was trying to keep Sunny from doing what she wanted, which was to get rid of all of us.

My eyelids were heavy. Was I going to pass out? I shook my head to try to clear it, but that only caused pain from where Sunny had headbutted me. That was going to hurt much more later. If I stayed alive.

Someone grabbed my legs and tugged me away from the window. I knew it wasn't the cats, so must be Sunny. Wow, my thoughts were weird. Was it from what Sunny had done to me? I wanted to fight her off, but I couldn't manage it. My whole body felt tired, used up like I had no energy at all. The cats meowed loudly in my ears, as I progressed slowly across the floor. Poor little guys must be following me. They'd be so scared.

From behind me, the door burst open.

Sunny gasped above me. "How did you get in here?"

Pounding footsteps came toward me. "Molly? Are you all right?"

It was Jillian's voice.

I smiled. "Never better."

"What?"

I cracked open one eye. Her long hair hung down, nearly touched my face. "Sunny cracked my head with hers. It kind of hurts."

"Oh, no." She lightly touched my cheek. "Don't worry. We'll take care of her."

Then I noticed two people scuffling over by the counter. It was Sunny. And Hank. I let out a breath. Thank goodness.

"Do you think you can sit up?" asked Jillian.

"Yeah, with help."

She took one of my hands in hers and placed her other behind me, pulling me toward her. "Are you dizzy?" she asked.

I blinked. "A little. Not too bad. Thanks for showing up." I frowned. "Hey, how did you get in? The door was locked."

"Jed is outside. He showed up right after we did and unlocked the door."

"Why is he outside?"

"He called Sheriff King."

I let out a breath. "Thank goodness you guys came when you did. It was scary in here."

"I know, honey. But it's going to be okay now."

I realized that since Jillian had found me, I could no longer see my cats. Panic shot through me. "Where are Percival and Jasper? She said she was going to hurt them. Or worse. Are they...."

Evan appeared beside me, holding my cats, who clung to him. "They are perfectly fine, Molly. Don't worry. Would you like to hold them?"

"Yes. Thank you, Evan." He placed them in my arms. They purred and gave me nose kisses on my face. When they patted my forehead, I winced, but didn't stop them. I knew they were as glad to see me as I was them. "I'm so glad you're okay, you guys. Mama was worried."

A siren sounded right outside the door, as if the sheriff had left it silent until the very last minute. I closed my eyes at the noise, which reverberated inside my head. "Ouch," I said.

Jillian patted my shoulder. "We're going to get you checked out by a doctor and get you something for the pain."

"I don't need a doctor, Jillian."

"Yeah," said Evan. "I think she's right. You do, Molly."

I groaned. There was no way I was going to get out of this with those two on the case.

"What's going on here?" boomed out the sheriff. "I got a call from Jed to hurry over."

He walked toward me. "Oh. Should have known it involved you, Molly.

Why can't you stay out of trouble?"

When Jasper let out a hiss, Sheriff King gasped and backed away a couple of steps. "Keep those creatures contained, will you?"

A door closed from the back area. Hank came out and waved the sheriff over. Jed had come in too and followed the sheriff.

Then Hank saw me and rushed across the room. He knelt beside me and embraced me and the cats in one giant human, kitty hug. "Oh, Molly. When I heard something was going on over here, and that you might have been in danger, I was so worried. I couldn't get here fast enough." He kissed me gently on the lips. "Are you okay? Really okay?"

"Sunny banged into her head," said Evan. "We think she needs to be checked out."

Hank studied my face and head, gently running his fingers down my cheek. "Yeah, good idea."

"Hey doc, I appreciate your bedside manner, but I'm not a dog."

"I know that very well." He winked.

I shook my head, but it hurt, so I held still. "Where is Sunny now?"

"Don't worry about her," said Hank. "She's rather, um, tied up."

I whipped my head around to see him better, then wished I hadn't. "You tied her up?"

Hank patted my shoulder. "Well, yes. She put up a great fight. I have arm scratches to prove it."

"Join the club," I said.

"But," he went on, "I'm a lot bigger than she is and was able to grab both of her hands. There was a rope sitting right there on a chair. I think maybe she had those out for you, Molly."

I swallowed hard. "Thank you, Hank."

Jillian clapped. "Yay, good for you, Hank."

"Way to go," said Evan.

Once Sunny was led outside, yes, still tied up, by the sheriff and Jed, I nearly wilted.

"Hey there," said Hank, "let's get you out of here, all right?"

"Yes. Please."

Once we were all outside, I had to shade my eyes against the sharp rays of the sun. Jillian led me to a vehicle and helped me to sit in the front seat of Hank's. He got into the other side and started the engine.

"Wait." I pointed toward the building. "The cats."

He patted my knee. "Jillian and Evan have them. They're okay."

"But how did you all even know where I was?"

"That was thanks to Veronica. When you didn't come back, she called Jillian, who went right over to Fabulous Felines. After a short discussion, Jillian called me and Evan. And here we are."

I sighed and slumped down a little in the seat. "Thank goodness for amazing friends."

"Yeah, you have a lot of those. Now let's get you to the doctor and get you checked out."

Chapter Thirty-One

Two days later, when my head stopped feeling as if I'd been kicked by a cow, Veronica arranged for our friends to come and celebrate all of us pitching together to find Carlotta's murderer. I could have arranged the get-together, but Veronica had been a mother hen to me ever since my unfortunate altercation with Sunny Wether.

I'd seen a few kitty clients today, but it was a light schedule. Again, that was Veronica's doing. But I didn't mind. She was a treasure, and if she wanted to watch over me after all that had happened, I wasn't going to complain.

She'd gotten out one of our large folding tables, covered it with a tablecloth, and enhanced it with vases of lovely roses. We, of course, wouldn't allow the cats anywhere near the flowers since it wasn't good for them, but the rest of us could enjoy them while we ate what she'd dished up from Leaning Tower of Pizza.

Once we were all seated and Percival and Jasper were sitting beside their full kitty dishes, we were ready to eat. Even though the food had come from a restaurant, the way Veronica had plated the meals so they looked homemade and delicious, was inviting.

Hank was seated on my left, with Jillian on my right. Evan, Veronica, and her husband, Jerome, were also there to celebrate. Once we were finished with our meals and Jasper and Percival had found a space on a shelf to take a nap, I tapped on my glass to get the others' attention.

"I just wanted to thank you all for being here. And to show my appreciation first for Veronica organizing this amazing evening." I smiled. "And the big thanks goes out to everyone for being a part of catching Carlotta's killer."

Hank grabbed my hand. "Molly, we're all so glad you're okay." He shook his head. "I can't...I can't imagine if things had gone differently and..."

I squeezed his hand. "It was due to every single one of you here, in helping me get out of that terrible situation."

Jerome gave me a wave from down the table. "I don't think I belong in that description."

"Yes you do," I said. "Because of you, Veronica can help me here at Fabulous Felines, where sometimes our schedules get downright crazy. If she hadn't been here waiting to hear from me when Jillian came by...well, it all worked together."

Veronica winked at Jerome. "She's right, honey. You do so much at home, so I'm able to work here."

Veronica was near retirement age, but had no plans to do so any time soon, thank goodness. Not sure how I'd manage without her there. Her husband, however, had retired from his career and now loved his role as stay-at-home dad to their menagerie of pets, as well as taking over the care of their home.

Jillian nodded. "Absolutely, to all the above. Everyone here played a part, and we should all be proud of each other."

Evan leaned closer to Jillian as he watched her. Did he even realize he was doing it? Jillian, however, sensed his nearness and gave him a shoulder bump with hers.

When I glanced at Hank, he was grinning at them, then nodded at me. We'd agreed that those two were on the right track for a great romance.

After Jillian and Evan finished making eyes at each other, she reached into her pocket and produced a folded-up paper.

"What's that?" I pointed to it. "Homework? Do we have to take a test?"

Jillian rolled her eyes. "Haha. Actually, it's something we've already talked about, Molly."

I watched as she unfolded the paper. "Oh. It's the list."

"What list?" asked Jerome.

Jillian smoothed the paper out on the table beside her plate. "When Carlotta's body was first discovered, Molly and I discussed daily who might have had motive to kill her. I said I'd put it on my list."

I laughed. "I said I had one, meaning in my head. My librarian friend, however, went a step further."

She shrugged. "It's what I do. It helps me think."

I nudged her hand. "I'm teasing you. It's perfect."

She sat up straighter in her seat, although she already had the best posture of anyone I knew, so it seemed nearly impossible she could improve on that.

I reached over and tapped the page. "I assume you're going to read what you have written down?"

Her eyebrows rose. "Of course."

Evan propped his chin on his hand and looked at Jillian. "I, for one, can't wait to hear your theories on the suspects."

Jillian giggled.

Oh brother, it really was getting deep in here. I waved my hand to get Jillian's attention. "I know you and I talked about all the people you'd written down, but I bet some of the others here would like to hear it too."

"I sure would," said Hank. Even though I'd kept him up to date on everything, he'd want Jillian to read it for everyone else anyway. Plus, with the way Evan was making gooey eyes at Jillian, we'd be here all night if things didn't get rolling.

Veronica nodded. "Definitely. Jerome and I have been discussing all the happenings lately, too. Molly keeps me updated, but I want to make sure there wasn't anything I forgot to tell him."

Jerome grinned and winked at his wife. Those two were so sweet.

"All right," said Jillian. "Now." She held up her hand. "I've written down what's happened so far, but please, if anyone has anything else to add, jump right in and tell us."

When a furry paw touched my leg, I glanced to my left. Percival wanted on my lap. I patted my thigh as in invitation, and he jumped onto my lap, making biscuits with his paws before turning in a circle to settle down.

Jillian smiled at Percival. "Aww, he wants to know what's going on, too. Anybody else?"

Light pattering paws approached from behind me. Jasper sat on his haunches, frowning that my lap was already occupied.

Hank looked at me. "Need some help?"

"Yes, please."

He reached down, expertly scooped up my other baby, and placed him on his own lap. Jasper, not at all upset at the recent change in venue, purred, closed his eyes, and mimicked his brother's biscuit-making skills on Hank's leg. "Well," said Hank, "since the cats were instrumental in bringing down the real killer, they should be here too."

Every head nodded.

"Oh, by the way," said Jillian, "I heard something today from the ladies about the sheriff."

I sat forward. "Really? What was that?"

"They were in the library checking out books. They'd seen the sheriff outside the building, running away from a kitten some little girl was playing with."

My mouth dropped open. "Ran away? I knew he didn't like my cats and was maybe even a little scared of them, but a tiny kitten?"

"I know. That's what I thought, too. But when I questioned the ladies further, they had an explanation. Apparently, when Sheriff King was a kid, his older sister had lots of cats around. His sister used to tease him mercilessly, and one time even tossed a cat at him, right at his head. The kitty ended up perched there, digging in its claws. The sheriff hasn't wanted to be around cats, or any animals, ever since."

"Wow, I hate to hear he went through that," I said. "Now I feel awful for teasing him myself about it."

Jillian touched my arm. "You weren't the only one, Molly. I did it too. But I won't anymore."

"Right. Neither will I. But wait. How did the ladies know about that?"

"Those two? They know everything. They remember Sheriff King's family when he and his sister were growing up. And that he got teased by everyone after they heard about what happened."

I shook my head. "Well, I'll try to be kinder and gentler around the sheriff from now on." It made me glad that when I had the occasional cat hat, at least it wasn't usually painful.

"Same here," said Hank. "I think we all will be kinder. That's a terrible thing for a person to go through."

Everyone nodded.

"Wait." Veronica waved her hand. "Speaking of Florence and Lottie, why aren't they here tonight, since they were the ones accused in the first place?"

I chuckled. "I invited them, but they said Helga and Eleanor would be taking naps right about then, and also it would interfere with their liquid supper time."

"Liquid…" Jerome's eyes narrowed.

"I'll tell you later," said Veronica.

"On to the list." Jillian held it up, then paused. "First, however, I wanted to thank Veronica."

"Me? Whatever for?"

"Because of your diligence and quick thinking, you called me because of your concern for Molly. You couldn't leave the shop with cats temporarily housed there, which I understand. Thank you for alerting me to your suspicions."

Veronica's eyes misted. "I'm just glad you were able to go to the bookshop and check on things."

Jerome patted his wife's hand.

Jillian smiled. "Now, let's look at who we all thought might have been Carlotta's killer. I'll start with Valene and get that one over with. It's a little painful to have thought my employee might have been responsible for a murder, but at the same time, she had a motive."

"And that video," I said. "I couldn't believe my eyes."

"What exactly happened in the video?" asked Hank. "I never got to see it."

Jillian got out her phone, pressed a few buttons, and handed him the phone. "Feel free to pass that around for anyone else to watch. It's not pretty."

Hank stared at the phone for a few seconds. "Wow, I knew something happened, but…"

"Right," I said. "Like Jillian said, definitely not pretty."

"So," Jillian waved her list. "Valene had a thing for the same guy Carlotta liked. Dalen Sparks. It was, and Molly agrees, and all-out catfight for a man."

I nodded. "But the ladies actually gave Valene instructions on how to get her man."

"I bet that was a show." Evan snorted a laugh.

"It was. Too bad I didn't get that on video, too. Not that I would have shown anybody but you guys."

"Did it work?" asked Veronica. "I mean, did Valene get her guy?"

"Time will tell." Jillian shrugged. "Apparently, while Valene had them practically married in her mind, Dalen was clueless that she even liked him. But last I heard, Valene called him up and they're getting together later this week."

Hank smiled. "That will make Valene happy. And Lottie and Florence as well. Who's next, Jillian?"

"Let's see. Next is… Mrs. Kelper. Molly, you were the one to talk to her the most. Want to add anything?"

"When I was there for a mobile grooming visit. She was spouting off about her award-winning Kelper-doodles."

Jerome's eyebrows lowered.

"Cookies," I said.

"Ah. Thank you."

"She had all kinds of awards for winning prizes for them from the county fair every year. Apparently, this year, her serious competition was Carlotta. Mrs. Kelper had even purchased for herself, ahead of time, a first-place trophy for her cookies."

"Ahead of time?" Evan's eyebrows rose. "Wow, that's confidence."

"Yes, it is," agreed Jillian. "But at the time, Molly felt it pointed more toward a motive for murdering her."

I shifted in my chair. "Yep. And she even had her cat Cleo wearing an apron that said, My Mom Won Again."

"Still weird that she bought her own trophy beforehand," said Hank.

"I agree." Jillian nodded. "While I admire a confident woman, that went beyond common sense."

Leave it to my best friend to mention common sense. "Who else do we have?" I glanced at the paper.

She looked down. "Next up is Lenny Griffith. The ladies were very helpful in giving information about Lenny's relationship with Carlotta."

"That's right," I said. "They'd been neighbors as kids. Carlotta knew a secret about Lenny that would have threatened his reputation later on when he wanted to become a town councilman."

Evan groaned. "Yeah, I got hit up to give him money for his campaign fund. I declined. Now that Carlotta is gone and he's in the clear, so to speak, I'm assuming he'll still run for office?"

I rolled my eyes. "Yeah, that's my take on it. Just, if you see him coming and you don't have spare cash to give away, run the other direction."

Laughter came from around the table, waking Percival. He looked up at me, yawned, then returned to his lap nap.

"I'd really wondered if the murderer was Lenny," said Evan. "When he came into my studio that day, he gave off the really weird signals."

"That's true," I said. "I was there that day. That guy is strange. And intense."

"But apparently not a murderer," pointed out Jillian.

"True enough." Evan nodded.

"By the way, show of hands, who all thought Mrs. Kelper or Valene might have been guilty?"

Veronica held up her hand. "After talking it over, Jerome and I both put bets on Valene. Sorry, Jillian."

"No, don't apologize. I thought so at the time, too. Just glad it wasn't true. What about Mrs. Kelper?"

I raised my hand. "Yeah, she was definitely on my radar. That woman takes getting a first-place trophy way too seriously."

"Especially when she buys the prize herself," added Hank, lifting his hand.

"Next," said Jillian, "was Jed. With him having been married to Carlotta at one time and them in a terrible court fight over money, he seemed a likely suspect too."

I nodded. "Definitely. Especially after I overheard him yelling at Sunny that day in their shop. But then, Sunny had me snowed when she described their relationship as something way different than it was. I was completely fooled."

"Don't worry." Hank patted my arm. "We all were. She always seemed harmless. A little chatty, but not a troublemaker."

"And Dalen Sparks." Jillian held up her list. "Anybody think he was guilty besides Molly and me?"

"I did," said Evan. "Florence and Lottie had also told me about being there during a bad argument between him and Carlotta. It sounded like he'd had reason to want his ex out of the picture."

Jillian's lips rose in a half-smile. "Yes. I know that ladies can embellish stories...."

"A lot," I added.

"Yes, a lot, but that sounded like a really bad scenario."

I pointed to her list. "So that leaves, Trixie, right?"

"That's right. The dancing queen."

Jerome's eyebrows shot up. "I don't think I heard about that part."

Veronica sighed. "That's my fault. I witnessed it one day through the shop window," she pointed toward the front of Fabulous Felines,"but forgot to tell you. Apparently, she was dancing all over town with glee that Carlotta was dead, following being seen at work and at other businesses looking unkempt and, from what I hear, not smelling great."

"Huh," said Evan, "sounds like one moody girl to me."

"She is," I agreed. "And she gives frightening manicures."

Evan frowned. "Frightening? I knew you weren't fond of her work, but..."

Jillian shivered. "I'll fill you in later. Remember to ask me about the eyes."

His mouth dropped open, but he snapped it shut. I gave Jillian a grateful smile. I really hadn't wanted to talk about it anymore either.

"Anything else to add?" I glanced at the piece of paper.

"No, that's all I had." Her expression turned serious. "I'm just so glad you're all right, Molly."

"Same here." Hank leaned over and kissed my cheek. My heart nearly melted.

"Us too," said Veronica, tilting her head toward Jerome. "We need you, Molly. I couldn't herd all those cats in the shop alone." She winked, but I knew she loved me like her own family.

Evan clasped his hands together on the table. "I'm so very grateful you're okay, Molly. And that we've become friends."

How was I so fortunate to have so many wonderful, caring people in my life? "Thanks, everyone. It was a group effort. Every single one of us played a part."

A stirring came from my knees. Percival jumped up on the table and sat, facing me. Jasper, seeing his brother was no longer asleep, crawled away from Hank and climbed up as well.

I placed a hand on each cat's chin. "And you guys were amazing. I couldn't have done any of this without you."

If the kitties' purrs were any indication, they were grateful I was all right, too.

About the Author

Ruth J. Hartman spends her days herding cats and her nights spinning mysterious tales. She, her husband, and their cats love to spend time curled up in their recliners watching old Cary Grant movies. Well, the cats sit in the people's recliners. Not that the cats couldn't get their own furniture. They just choose to shed on someone else's.

Ruth, a left-handed, cat-herding, farmhouse-dwelling writer uses her sense of humor as she writes tales of lovable, klutzy women who seem to find trouble without even trying.

Ruth's husband and best friend, Garry, reads her manuscripts, rolls his eyes at her weird story ideas, and loves her despite her insistence all of her books have at least one cat in them. See updates about her cozy mysteries at Ruthjhartman.com.

AUTHOR WEBSITE:
  https://www.ruthjhartman.com/

SOCIAL MEDIA HANDLES:
  https://www.facebook.com/ruth.j.hartman
  https://www.facebook.com/profile.php?id=100063631596817

Also by Ruth J. Hartman

Brushed Up on Murder (Book 1 in the Mobile Cat Groomer Mysteries)

Purrfecty Framed (Book 2 in the Mobile Cat Groomer Mysteries)

Butterfly Betrayal (Book 1 in the Seneca James Mysteries)

Murder at the Painted Wings Café (Book 2 in the Seneca James Mysteries)

Dial M for Meow (Book 1 in the Kitties Bookshop Mysteries)

Murder She Meowed (Book 2 in the Kitties Bookshop Mysteries)

Hairballs and Homicide (Book 1 in the Kitty Beret Café Mysteries)

Felines and Fatalities (Book 2 in the Kitty Beret Café Mysteries)

Meows and Mayhem (Book 3 in the Kitty Beret Café Mysteries)

Claws and Conflict (Book 4 in the Kitty Beret Café Mysteries)

Ring of Death (A Dorey Cameron Mystery)